THE SECRET MINISTRY OF FROST

NICK LAKE

D1392220

SIMON AND SCHUSTER

First published in Great Britain in 2009 by
Simon and Schuster UK Ltd
A CBS COMPANY

Simon & Schuster UK Ltd
1st Floor, 222 Gray's Inn Road
London WC1X 8HB

This book is a work of fiction. Names, characters, places
and incidents are either the product of the author's imagination
or are used fictitiously. Any resemblance to actual people living
or dead, events or locales is entirely coincidental.

A CIP catalogue record for this book
is available from the British Library.

ISBN 978-1-84738-309-9

1 3 5 7 9 10 8 6 4 2

Typeset by M Rules
Printed by CPI Cox & Wyman, Reading, Berkshire RG1 8EX

www.simonsays.co.uk

—NL

. . . the secret ministry of frost
Shall hang them up in silent icicles,
Quietly shining to the quiet Moon.

Frost at Midnight, Samuel Taylor Coleridge

*örðin ok steinarnir ok tré ok allr málmr . . . þessir hlutir
gráta þá er þeir koma ór frosti ok í hita*
the earth and the stones and the trees and all kinds of
metal . . . these things weep when they come out of frost
into warmth

Gylfaginning, Snorri Sturluson

Part One

Home

Chapter One

Light

Light was woken on the morning of her father's funeral by a pneumatic hiss. She rolled to the side but she was too slow.

Whump.

A heavy steel and glass message tube landed on the duvet above her stomach, knocking the air out of her.

Ow.

Light coughed and spluttered, picking up the tube.

Stupid message system.

Her family had a history of eccentricity, and this was her great-grandfather's contribution: a system of wide brass pipes laid through the house, by which rolled-up notes could be sent from room to room. Subsequent generations had kept the tubes, despite the advent of mobile phones and intercoms. It felt right, somehow, a part of the house's soul. If Light wanted to say something to someone without leaving her room, she simply wrote a message, rolled it up, put it in a tube (there was a pile by her bed for this

 3

purpose) and then held it inside the left pipe using the slot provided. Some invisible force she did not understand (science was not Light's forte) would take the tube and whisk it down to the kitchen, or to another room, or to the hall.

Light opened the tube that had just landed on her bed and unrolled the message inside:

Good morning.
You'll get through this.
Love, Butler

Light smiled. Even now that she had moved rooms, Butler always found a way to wake her up in the morning. She had a wing of the house to herself now – something she would have been excited about a few years ago, imagining herself sliding down polished corridors in her socks, and having midnight feasts every night with . . . well, with Butler, she supposed. But Light found that, with her father gone, the magic had gone out of these dreams.

Light added the message tube to her pile and slid out of bed. The window was covered with a light filigree of frost which formed swirling patterns on the glass. But the morning was bright – late-autumn sunlight played magician's tricks on the world outside, causing patches of the lough to shine like polished silver. Light narrowed her eyes against the glare and peered out at the grounds and the lough – a lake that stretched to the horizon, almost the whole way across Northern Ireland. She was three floors up, at the top of the old mansion, and she could see all the way down to the lush green trees by the shore and the red-brick, crenellated folly one of her ancestors had built. On the seamless surface of the lough, a pair of swans glided sedately. Far away over the water, black clouds boiled.

In the early morning, with the sun shining, Light could just about forget it was her father's funeral today, or at least trick her mind into not thinking of it. She was enjoying the view of the lough and the gardens when something strange caught her eye. Standing together on the lawn below her window was a group of ravens, arranged in a perfect circle. They were big – Light wasn't sure she'd ever seen such big ones, even when she'd visited the Tower of London with her father – but that wasn't the only strange thing about them. They stood perfectly still, as if keeping watch over the house, or waiting for someone within it to come out and meet them. Light stared at them for some time, but they showed no inclination to move, only stood, heads cocked, eyes sharp, as if awaiting instruction.

Light turned away from the window, feeling disconcerted. She took her funeral outfit from the wardrobe – a simple black skirt-suit with a white blouse. She hung the suit on the brass knob on the wardrobe door, then laid her black patent-leather shoes on the floor beneath it. The effect was a little uncanny: as if an invisible girl was standing there. Deciding that her imagination was definitely on overdrive this morning, Light took off her pyjamas and put on the blouse, then shrugged herself into the jacket. She looked at herself in the ornate mirror set into the wardrobe which was a relic of the seventeenth century when the house had been built. Silvery tarnish marked the corners of the mirror, framing Light's face. The contrast between the black fabric and her snow-white hair was startling. Her skin was white and glowing as the moon.

Because Light was an albino, she usually disliked dressing in black, but for the funeral she was making an exception. Putting on the skirt, she thought she looked like a black and white photograph – where her mother and father had been invaded by the colours of the world (the blue of the sky was in her father's eyes, the green of the earth in her mother's) she had been left untouched, white, with only a touch of pink in her eyes. An observer would notice that those eyes were usually shining and intelligent – except occasionally when they would go blank, as if Light was tuning into some private, internal channel.

As satisfied as she would ever be with her appearance, Light took off the funeral outfit again, and put on her usual tracksuit and T-shirt.

The suit was itchy.

It could wait.

She left the room and headed down through the old house to the front door. Given the brightness of the day, she picked up a pair of sunglasses from the hall table to protect her sensitive eyes.

There were no tears, despite the approaching funeral. She was aware that the staff talked about her, that some of them thought she didn't care about her father just because she didn't cry all the time. But Light *did* care: she simply had to remain strong because at the edge of her mind was a terrible, vacant grief that demanded to be let in. And mixed in with the grief was fear – abject terror at the idea of being left alone. This maelstrom rushed around the borders of Light's consciousness like high-altitude winds, and she was dimly aware that if she let it in, if she cracked open the door of the pressurised plane that was her personality, it would rip apart everything within, pulling it around and out.

Light needed a moment outside before facing anyone. She wanted to delay the start of the day – delay the moment when her father's empty coffin would be lowered into the ground. She opened the heavy front door of the house and stepped out onto the lawn, shivering slightly at the cold. The crows were still standing on the lawn and now they turned to look at her. She frowned at the black birds, unable to remember ever seeing so many of them in one place. As one, silently, the birds flapped their wings and took to the sky, sculpting for a moment a twisted black silk flag that hung, shimmering, in the air, and then flew off over the lough.

Light set out across the lawn – emerald-green and so perfectly flat that you could play croquet on it if you wanted to.

Light didn't.

Before her lay the woods. To her left, the gardens of the estate ran all the way down to Lough Neagh; to her right, they rose until they merged with Mount Carmel, a medium-sized hill with delusions of grandeur. At this time of year, the hill was covered with purple bracken – in combination with the green grass, it reminded Light of a lump on some-one's head. Lough Neagh, on her left, was grey and still, vast and foreboding. They said that the lake had just appeared one day, back in the time of the Celts. A flash flood. They said there was a village drowned underneath it, and that on a clear day when the water was still you could see the houses. Light had never seen them.

She walked to the lough and sat down on a rusted iron bench that looked over a grey, pebble beach. The water hung over the stones clear and pale blue, wavering like gas flames. The dark clouds over the lough seemed closer and higher, threatening heavy rain later. To her right and in the distance, Light could see the squat buildings and church spire of the village of Toome. The village had a town hall and an eel fishery, and little else.

It was a beautiful place, Light's home, but it was deathly dull.

Light took a deep breath, preparing herself for the day ahead. In a barely acknowledged part of her mind, the black birds had disturbed her, reminding her of the bizarre circumstances surrounding her father's disappearance. Nearly nine months before, her father had left to go to the Arctic, for research purposes. It had been six months, three weeks and four days since he had last been heard from. He wasn't an amateur, one of those foolhardy explorers who get themselves killed as a short cut to a reputation. In fact, he'd been to the same research station more or less every year since before Light was born, conducting experiments to measure the impact of rising CO_2 levels on the sea water of the far north.

This time, taking his cue from research which had been done in America, he had packed several cases of iron filings. In theory, dropping these into the sea would increase the plankton population, which in turn would remove carbon dioxide from the water. Sadly, it remained a theory, with no evidence that Light's father had carried out his research.

Since his disappearance there had been no emails, no satellite phone conversations. The high frequency Morse code paddle and receiver he had installed in Light's room had gone dead. Worse, his blog entries had ended. Light could no longer turn on her laptop and read her father's musings – could no longer think about the blog, in fact, as the memory seemed to have grown thorns and she could no longer touch it.

After some months had passed, her father's lawyer had recommended declaring him dead. Usually, when someone disappeared, the family had to wait seven years before the law would consider them officially deceased. But in exceptional circumstances an earlier application could be made. Since Neagh House was run – and the salaries of its staff were paid – from Light's father's accounts, the circumstances were deemed sufficiently exceptional. And anyway, the Navy had searched his research station and the surrounding ice. If he was alive, they would have found him.

When death had been declared Butler had become Light's guardian, and the executor of her trust fund – it seemed that her father had drawn up a will and left it in his solicitor's care. The will specified quite clearly that in the case of death or disappearance, Butler was to have custody.

Light had asked Butler if he thought her dad was really dead. He had mumbled an answer that was intended to be positive – something about resourcefulness, and pig-headedness – before seeing the hard look in Light's eyes and trailing off into a silence that spoke more honestly of Light's father's fate.

Once it was decided that Light's father was officially

dead, Butler told Light that they would hold a funeral 'in absentia'. She'd asked why they couldn't just have it at the church in the village, and he had smiled – the only time in those first months that she saw him smile – and told her that it meant a funeral without a body.

Light's mother Amaruq had died years before, and Light had never known her except in three photographs that stood on the fireplace in the front room. These images – one a simple portrait, the second a shot of mother and baby and the third a candid photo of Light's parents dancing – showed a beautiful young woman with green almond-shaped eyes and skin so pale as to be almost translucent. She was beautiful.

Light knew her father missed her mother terribly. He had never married again, or even had a relationship, to the best of Light's knowledge. Her mother had been the love of his life, and he had no intention of replacing her.

Light's mother had also been taken by the Arctic, after wandering from the station and freezing to death on a much earlier research trip with Light's father. They had never recovered the body – her father had found her and gone back to the station to get a snowmobile and a stretcher. But by the time he came back she was gone, perhaps taken by a polar bear. It was strange that she should have been so careless – because Light's mother was an Inuit, and knew the snow well. Light's father had met her in Iqaluit, on one of his earliest research trips, when his ship stopped for provisions before entering the iceberg-filled bays leading to the fabled Northwest Passage. He had left Iqaluit with tinned food, a rifle, several furs and a wife. They had spent the whole of one dark winter together, on the ice. When they realised that Amaruq was pregnant, they knew immediately what the child would be called – they chose the name that, in the permanent darkness and cold, represented to them what they most missed.

When they came to Northern Ireland, Amaruq was close to giving birth. The villagers had never taken to this Inuit woman – and only reluctantly to Light herself. There was much whispering after Light's mother's death. 'Imagine,' people said, 'an Eskimo freezing in the snow!' And at Light's school, the playground chants had made themselves:

Your mum is an eskimo.
Got frostbite and lost a toe.
Got frostbite and died, oh no!
Your mum is an eskimo.

Distracted by grief, Light's father had brushed off the tales of her bullying, saying that she would 'make friends eventually', as if the making of friends were an easy thing, like shaping clay on a wheel.

Light's mother had come from the territory now called Nunavut, in northern Canada, and this was the homeland of the Inuit peoples. Light's father had taught her these things at an early age, shown her slides and photos of the Arctic and spoken to her in Inuktitut, the guttural, liquid language of the North. Light spoke Inuktitut pretty well, though she was far from fluent. It was a language of strange sounds and long words, all the consonants seeming to come entirely from the back of the throat, as if the early Inuits had invented the language when their tongues and lips were numb with cold, forcing them to speak in Gs and Ks.

Yes, Light knew the Arctic well.

It was just that she had never been there.

It was strange, really: her mother came from the Arctic and her father went there often, but Light had never seen it with her own eyes. She could speak its language, knew some of its customs – yet had never so much as felt its snow beneath her feet.

The school in the village had not worked out, of course. Light was too unconventional, too different-looking with her white skin and pink eyes. But she enjoyed her home-school lessons with her father and Butler – they were interesting teachers who covered an eclectic range of subjects: philosophy, map-reading, mathematics, languages. One day Light might be conversing in Arabic with the slightly bemused owner of one of Belfast's Lebanese take-aways, specially flown in by helicopter for the day. The next she might be orienteering through the woods, avoiding dummy landmines. She could locate a book in her father's library using the Dewey Decimal system, which she knew by heart, but she could also drive a jeep through a bog – and dig it out if it got stuck. It was an interesting education.

When Light entered the kitchen later, Maeve, the cook, grabbed her and raised her eyebrows. 'Into the drawing room with you, child! Butler is looking for you, and he's in a bit of a kerfuffle.'

'Oh, no,' said Light. She helped herself to a pastry from Maeve's table.

'Oi! Hands off that. It's for the wake.'

'Sorry Maeve. S'very good.'

Maeve was dressed as usual in a stunning ensemble: a midnight blue dress and sparkling vintage heels. She was fashionable at all times, even when cooking – something which men were largely oblivious too, and women enviously admired.

She was also beautiful. Something men were not at all oblivious to.

She was tall, with pale blue eyes and delicate features, and Butler became comically tongue-tied in her presence.

Maeve had been hired in the upheaval of six months ago, in order to take up some of the cooking and cleaning while Butler was engaged in the search for Light's father.

Light had expected a round, rosy-faced mothering type, kindly and possibly corpulent. Instead, on the day Maeve arrived, Light met an impossibly elegant young woman with film star looks, dressed in a skirt, a cashmere cardigan and pearls.

This would have been less unusual if it had not been snowing heavily at the time, and the village a half hour walk away.

The home-help agency had sent Maeve to the house to meet them. Light and Butler had been having a snowball fight in the garden – both of them dripping wet and shrieking. Light had just chased Butler round the corner of the house and onto the front lawn, where she unleashed a hard-packed snowball aimed at his face. (She had been brought up by two men and could throw hard and true.)

But Butler ducked and the snowball flew over his head. At

precisely that moment an elegant young woman in designer clothes and high heels was walking up the gravel path towards the front door. The snowball hit her on the neck.

Light stared, horrified. The agency would have to send someone else.

Again.

But Maeve had simply dusted the snow off her collar, kicked off her high-heeled shoes and ducked down to form a hard, perfectly round snowball that two seconds later caught Light in the vulnerable gap between her jeans and her jumper, dripping cold slush down her legs.

'You must be Light,' she'd said. 'It's a pleasure to meet the lady of the house.' Then she'd stooped to gather up more snow.

'Pleased to meet you,' said Light, making a snowball of her own while skirting around, keeping herself a moving target. Butler was moving fast too, piling an arsenal of snowballs into the crook of his left arm.

Soon afterwards, all three of them had been soaked.

There was an interview of sorts, later, around the fire – with Maeve swamped in a pair of Butler's trousers and one of his T-shirts. Maeve made her way through three hot chocolates. 'Chocolate,' she said, conspiratorially, 'is a weakness of mine. Well, that and snowball fights.'

Butler had asked a few half-hearted questions about food and cleaning, but she had really been hired as soon as that snowball left her manicured hand.

Back in the kitchen and the present, Maeve waved her hand in front of Light's face.

'You're day-dreaming,' she said. 'Go and make yourself useful.'

Light put down her cup and wandered over to the drawing room, where Butler was leaning over the table, pushing small bits of food around on a silver platter. He was wearing a morning suit: bow tie, black pin-striped trousers and a long black jacket that split into a tail at the back. He looked like an enormous blackbird. At the moment, his smart outfit was ruined a little by his rolled up sleeves, which revealed the elaborate tattoos running up his forearms. These tattoos were abstract and tribal, and Light could never be sure what they represented – sometimes they looked like blackbirds, sometimes like sea creatures or thorns. As a child she had been convinced that they moved slightly when she wasn't looking.

Light wasn't sure where Butler was from: his features were vaguely oriental, but she didn't think he was Japanese or Chinese. It was possible he came from the North, like her mother, but she hadn't dared to ask: from a young age, she'd seen the way his voice went sharp if someone asked and he would always say, 'Northern Ireland. Like you.'

'Hi, Butler,' Light said. 'What are you doing?'

Butler turned. '*Vols au vents*,' he said. 'For the wake.' He looked her up and down. 'You're still in your tracksuit and T-shirt. As outfits go, it's a little irregular.'

'Actually,' said Light, 'I wear it almost every day.'

'Very amusing,' said Butler, witheringly. 'Perhaps when you have a successful career as a stand-up comic, you can support me in my dotage.'

'Don't be silly, Butler. I'll just put you in a home.'

Butler feigned a hollow laugh. 'What are you doing here, anyway?'

15

'Maeve said to make myself useful.'

'Well then, go and get dressed,' he said.

And with that, Butler turned and swept out of the room, his coat tails swishing.

Chapter Two

No body came to the funeral

Half an hour later, the funeral party walked down the Corpse Way. They passed through a copse of pale trees. It was a between time of the year: at this hour of the afternoon frost had started to dust the grass, but the leaves on the trees were still green. Looking at the countryside in autumn was like looking at a man whose age you couldn't guess – one who's young in the face but going grey.

Light loved to look at the plants and flowers in the hedgerows but had deliberately chosen not to learn their names – she thought it left more mystery that way. She'd heard that giving something a name gave you power over it, but she didn't think that was exactly right. It was more that giving something a name took the power *out* of it, made it ordinary and classified, no longer unique.

Butler carried the coffin on one shoulder, his head tilted to one side to accommodate its bulk, his gait slower

17

and more deliberate than usual. Butler's right arm easily supported the weight as it rested on his shoulder, but it was still an awkward shape, and he had to shuffle forwards in a sort of crablike motion. Maeve, as well as several people from the village and the estate, followed behind.

Butler tapped a torch against his left leg as he walked.

'What have you got that for?' Light asked.

'It may be dark when we come back, if that storm breaks.' He used the steel torch to point at the dark clouds over the lough. In the fields that sloped down to the water hung a delicate evening mist, shimmering above every object as if the grass, fences and sheep were giving up their ghosts.

As they walked through the copse, Light heard a rustling sound and looked up. In the branches of the pale ash trees, dozens – maybe hundreds – of black ravens sat watching the people below. Light stopped. The bird closest to her fidgeted on its perch, keeping its shining black eyes always on her. Light felt scrutinised, *regarded*, but also strangely protected. She could feel that the crows would not harm her. Light realised that she'd fallen behind – she took a last look at the crows in the trees and hurried to catch up.

The procession came out of the copse and into the fields, following the narrow path down which, since time immemorial, family bodies had been carried to their resting place. The family Corpse Way led through fields owned by different farmers, a thin strip of countryside no-man's-land leading directly from the house to the church, bordered on both sides by fences, no more than a metre across. There were dozens of Corpse Ways, one for each major family, radiating out from the church like a cobweb. Historically there had been long conflicts over land in these parts, and the overlapping claims meant that it was impossible to reach the church from any angle without crossing several boundaries. But no matter what disputes they might have, every landowner respected the right of his neighbours to take their bodies for burying, and so the Corpse Ways had been drawn up. Each landowner had allowed these rights of way across his land, knowing that when he had to cross other fields to bury one of his own, the same courtesy would be extended to him.

The sky over the lough was black now. Lightning flashed intermittently, thin jags of white, as if the sky had been laid out on an X-ray table, and the flashes were revealing its bones. Light scanned the sky nervously. Clouds raced overhead, casting black shadows that moved along the hills as if they were alive – or as if some creature that fed on light were running through the fields, plunging them into darkness as it passed.

By the time the coffin was lowered – more easily than usual – into the grave, it was raining heavily and the mourners were drenched. None of them had brought umbrellas, feeling that it would be rude, somehow, to take care of their own comfort in the middle of a funeral. Cold water trickled down Light's back, crawling like fear down her spine. Her feet were wet and clammy inside her black leather shoes, squelching when she moved her toes.

Light, overwhelmed by the drama of the scene, thought that it might break through the barriers she had erected in her mind, causing her sadness to come flooding out and drown her mind. At the head of the grave, the priest was declaiming in Latin, lit in the false darkness of the storm by the torch Butler had thought to bring along. He was wearing robes that looked black in the darkness, like bat's wings. Unfortunately, the effect was slightly ruined by the man's voice, which was high and strident, not at all the stentorian boom that would do justice to the dramatic weather. Light half listened to the words of the mass, glancing down at the programme in her hands to read the English translation. '. . . *gratia tua illis succurente mereantur evadere judicium ultionis, et lucis æterne beatitudine perfrui.*' 'By your grace may they deserve to avoid the judgment of revenge, and enjoy the everlasting blessedness of light.'

Light sent her own blessings to her father, wherever he was, alive or dead.

The graveyard was on a small hill next to the lough. There was an undeniable power and atmosphere to the place, with its gnarled yew trees, its old, crumbling headstones, and the sweep of the hill down to the pebble beach of the lough. The lough was choppy today, making it look like grey, corrugated iron. Light shivered – there was something about the water of the lough that made you feel cold to the very centre of your being. Not a normal cold, but a cold that struck to the soul, making it feel as if you would never be warm again.

Like all the family's graves, her father's was situated in the very centre of the graveyard, next to the grave of the sixth lord, who, it was said, was smothered in his bed by his own son. It was this sixth lord who had installed the message tubes. Nearby was the grave of Mad Eric, the first lord of the manor – or at least, the grave of half of him. He had been torn in two during a peasant revolt, and only his lower half had ever been recovered. Her father's black granite gravestone was already in place. Below the name, Gordon Fitzwilliam, were the dates of his birth and disappearance. Below that, a poem had been inscribed, the chisel marks so new and their white filling so fresh that the text looked like chalk on a blackboard.

HE SLEEPS BENEATH HIS NATIVE EARTH
SO NEAR THE SPOT THAT GAVE HIM BIRTH
BENEATH THE WEEDS AND FLOWERS THAT BLOOM
SO SILENT IN HIS EARLY TOMB

The priest had chosen the inscription. Light thought it was stupid – her father certainly *didn't* sleep beneath his native earth. If he slept anywhere, it was on the sea ice of the cold Arctic, or under it, in the freezing blue-black sea. As Light's gaze lingered on these meaningless words, she was startled by the sudden appearance of a jackdaw, which flew in fast then landed neatly on top of the gravestone. It folded its wings fastidiously, with a slightly prim air, then cocked its head and looked at Light. The jackdaw was smaller than the ravens Light had seen earlier, but its eyes – acute, shining – seemed to fix her with the same intensity. Light stared back, curious, and noticed that Butler was watching the bird too.

A wet *thock* brought Light's attention back to the black

 21

hole in the ground, and the jackdaw took to the air, startled. Someone had just thrown a clod of sodden earth on the grave. Butler followed. There must have been a stone in his lump of earth, because from the grave came the sound of a knock on a door – a loud reminder of the coffin's hollowness. Light looked at the grave, stricken, stunned by how loud the noise had been. It seemed to her that she would never hear again. She felt like a struck gong.

Moments later, though, she heard the priest's voice, still intoning the words of the mass. '*Lux æterna luceat eis, Domine.*' She didn't need to look at her programme to translate.

'May everlasting light shine upon them.'

She wished it fervently.

Glowing white lights swam in front of Light's eyes and she felt a strange weightlessness, as if someone had replaced her blood with helium. She swayed and twisted the heavy gold ring on her left index finger – her father's wedding ring, which he had given her before leaving on his trip. She felt sick, all of a sudden, and weak. The wet, black earth on the coffin's lid, the priest in his robes, the lightning . . . it was all too much. Right then she was struck by a realisation that made her knees tremble and threatened to pitch her forwards into the open grave. *My father is never coming back.* She had known this before – but now she *understood* it. It was if she had, throughout her life and in violation of all logic, entertained the assumption that after a person died they would still be available for conversation.

She began to breathe rapidly.

 22

At the head of the grave, she saw Butler's torch flash on and off.

-.-. — .. -. .- — . / .-.. .. - - .-.. / — -. .

Courage, little one.

The priest faltered in his reading, distracted by the flashing light. Light smiled, feeling the strength return to her limbs, rooting her to the ground as if she were a tree drawing up water, though the only thing she was drawing in was Butler's support. Light's father had taught her Morse code when she was young, and now it was coming in useful again.

Luckily for her, she didn't know *how* useful it would soon prove to be.

When it came to Light's turn to throw earth on the grave, she shook her head. Her father had disappeared – she wasn't going to bury him too. She found her feelings impossible to sort out: grief, she had realised, was not a single emotion but a mess of contradictory sensations. Sadness, anger, loneliness – and guilt, too, when you felt happy or something made you laugh.

We are not broken by tragedy, only changed – like a tree struck by lightning, and made to grow in a new and painful direction.

Light was no exception. She felt a usurper in her own skin, looking out through the windows of her eyes onto the familiar but foreign contours of her body. The old Light had been light-hearted, easily amused. Now she was a heavy lump, a mass of nerves.

No one had much to say, and so the group drifted apart,

 23

heading down the lough-side path to Toome for food and drink at the pub, most looking forward to getting into the dry but not wanting to hurry in case it looked unseemly. Yet, at the same time, no one wanted to dawdle in case it looked like they were enjoying their stroll, so most had compromised on a purposeful, steady stride, keeping their heads down.

The Wriggling Eel in Toome was a dour, square building of grey stone, standing just next to the flood gates and commanding an impressive view of the River Bann's mouth, where water from the lough began its journey to the Atlantic. The view was by far the pub's best attribute. Next door stood the shell of the old Paint Works, a massive red-brick construction whose broken windows were sometimes jagged-toothed mouths, and sometimes sly, peering eyes. The schoolchildren dared each other to go inside. Light never had – she had never been brave or intrepid.

In a wood-panelled, dark room at the back of the pub, the wake got under way. Light's eyes stung from smoke and sadness, and she stood unnoticed in a corner. Butler handed out his *hors d'ouevres*.

The atmosphere was awkward, with a handful of stilted conversations starting and stopping abruptly. A woman from the village – Light thought she might be the librarian – glided past and murmured, 'I'm so sorry for your loss.' Before Light could respond, the woman had moved on, shaking her head slightly in apparent disapproval of a world that left twelve-year-old girls without fathers.

'The eel men are here,' said Maeve.

Light turned. In a corner of the pub sat a group of eel fishermen, conspicuous by their hard muscles and the open friendliness of their faces, especially when they looked at Light, which was often.

The fishermen were friends to Neagh House. When Light's father had first inherited, he had supported them in their fight against a paint factory – the very same one whose empty shell still sat next to the pub – that had been polluting the lough, killing off the eels and threatening the fishermen's livelihoods.

One of the fishermen, his face wrinkled and creased by a lifetime of wind and spray, nodded to Light as she approached. 'I don't know what to say,' he told her. She could see that his eyes were red-rimmed from tears. The men hadn't been at the funeral, and it was clear they'd spent the time drinking and remembering instead.

'Good,' said Light. 'I wouldn't know what to answer.'

The man nodded again. 'He was one of the best. A true gentleman.' And then, softly at first, he began to sing. The other fishermen picked up the refrain. It was a protest song from the time of the paint factory scandal, a song that Light had always seemed to know.

Come all you gallant Irishmen
And listen what I say,
I was a hardworking fisherman
From the shores of sweet Lough Neagh.
My father fished the deep at Doss
And knew its rocky shores,
But I have lost my livelihood
And cannot fish no more.

 25

They poisoned our waters
And they held us up to scorn,
Even though it was a heritage
To which we all were born.
The waters of Lough Neagh we fished
As our fathers did before,
But because of the Toome Paint Works
We cannot fish no more . . .

Light retreated to the front bar and sat down. Butler followed and sat down opposite. To look at his face, you wouldn't know he was grieving, but Light knew that he was suffering. His eyes and mouth were like a layer of permafrost: frozen, unmoving, but with bright and terrible things swimming underneath.

Now Butler held her hand. 'You can cry, you know,' he said.

'No,' said Light. 'I can't.'

Butler believed that a person mourning was like a bath that's been left with the tap on – you had to 'let it out' or eventually the bath would overflow. Light did not agree. For her, the missing of her father was more like a hippo in a bath: it squeezed out the water, leaving no room for anything else, taking up her entire being.

She had not cried once since her father left. Now she looked across the pub and saw Judith, the florist from Neagh, weeping openly. *How come she can cry and I can't?* thought Light. Her sadness ached in her throat like an illness, but would not come out.

'You need to get out of here, I think,' Butler said thoughtfully. 'This wake is worse than the funeral. Go outside, have a walk in the woods.' He smiled and Light smiled back, grateful for his advice. She was itching to get out of her suit and into her usual tracksuit trousers and T-shirt.

'Besides,' said Butler, pointing at a man who was climbing onto a table, 'I'm pretty sure the fishermen are going to start singing again. And believe me, most of their repertoire is *not* suitable for a young girl.'

Chapter Three

'Who could have frozen your poor daddy's heart?'

Light pushed through the undergrowth at the edge of the woods, passing a sign that had been painted on a wooden board and staked into the ground next to a narrow path. Barely registering the sign, Light took in its familiar words:

> *Poison ivy rampant.*
> *Unexploded mines.*

Light plunged further into the wilds of the woods. She had been out for at least an hour – the guests would have left by now, she hoped. Through the trees, she caught glimpses of the lough, which came right up to the woods on this side of the house. She could smell rotting leaves – the decay of autumn all around her. Reaching the edge of the wood she stooped and wiped her hands on some springy, wet moss, cleaning the mud from them. Dappled light fell through the branches of the trees, making leaves glow red and orange, illuminating lichen-covered rocks and creeping ivy. As a child, Light had seen faces in the trees and the stones. And still she enjoyed the beauty of her surroundings, felt herself in a magical world just to the side of our own.

But there were things that didn't belong in that magical world. Light found what she was looking for at the edge of the woods: a fox trap, as inhumane as they came. It was nothing more than a thin noose of sharp wire, hanging over a barely visible and tiny path through the bushes that an expert tracker would recognise immediately as a fox trail. Light wished her father was still here to help her sabotage the shooting season. When he'd inherited the estate he had not felt up to calling off the traditional shoots – they brought money to the local community – but he had gladly joined Light as she waged her endless guerilla war against traps. These were designed to protect the game birds, but they did so by killing foxes, birds of prey and weasels – and usually in particularly unpleasant ways.

Drying her hands on her trousers, Light crouched in the mid-afternoon sunlight and began to untie the noose. The key was to ruin the slip-knot without disturbing the trap, so that the gamekeeper wouldn't get suspicious.

Engrossed in her work, Light zoned out the noises of the woods – the birdsong, the creaking of the branches, the constant murmur of the lough. She concentrated totally on the task at hand, using her fingernails to prise the wire knot open. Then a small black bird landed on the ground just in front of her, near enough to touch. It cawed at Light. She sat back on her heels, surprised. The bird watched her with intense but friendly eyes.

'Are you the jackdaw I saw in the graveyard?' Light asked. The bird merely peered at her. On an impulse Light reached out, gingerly, to stroke the bird's head, and it submitted to her touch, but then cawed again, louder this time, as if repeating an important point. Light looked around her.

There was a thin crack and Light whirled to face the source of the noise. Something had just broken a twig. She scanned the woods behind her, and her eye was drawn to a movement. Twenty metres away, creeping through the trees, was the figure of a man. Light peered closer, but it was hard to see through the branches. The man was tall, angular, and walked with purpose – towards *her*. A frisson of elementary fear ran through Light – a wordless signal that she felt rather than knew.

Danger.

Run.

Light stood up, ever so quietly, and began pushing her way through the gorse. The jackdaw, having successfully warned her, flew alongside as she moved, occasionally landing on branches just ahead of her and waiting till she came level.

Light wanted to get out of the woods quickly. She didn't know who the strange man was but she could hear the odd crack and rustle as he proceeded through the woods, seeming to follow her. Something about the catlike poise of his gait, the predatory smoothness of his movements, had filled her with a stark and irrational fear. Thorns tore her trousers and cut into her arms. Her breathing was rapid and shallow.

Breaking through the bushes onto one of the larger paths that ran through the woods, Light passed another of her own, hand-painted signs. The jackdaw was sitting on it, patiently waiting for her.

> *Army munitions testing.*
> *Heavy ordnance.*
> *No access at any time.*
> *Risk of death.*

Light had planted signs like this everywhere the beaters and shooters might wander, and she liked nothing more than watching from the windows of the big house as some overdressed aristocrat quickstepped out of the woods, casting worried glances over his shoulder. She hoped it might slow down her pursuer, whoever he was – make him think twice about chasing her through these woods.

A few minutes later Light broke cover at the point where the woods met the gardens of the house, breathing a sigh of relief now that she was back on safe ground, the house visible in front of her with its soaring limestone elevations and its mullioned windows. Light's shadow – the dark, flat girl lying at her feet – was long and falling towards the woods. That told her it was nearly dusk. Light's father had taught her to tell the time by her shadow – he didn't like watches, saying that even as they dressed your wrist they stripped your connection to the earth and its spin, which was what time really boiled down to. Light felt her stomach rumble.

Something brushed her left cheek and then something small and sharp dug into her shoulder. She stopped, turned her head and saw the jackdaw sitting there, bold as brass on her shoulder, gazing at her. 'Careful,' it said.

'Huh?' said Light, shocked.

'*Caw, caw*,' said the jackdaw.

Light shook her head. For a second there . . .

The jackdaw didn't move, just looked at her, and she wasn't sure whether to brush it off or not. Would it bite?

Then Light saw a movement in the corner of her eye, by the side of the house. She spun, saw nothing. There was only the house, standing solidly before her.

'*Caw!* said the jackdaw, insistently. Light turned to look at it and again she felt a tug of movement in the corner of her vision. She snapped her head around and there it was – a large bird of prey careering with ungainly flight over the lawns. It flew clumsily, as if injured, rising high into the air above Light. The jackdaw took off, its claws cutting into Light's skin as it pushed itself into the air. It wheeled towards the woods and vanished.

Light raised her eyes, following the raptor's trajectory. She thought it was a hawk of some kind. The bird hovered above, maybe twenty metres up, its wings tattered and dirty. Then it folded its wings and dropped, suddenly sleek and fast, suddenly dangerous. Instinctively, Light took a step backwards, nervously scanning the ground around her. There must be a rabbit or a mouse somewhere . . .

There was nothing, and the bird was falling fast. She was conscious of a pair of black eyes, cold and malevolent. Then the bird was upon her, plunging, kamikaze-style towards her face. Its beak was hooked and cruel. There was a rush of air and a smell of rotting flesh and Light threw herself face down on the ground, feeling claws tear through her hair. The grass was wet beneath her face. She rolled, feeling the slick cool of dew on her face.

The hawk rose and banked. It hung in the air for a moment and then dropped into its dive again. Light scrambled to her feet, terrified. The bird came in for the attack once more and this time she waited till the last possible moment before diving to the side. The hawk crashed into the ground and there was a snapping sound. The head bent away from the body at an unpleasant angle and the wings flopped to the ground. Light took a small step, nervously, towards it.

'Don't touch it!'

Light saw Butler running towards her across the lawn from the house. His eyes seemed to blaze with an inhuman, yellow light but Light blinked and they were normal again, black and intense. He put an arm around her and started walking her backwards, away from the dead bird. Light was trembling but Butler was impassive, unflappable. His face gave the impression that he had already seen everything that was possible, and so it was impossible that anything could surprise him.

He raised a finger to Light's cheek and touched it gently – when he took his finger away, there was a drop of blood on the tip. 'Beak must have got you,' he said.

Light tried to say something but couldn't, her heart still hammering a rapid tattoo in her chest. Then a dark flock of birds appeared over the roof over the house, flapping and snapping like washing on a line. They were black birds of all sizes, crows and ravens and jackdaws, and they flew towards Light with quick, deft purpose. She sensed no threat from them, though, and Butler did not move as he watched them approach, only stood calmly and waited.

The first bird, a raven, landed on the grass between Light and Butler and the carcass at their feet. Seconds later, it was joined by dozens of others, crows and jackdaws, mostly. The crows were jet black, but the jackdaws wore hoods of shimmering blue and grey.

Cawing and grumbling, the black birds lined up into a neat, straight cordon between Light and Butler and the dead bird. Light thought of riot police, holding back a crowd. Then the birds moved forward in formation. Light stepped back, startled, but Butler gripped her arm. 'Do not offend them,' he said. 'These birds will protect you with their lives.'

From the centre of the line, a large magpie broke away and came closer to Light. It bowed, sweeping its wing before it like a page keeping his coat out of reach of the grubby ground. Automatically, as she had been taught by her father, Light said, 'Good afternoon, Mister Magpie. How are your wife and three daughters?' Then she turned around three times on the spot. She felt like an idiot, and was preparing for some light mockery from Butler when, to her surprise, Butler patted her shoulder encouragingly and nodded at her with grave approval. The magpie nodded too, in acknowledgement.

Butler bowed to the birds and gave a sudden, harsh cry, almost like a squawk. Light stared at him, utterly confused, not understanding what was going on.

Then a movement behind the magpie caused it to whirl around, chittering. The dead hawk stood up, slowly but jerkily, like a clockwork toy that has been left to wind down. The bird was facing away from Light but there was a series of gruesome *ticks* and *tocks* as the bones in its neck cracked, and then its face turned unnaturally to face her. One eye was hanging down, while the other side of its head was completely caved in.

Finally, to Light's horror, the bird started to sing. Its voice was a rumbling creak, as deep and booming as the slow movement of a glacier.

Who could have frozen your poor daddy's heart?
Who could have made his blood run cold?
Who could have iced up every part?
Who could have been so bold?

Light felt goosebumps appear on her arms. Something about the hawk's jerky movements and its croaking voice set off a butterfly buzz inside her and liquefied her legs. Her balance faltered and Butler's grip on her arm tightened. With his other hand, he made a small but deliberate signal to the magpie which had bowed to Light.

The hawk opened its mouth to continue singing, but the magpie gave a quick squawk of command, and the crows, ravens and jackdaws fell on the moving corpse, cawing loudly. With sharp beaks and claws, they reduced the large bird of prey to feathers and blood in seconds. Butler slung Light over his shoulder and strode back to the house.

As Butler carried her to the door, Light watched the woods for movement. Nothing. She closed her eyes. Whatever had been chasing her was gone.

Chapter Four

Invasion

'This might sting,' said Butler, soaking a ball of cotton wool in TCP. He paused. 'Actually, that's a lie.'

'It won't sting?'

'No. It definitely *will* sting.'

Light glared at him. Butler gently cleaned the wound on Light's cheek and, sure enough, she had to clench her teeth against the hot, sharp pain.

Butler and Light sat at the kitchen table, sipping hot, sweet tea. Luckily for them the funeral guests had left before Light's little adventure – and Maeve had gone to pick up the leftover food from the pub.

Light looked at Butler as he prepared a bandage. 'I think someone was following me, in the woods,' she said. 'I ran away and that was when . . . when the bird attacked me.'

Butler looked up sharply. 'Who was following you?' He sounded – and Light could hardly believe this – *frightened.*

'I don't know. I didn't get a good look. It was a man, I think. Very tall. He moved . . . kind of weirdly.'

Butler narrowed his eyes., 'Weirdly how?'

'I don't know . . . like . . . as if it wasn't really a person, just something that looked like a person. Like it was a *thing* wearing a person suit.' She looked at him. 'I'm not describing it very well.'

Butler started to wrap the bandage around Light's wound. 'Nevertheless your description unsettles me. There shouldn't be anyone in the woods, not today. I fear that—'

Butler cut himself off as Maeve walked in, earlier than expected.

She surveyed the horrifying tableau before her: blood, TCP, bandages.

Butler waved a hand in a calming motion. 'It's OK Maeve, really. Just a scratch. No one's hurt.'

'*I'm* hurt,' said Light.

'No one's *badly* hurt,' said Butler.

Maeve recovered some of her composure. She had changed out of her funeral outfit but as usual she was impeccably dressed, in a pale trouser suit and high heels, over a silk blouse. Nevertheless, she hugged Light without hesitation, ignoring the blood that stained her clothes, and stroked her hair. 'My poor girl,' she said. 'What on earth happened?'

'A hawk attacked me,' said Light.

Maeve gasped. 'Really?' she asked.

Butler sighed and explained.

'Well, shouldn't you call someone?' Maeve asked, looking at Butler. 'I don't know . . . the RSPB or something?'

'It's dead. It doesn't need protecting.' Butler stood up and began clearing away the first aid kit and the cotton balls. 'Listen, Maeve, Light and I are tired. Why don't you take the evening off? Perhaps you could take tomorrow off as well.'

'Well . . . I am quite tired, but—'

'But nothing,' Butler insisted. 'You've had a long day. Go home. Come back tomorrow – or the day after tomorrow even. You deserve a rest.'

'I had my day off on Sunday,' Maeve said, clearly seeing the idea of going home as a dereliction of duty. 'I couldn't possibly take another one. What about food for the two of you?'

'We'll be all right, Maeve, honestly,' said Butler. 'We're really not hungry. And if we do feel like something to eat, I'll make some sandwiches later.'

'But you need something hot, after standing outside in the rain like that,' said Maeve. 'Light especially.'

'Then I'll make something hot,' said Butler, a little sharply. 'And besides,' he added, his voice turning gentler, 'I think Light and I need some time alone, to remember Gordon.' Light was sure she saw his eyes flash as he looked at Maeve – they lit with a momentary glow, and Light saw a flicker of confusion cross Maeve's face. Her expression changed from determination to mild puzzlement. She still didn't look happy about the idea but she backed down, giving Light a smile of sympathy. 'All right then. I'll . . . let me see. Where were you? Oh yes. I'll see you both tomorrow, then?' She stroked Light's hair again. 'Feel better, my girl.'

When Maeve left the room, Light hissed, 'What's going on? What did you just do to Maeve?'

Butler silenced her by holding a finger to his lips. He sat perfectly still for several minutes. Then from the hall came the sound of the main door opening. 'Bye then!' called Maeve.

'Bye!' called Butler.

The door slammed and Butler lowered his finger. 'We need to make the house secure,' he said.

'I'm sorry?'

'We need to make the house secure. Come on.' He strode into the hall and dead-bolted the front door. Then he started working his way around the lower floor, locking all the windows. He was a muscular man, and he moved now with grace and purpose.

'Butler,' said Light. 'What's happening? Why did you send Maeve away? You know something about the man I saw in the woods, don't you? Does it have something to do with the bird that attacked me?'

Butler raised a hand to stem her stream of questions. 'We're in danger,' he said. 'That's all I know. Someone bad may be coming.'

'And how do you know that?' Light stopped, one hand on her hip, frowning. Butler didn't reply, just turned and went back to the task of locking windows, checking entry points. Light went to him and grabbed his arm, forcing him to stop. 'Look, Butler,' she said. 'We need to talk about this. What on earth happened with that hawk? It *sang* to me, Butler.'

Butler's shoulders sagged. 'I honestly don't know, Light.'

'And the crows? I've been seeing crows all day. And ravens, and jackdaws. All kinds of black birds.'

'I don't know.'

'You don't know? It seemed like . . . Like you talked to them, or something.'

'Talked to them? They're *birds*. Birds don't talk.' Butler's tone indicated that the conversation was over – yet Light didn't believe a single thing he said.

Butler sighed. 'For now, we protect ourselves. Later, I'll explain. OK?'

'Fine. Whatever you say,' said Light.

Butler sighed and kissed her forehead. 'Something bad is happening, and I need to protect you – the lady of the house. That's my priority right now.'

Light smiled warmly. 'Well, you do know how to make a girl feel special.'

They sat in the drawing room, on the window seat, Butler with a shotgun in his lap. Minutes before a blazing sunset had shafted through the woods outside, making the room glow with red and orange light. Now the sun had dropped completely over the horizon and the room was plunged into a spooky penumbra, shadows criss-crossing the floor and obscuring Butler's features, making them threatening and strange. His face was set in an expression of grim determination. But in the darkness his eyes shone, as if an inner store of light were available to him that was denied to the rest of the world.

In the corner of the room, the old grandfather clock ticked very softly and discreetly, as if to suggest that the passage of time was a vulgar concern that should not be attended to.

But as soon as Light noticed the sound, it seemed to fill the room, tick, *tock*, tick, *tock*, becoming louder and more insistent – quicker, too, as if the house's heartbeat were quickening with anticipation.

41

The door between the drawing room and the hall was locked, enabling the pair to survey the front of the house through the window, while protected by two locked doors between themselves and the outside. Suddenly Butler sprang to his feet, peering out of the mullioned window that gave onto the lawns. Light peered out too, and saw Maeve trudging towards the door of the house. In her hands was a large casserole pot, wrapped in a dishtowel. Steam rose from it in the cold night air.

Butler shook his head. 'Oh, Maeve,' he said.

The window was bay-shaped, which enabled them to follow Maeve easily with their eyes, even when she was standing on the porch. The porch light illuminated her perfectly. She raised her hand to ring the doorbell and—

Crunch!

There was a sickening impact that seemed to ring in Light's teeth as a dark, tall figure ran into Maeve at full tilt from the side. The figure lifted her easily and slammed her into a marble pillar supporting the porch.

The casserole dish dropped to the ground and smashed.

Butler gasped as if in pain. Light gasped too – she had seen this man before. It was the figure that had stalked her through the woods.

Light heard a high-pitched scream, a long word in the language of terror – all vowels and no consonants. It was several moments before she realised the scream was coming from herself, and even then only because Butler clamped his hand over her mouth. 'Stay here,' said Butler. 'Don't move.' He handed her the shotgun and unlocked the door to the hall. 'I'm going to get Maeve.'

'Wait—'

'Yes?'

'That man . . . he's the one I saw in the woods.'

Butler simply nodded as if this confirmed some previously held suspicion. His face was set in a fierce expression of anger, and when he rolled up his sleeves Light could swear she saw the black tattoos on his arms writhe and move, sliding inkily down towards his hands. She blinked in surprise and Butler let himself through the door and padded, silently, to the front door of the house. Light watched him go, unconsciously hugging the shotgun.

It was only when he had already left the room, locking her in, that Light thought to wonder how he would defend himself. 'What about your gun?' she asked the empty room. She slumped into the window seat. Maeve had been hurt and now Butler was walking into danger armed with nothing more than his fists. Fear had taken root in her body, inside and out, and the effect was extreme enough that she almost giggled in wonder. Her heart hammered in her chest and her stomach *swooshed* unpleasantly, as if her viscera had turned to liquid. Her hands and legs shook violently.

Light pushed her face up to the window. She could hear Butler creeping towards the front door. On the porch, the figure stood, stretching its body with apparent pride, like an athlete after a good performance. It was a man – or something like a man – with a tall, heavyset body and long, thin arms that contrasted oddly with the muscular bulk of the torso, like ivy hanging from the trunk of a massive oak. It – *he* – was wearing furs of some kind. What was this thing doing on Light's porch, in the twenty-first century? The figure took a step towards the bay window

43

but at that moment Butler burst out of the front door, seeming somehow taller and larger than Light remembered him. The figure whipped around and then, apparently unintimidated by Butler, cackled throatily. It lashed out with one of its slender, elongated arms.

Butler ducked under the punch then surged forwards, barrelling into the strange figure. He immediately lifted his feet off the ground, carrying his body over the other man in an elegant somersault. His feet, arcing above his twisting body in a smooth parabola, smashed into the hanging light bulb, plunging the porch into darkness. Light peered out of the window, trying to make out what was happening. She got a vague impression of a large, swirling black shape, like a cloak (*or wings*) and then there was nothing. Butler and the man had both disappeared completely.

Light cupped her hands over her eyes and tried to distinguish movement in the darkness. Where was Butler? Was he hurt? All she could see was her own reflection, pale and wavering, as if the window were showing her what she would look like as a ghost.

Then where her face had been was suddenly another – this one the face of the strange man, its features white, gaunt and angular. Light screamed in terror.

Impassive, the thing gazed in. It spoke, its words sounding clearly through the ancient, single-paned window. 'Spying on me, little girl? Tsk, tsk.'

The man spoke in a strange, lisping voice and said 'tsk' the same way it was written – as if he wasn't all that familiar with human language, and was reading from a script. Light staggered backwards with fear. What was this thing?

Then the man smiled and blinked and Light gasped.

Because his eyelids moved sideways, just like a cat's. The irises – too narrow, too vertical – were the cold, pale blue of an iceberg.

Her mind disconnected by terror, Light pointed the shotgun automatically at the face. Her finger – operating on its own – pulled the trigger. Light was instantly deafened by the gun's detonation, and the stock recoiled painfully against her shoulder. The glass of the window shattered outwards onto the lawn and the leading twisted, leaving a gaping hole.

But in the chaos of the noise and the muzzle flash Light couldn't see whether she'd hit him or not.

Just as her hearing began to return, the intruder crashed through the newly opened hole, landing on all fours on the drawing-room floor, before springing to his feet. Blood poured from multiple cuts on his face and hands, but it was impossible to tell if these resulted from the gunshot or from breaking through the glass. His skin was chalky white, his eyes large as eggs and his teeth sharp – filling a mouth that was fixed in a rictus grin devoid of humour. The structure of his body – of his facial bones – was almost, but not quite, human.

'What do you want?' Light asked, her trembling body betraying her, making the words come out in a weak vibrato.

'I want *you*,' the man replied. 'You were supposed to come to us. But you did not come. Now we have come to you.'

Light's eyes widened with shock, making the room appear suddenly brighter. The attacker smiled sardonically and flashed sideways, a blur of movement, and then was standing in front of Light, the gun no longer in Light's hand but in his. He reached out his free hand to touch her face.

Light whipped her left hand out and blocked him, the speed of her own reflexes taking her by surprise. Unfortunately, she had not the slightest idea what to do next. She could feel the man's tendons and muscle moving like snakes under his skin, and she didn't have the strength to hold him for long. His skin was cold and surprisingly hard – as if he were a simulacrum made of porcelain, or milky ice. Feeling a rush of dread in her stomach (*that's not real skin that's not real that's not living skin*) Light was powerless to maintain the grip of her fingers.

She let go.

A smile appeared on the man's face.

In that split second of his distraction, Light let her right hand shoot out and grabbed the gun, twisting it out of his hand.

Shotguns have two shots, don't they?

They'd better *have two shots.*

She was not aware of thinking about the stratagem. She simply let her body become deadweight and dropped hard, backwards, to the ground.

Now she was lying on her back, looking up at the startled intruder. She brought the gun up to a near-45-degree angle and fired, hitting the man in the chest and blowing him backwards. He was driven with considerable force into the back wall of the drawing room, smashing through it and disappearing from the waist up into the dark gap behind. Brick dust and lumps of plaster rained down on his legs and feet, which flopped over the hole in the wall like the limbs of a discarded puppet.

The recoil from the shotgun had ploughed the stock into Light's diaphragm, winding her badly. She gasped for breath, dropped the gun and clutched her throbbing trigger finger, which had been twisted by the force of the gun's backwards movement. Once again, her ears sang with painful, metallic resonance. In the watery rushing of her deafness, three words flashed again and again through her mind.

I killed someone. I killed someone.

Paralysed, Light could only lie helpless. She felt sick – with the adrenaline, but also with what she had done, even if it was in self-defence. Even flies she would try to catch rather than kill.

She heard the tinkle of falling glass, made distant and ethereal by the thick muffling of the gunshot that still echoed in her ears. She tried to sit up but her stomach muscles wouldn't lift her. Then a face loomed over hers: it was the same man. He'd survived a point-blank shotgun blast and now he'd come back for her and—

No. Not the same man: this one didn't have cuts on his face. This was a different man, one who must have just climbed in through the window. He only *looked* the same.

'Brave girl,' he said. 'You kill my friend.' His accent, like the other's, was guttural and liquid, as if he were speaking underwater. He looked over at the fireplace where the body had landed. 'Actually, no.'

'He . . . he's not dead?' Light asked, weakly.

'Oh, he is dead.' The man smirked, his white flesh stretching, becoming almost translucent around his mouth. There was a powerful smell of the sea coming from him, of fish and salt water. 'But he is not my friend. Only my . . . what would you say? My fellow worker-person.'

47

'Your colleague?' Light suggested, a little voice at the back of her mind screaming at her to *shut up shut up run run run.*

'Yes, that is right. Now you come with me.'

Light started scrabbling at the thick Persian carpet, trying to pull herself backwards, her body still trying to save itself even as her mind told her there was no chance. She didn't know where this thing wanted to take her, but she knew it couldn't be good. The creature gave a couple of those sideways blinks – almost like applause – and smiled down at her with approval. 'Brave, like I say. I tell you, to me it is seeming an impressive thing, this shooting of my colleague. But I am thinking that Frost will be angry with you.' He hugged himself and shivered, making a *brr* sound like someone trying to warm themselves up. 'This is sad for you.'

Something about this little speech filled Light with horror and she made one last, enormous effort – and managed only to prop herself up on her elbows. The gun clattered to the floor beside her, and the man casually reached down to shove her to the ground again. She felt tears welling up in her eyes.

There was a crash from the door to Light's right and at the same time it seemed to her that the odour of fish increased dramatically, going from a smell to a stink. A vast bulk filled her peripheral vision, striding quickly towards the man who was no longer leaning over her but standing, perplexed and – Light thought – frightened. Then something happened too fast for her to see and the intruder was still standing but his head was gone, and then the tall body wavered from side to side and fell, straight as a tree, to the ground.

48

Light screamed and closed her eyes, seeking solace in blindness. When she opened them again, the newcomer was leaning over her.

Light stared, too scared to move or speak.

The thing above her was only a man from the waist down. He didn't even have a neck – above his shoulders was only the smooth white expanse of a huge shark's head, pock-marked and glistening. Light registered, with numb shock, that there was no visible point of attachment, no obvious sign of how the costume had been made. The shark's head and the man's skin were joined seamlessly – although criss-crossing the border between them were pale pink scars that looked like the ghosts of old, thick stitches.

It *wasn't* a costume. Light had known that at first sight.

The shark's mouth opened, revealing rows of gleaming, serrated teeth.

Light was filled with raw, atavistic fear – what the deer feels when it sees the shadow of the wolf. She froze, as the jaws opened wide.

Then Light heard quick footsteps and Butler came running into the room, stopping dead when he saw the man standing over Light. The shark's head raised and turned towards Butler, the tip of the nose seeming to quiver. The man took a step towards Butler, arms outstretched.

Light fainted.

Chapter Five

Mission

When Light woke she was lying on one of the couches in the living room, covered with a woollen blanket which itched the bare skin of her arms. Butler was sitting beside her on a chair, looking at her with a concerned expression. He had filled the room with little lamps and candles, which cast a warm, flickering glow on the bookcases and comfortable furniture of the cosy room.

Light felt a flood of relief, mingled with confusion. How had Butler possibly survived against the shark-headed man?

She looked at him, sitting there, unfazed as always. 'You're alive,' she said. Then she began to babble. 'Thank God you're OK, I was so scared, and I didn't know what to do and I couldn't lose you as well and . . .'

'Sssh,' Butler said. 'You're all right now.'

Light suddenly remembered something. 'Maeve?' she asked, urgently. 'Is she . . .?'

'She's fine. Shaken, but not badly hurt. A couple of broken ribs. I called an ambulance to take her to the hospital. She believes that we were the victims of a robbery, but for obvious reasons I have not called the police.'

Light felt hot tears on her cheeks. 'I thought you'd been *killed*,' she said. 'I was so scared.'

'I apologise. I should not have left you for so long. Though it looks like you handled yourself well. There is a rather large hole in the wall of the front room.'

'Sorry. I just . . .' Light felt a choking sensation in her throat, as realisation sank in. 'I shot someone. I *killed* him, Butler.'

'He was trying to kill you,' Butler said gently.

'It doesn't matter. He was *alive* and he could *speak* and . . .' Her tears flowed now, strangling her voice as she spoke. 'And I was so scared . . . you weren't there, and I shot him dead, and then another one came in but he died and then there was a monster in the room and I thought it would kill you—'

'Ah, yes,' said a voice from Light's other side. 'I'm sorry for startling you.'

Light turned. Standing, one hand on the back of the couch, was the man from the front room.

He *still* had a shark's head.

Light screamed and rolled away, falling off the couch and onto the floor. She scrambled to her feet, trying to run, but Butler snapped up from his chair and held her round the waist. She struggled to get away.

'Don't worry,' Butler said, calmly. 'He's a friend. He saved you from the attacker.' Turning to the stranger, Butler glared. 'That's what you call *breaking it to her gently*?' he hissed.

In her mind's eye, Light saw her assailant in the front

51

room leaning over, threatening – then the sudden movement, an impression of heavy bulk in motion, and his body suddenly swaying, headless, before toppling to the ground. Was it possible? Had this monster only wanted to *help* her? He had killed the other man, it was true . . .

'You . . . you . . . you have a shark's head,' said Light, a little lamely. She was sure that she would wake up again in a moment and Butler would be dead and the world would be cold and grey and empty of such miracles.

'Yes,' said the shark-man, through a mouth full of teeth. Light marvelled at the way the man's voice came from that great, inhuman head. The opening and shutting of the mouth didn't seem to correspond exactly with the sounds coming out of it, as if the voice were generated magically, and not by any of the usual vocal apparatus – vocal cords, tongue, throat. The accent was American, or Canadian maybe, with no hint of the glutinous quality so evident in the voices Light had heard from her attackers.

'This . . . man . . . comes from the Far North, like your mother and me,' said Butler. 'I'm sorry. This is a lot for you to take in.'

'That's not a man, Butler,' said Light, who was having trouble dealing with a world in which men went around with sharks' heads attached to their bodies.

'No,' said Butler. 'But once he was one.'

Light turned to the monster. 'What—'

She'd been about to ask, 'What are you?' but she decided that was rude, so she switched mid-sentence and turned it into, 'What are you called?'

The thing smiled, showing its sharp teeth. The result was disquieting.

 52

'You can call me Tupilak,' it replied, not precisely answering Light's question. Somehow, the answer seemed to say more than the words alone – implying, with mere inflection, that the man with the shark's head had other names; that Tupilak was a simplification of sorts; and that names, anyway, were less than entirely necessary.

Tupilak stepped forwards into the circle of golden light cast by one of the table lamps. 'I am honoured to make your acquaintance, Lady Fitzwilliam.'

'Light,' said Light, weakly.

Tupilak nodded, his massive head moving slowly. 'Light,' he said, as if to test the word on his tongue. 'A good name.'

Light examined Tupilak. She had only noticed the head before – now she realised that his legs were not human, either. They were covered in white fur.

'Polar bear,' said Tupilak, following her eyes.

Tupilak was at least seven feet tall. On the skin of his head, drops of water shimmered in the lamplight, slowly descending the face before dripping to the floor. Black, knowing eyes gleamed above the powerful nose – below it, the mouth was twisted into what could have been intended as a smile. Towards the base of the head, nearly overlapping with the human skin of the neck, a neat row of parallel wounds slashed the skin, as if inflicted by a large animal's claws. Then Light realised – those weren't wounds, they were gills.

He took another step forwards and Light jerked back instinctively. Butler looked into her eyes. 'I promise you, Light. You are safe. This man saved your life.'

'I know,' said Light. 'I was there.' She gave him a weak smile.

'You must be wondering what's happening,' said Tupilak. Light looked at him, then at Butler. 'You could say that.'

Tupilak paced up and down. Any doubt Light might have had that the impossible head might be anything but a costume vanished when she saw him move. She could see the muscles working under the pale, pock-marked skin of the head, could see the little black eyes following her own. On the powerfully-muscled torso, tattoos similar to Butler's swirled, covering all the exposed skin, acting almost like clothing. Spirals, abstract shapes that could have been deer, birds and fish and whales. The human part of the body, too, was powerful. Muscles moved thickly and gracefully under the tattooed skin – snakes gliding under carpet. Tupilak seemed unsure how to start, so Light prompted him. 'Who were those men who attacked us?' she asked.

Tupilak shook his head. 'I am sorry. I don't know.'

'You don't know, or you don't want to tell me?'

He cocked his head to one side, looking at her. 'I don't know. And I don't think we could ask them now.' An image sprang, unbidden, into Light's mind: the headless body, blood gouting from its neck. She felt sick. Exhausted, she sat back down on the couch. 'I believe,' went on Tupilak, seeing that she was upset, 'that they were . . . there is no word in your language. *Kivigtok*. Bad men. No longer men, really. They are creatures who leave the human world behind, and depart for the wilderness. Soon, the wilderness is in them as well as around them. They are better off dead, I assure you.'

'But what were they *doing* here?' insisted Light.

'They wanted you,' said Tupilak, simply. 'I was sent here to stop them.'

'What? Who sent you?'

'Sctna entrusted me with this mission of saving your life. It is a great honour.' The way he said it made it clear that the honour lay in being trusted by Setna, not in saving Light's life.

'*Setna?*' she asked.

'Yes, Setna. My creator – or my saviour, perhaps. She is a woman . . .' He twirled his hand in the air, as if trying to think of a word on the tip of his tongue. '. . . A goddess, maybe . . . who lives under the sea and controls all the creatures of the deep. She determines the result of fishing expeditions – when men wish to catch a fish or a whale, it is Setna who decides when they will succeed and when they will return home with nothing but empty nets and unbloodied spears. And she decides when Tupilak must cross the ocean and come to visit you.'

'I know who Setna is,' said Light. Her father and Butler had told her a story once about this strange Inuit goddess of the sea, kindly but bloodthirsty, wise but cruel. She lived on the sea floor, sitting on a throne of whale bones. That someone should mention her as if she were a neighbour, or an employer – a thing of casual existence – was an absurdity.

Worse, a monstrosity.

'I just didn't think she existed,' Light went on. 'I thought she was . . . you know . . . a story for children.' Looking at the very real jagged teeth of the shark-headed man in front of her, Light felt the ridiculousness of what she had just said. This man didn't come from a children's story. He came from a world Light hadn't known existed – a world where life and death and magic and gods were just there, on the other side of the air. A world of blood and snow and cold, grey sea.

Then something Tupilak had said struck her.

'You crossed the *ocean* to visit me?'

'Yes,' said Tupilak, simply. 'In my kayak.'

'In a *kayak*? That must have taken days. Why would you do that?'

Tupilak looked at her blankly, his round, black eyes unblinking. 'Because Setna told me to. Luckily, the lough connects to the sea. I paddled up the River Bann.' He looked down at his furry legs. 'At night, obviously.'

'OK,' said Light. 'But *why* did she send you?'

Tupilak brought his hand up and scratched his – well, his chin, she supposed. 'In the towns of the North – in Alaska and Nunavut and Canada – a great many people have gone missing. This is peculiar and sad, of course, although Setna does not as a rule concern herself unduly with people. But then the seals started to disappear, too. Setna is fond of seals.'

'Charming.'

Tupilak ignored her. 'Something bad is at work in the Arctic – a monster. This monster has been spoken of for many years. Many centuries. But even Setna has never seen him. He is called Angutagiuppiniq.'

Light processed the parts of the Inuktitut word. 'Snow . . . man?' she ventured.

'Frost,' said Butler. 'That's what the English-speaking Inuit call him.' He shuddered involuntarily. 'But most avoid mentioning his name. He does not appear in any of the Inuit tales, for fear that invoking him might attract his attention. He is . . .' Butler searched for the words. 'He is worse than a monster. He is the cold. And he is Death. To meet him is to be lost. This is why none can say what he looks like.'

'All those years you and dad taught me, and you never told me you were Inuit,' said Light to Butler, reproachfully. Now that she thought about it, it made sense. Those vaguely Asian features, his facility with Inuktitut . . . but she had never had it confirmed before today.

'My past is . . . That is to say . . . there are things I would rather forget,' said Butler. 'I would have told you, eventually.'

Light could never stay angry with Butler for long. 'You met my father on one of his research trips?'

Butler nodded. 'He is my greatest friend. When he moved back here, with your mother, he asked me to come too. I never regretted it. You have been as a daughter to me.' His voice broke a little.

Light smiled at Butler. 'I know.' She glanced at Tupilak. 'You two . . . know each other?'

Butler shook his head. 'No. But I have heard of the creature called a *tupilak*. It is made of different animals, joined together – a patchwork monster. Like you, I didn't think these things were real. Besides, in all the stories, *tupilak* are dangerous, mindless things, created by bad shamans to destroy their enemies.'

Tupilak grinned and bowed. 'Your servant. But rest assured, I am only dangerous to your enemies.' Then he stepped forwards and took Light's hand. His hand was warm, soft and human. Light wasn't sure what she had been expecting, but the familiar skin seemed peculiar, as if the monstrous head should only exist with a monstrous body. 'Setna believes that only you can stop Frost,' he said. 'And save the people of the North.' He looked at Light, registering her skinny frame, pale skin and white hair. 'Why she believes this I do not know.'

Light didn't respond to the veiled insult. 'And what does Setna want me to do about it?'

Butler sat down beside Light. 'According to Tupilak, she wants us to go to the North. To the Arctic. She thinks that you can defeat Frost.'

'But she's never even seen him! I mean, if she exists, which . . . well, even that's crazy. This whole story is crazy! This . . . *thing*' – she waved at Tupilak, who looked wounded – 'wants me to go off to the Arctic and you' – she glared at Butler – 'don't even seem to think that's odd! I can't just . . . I mean, I'm supposed to be getting an education and—'

Light broke off, looking at Tupilak. 'What if I fail? What if I *die*?' She felt the kind of sloshing, thrilling fear that comes when you stand too close to a precipice.

'I'm sorry. I cannot predict the future,' Tupilak replied.

'Why not? You seem to know a lot about everything else.'

'Because I cannot predict a future that does not exist. Do you think Frost will stop there, killing a few people and some animals in the Far North, where nobody cares what happens? No, if Setna is right, he will eventually destroy the world. He hates everything that is warm and living. He has been biding his time for many years. And now the cold is being pushed back – the ice is melting. It has made him angry.'

Light gaped.

'Light,' said Butler gently. He held her other hand. On either side of her, the shark-man and the old family retainer bent down, solemn, solicitous. 'Frost will find you, whether we go or not. Those men, tonight – it's likely that he sent them. Better that we go and face him, rather than wait here like prey.' He coughed. 'And . . . there's something else.' He nodded to Tupilak.

The tooth-filled mouth opened, close to her face, and reflexively Light flinched.

'Butler is right,' he said. 'There is something else. Something important.' He paused and Light stared at him, head spinning. 'Setna believes that Frost has your father.'

Light blinked. Hope was a hot tearing in her throat. 'My . . . is he . . .?'

'Yes,' said Tupilak. 'He's alive.'

Chapter Six

Fisherman

Light sat in the window seat in her room. She held a mug of hot tea, which Butler had brewed before going off with Tupilak to deal with the corpses. Light was amazed by the power of her mind to assimilate the impossible. Only today she had been attacked by a talking bird, then rescued from cat-eyed, lanky men by a man with polar-bear legs and a shark's head. And yet here she was, drinking a cup of tea and thinking seriously about travelling to the Arctic to rescue her father – who only recently she had given up for dead, after months of waiting by the phone – from a monster so terrifying that even the storybooks wouldn't mention him.

Her head swam. She looked at the image of her face in the surface of the tea, warped and wobbling. It seemed a reflection of the change that had come upon her, of the new, confused Light, trembling with fear and hope.

Light gazed out of the window at the lough. She wished she could go down there, but she was afraid that more of the sideways-blinking men might be out there, waiting for her. From the night sky the moon shone down, making a path of white light that ran from the pebbly shore all the way out to the shoreless horizon. Light wished she could follow it and get away from this place – from this decision, from these responsibilities she was being saddled with. The light of the moon always comforted her, touched a secret part of her inner being and evoked in her a strange feeling of pure emotion, of happy-sadness, something akin to looking at a photo of a loved one who is far away.

With one hand, Light traced the letters that were etched onto the corner of her window.

Lucas Fitzwilliam,
ob: 1624

Her father had told her the story. Lucas was a nephew of Mad Eric's, who had come to Neagh House to complete his education as a gentleman. Almost immediately, he had fallen in love with one of the maids. He had proposed, but she knew her place – and Mad Eric's infamous temper – and so had refused, though she did truly love him. Heartbroken, Lucas had cut his own brief epitaph into the glass before jumping to the gravel path, three storeys below.

Light had often thought of him, and the hopelessness that had pushed him to his extreme decision. Now she envied him his certainty: he had lost his love, so he had died. How Light wished that her choices were so clear! Should she go with Tupilak and Butler? They said her father lived . . . but they couldn't be sure. What if nothing could bring him back? Wouldn't trying – hoping – only make her grief all the worse in the end? Or should even a tiny possibility of his return send her on this crazy mission to the frozen North? She missed him so much that it was like a bird trapped in her chest, flapping wildly, looking for an exit.

In her hands, Light turned over the compass her father had given her before leaving. It was an antique – a fat, round masterpiece of brass and leather. On the rear was inscribed a dove, holding an olive branch in its beak. A scroll surrounded the image, bearing the Latin motto *Spero Meliora*. Light knew from her father that it meant 'I hope for more', and was supposed to be a sort of inspirational message.

On the front of the compass, the cardinal points were carefully inscribed around the edge of the dial in faded gold foil. One point was still gleaming, as if the gold leaf had only recently been applied:

North

As Light rotated the heavy, smooth old object in her hand – it felt so right, so warm – the needle turned always back to north. Her father had said, 'Whenever you look at it, it will point towards me. You will always know where I am.'

Light heard a knock on the door and quickly put the

compass away in her pocket, wiping away the tears on her face with her other sleeve. She turned.

'Butler told me you would be here, looking at the lake,' Tupilak said.

'It's a lough.'

'Lough. Lake. It's not enough for you that I speak to you in your own language?'

'Sorry.' Light looked out at the silver water, interrupted by the dark shapes of swans and geese, the weeping willows that lowered their branches to the water.

Tupilak took Light by the hand. 'Come. Show me the lough. You should not be inside, worrying.'

Light swallowed. 'What if those men are still here?'

'There are no men. If there are, I will bite them.' He snapped his teeth shut with a very final sounding *click*.

'OK, then.' She'd seen what those teeth could do.

Light led the way downstairs and out, through the front gardens, to the jetty. It jutted out straight into the water, long enough to appear narrower at the end. It glistened in the moonlight, strung with waterweed.

A question occurred to her, as she looked at the blank surface of the water. 'How did you eat? You said you came across the ocean in a kayak.'

'Sea creatures,' said Tupilak.

'Sea creatures? Like what? Fish?'

'Fish, yes. Some squid. A dolphin.'

'You ate a *dolphin*?' Light asked, shocked. She turned to stare at the big man with his shark's head. 'How *could* you?'

'Well, it wasn't easy. I had to tear out its throat. Then I

63

ate the fins. But the body was very heavy. It was necessary to strike a balance between eating too quickly, and making myself sick, or slowing myself down with the weight of the thing. Not easy, as I said.'

'That's not what I meant.' Light felt sick. 'You can't just go around eating dolphins,' she said. 'They're *friendly*.' It was axiomatic: sharks were nasty and dolphins were nice. Yet here she was talking to a friendly man who was half shark and thought nothing of eating dolphins.

'Why not?' asked Tupilak, looking confused. 'They eat fish.'

Light opened her mouth to reply but couldn't think of a word to say.

Tupilak sat down on the bench, suddenly serious.

'Why is it . . .' he hesitated, sounding embarrassed. 'Why is it that you don't look like your father?'

Light jumped to her feet. 'You *knew* my father?'

'Perhaps I knew him, perhaps Setna knew him. I cannot say.'

She caught the change to the past tense, and it made her wonder whether her father really was alive or not. 'You don't know, or you're not allowed to say?'

'I cannot say.'

Light whistled with irritation and sat down again. 'Never a straight answer.'

'And you – you didn't answer me. Why is your skin so pale? Why are your eyes so pink? And why is your hair so white?'

'All the better to confuse you with.'

'Sorry?'

'Nothing. A stupid joke. I'm an albino,' Light explained.

'My body doesn't produce pigment. Most of the time, outside, I have to wear sunglasses. The light damages my eyes. And my skin too.'

Tupilak stood, considering. 'Then it is good that you are going to the North at this time of year. The winter darkness is beginning.' He said this – that she was going to the North – as if it was a *fait accompli*.

Light shivered. 'I haven't made my mind up yet. For a start, I don't know anything about you.'

Tupilak gazed out at the lough. 'Ah, well, that is easy. First, you must understand that I was a man once. A fisherman, an Inuit like your mother. I was a very good fisherman. Whenever I killed – a seal or a white whale or a fish – I treated the *inua* of the animal with respect. That is the animal's soul, and it is important to treat it with reverence. For four days after the kill, I would close myself off alone, not talk to anyone. I would cleanse myself, keep myself away from knives or women. And I would leave the carcass by the sea so that the *inua* could return to the water and become another animal. That is why I was such a good fisherman.'

At this, Tupilak stood and dived off the jetty. Light was taken aback. She stood and peered over the edge, seeing a dark shape move under the water. She crouched, the wetness of the wood soaking through the knees of her trousers. She could smell the mineral scent of fresh water. There was no more movement in the water, no sign of the shadow that had been Tupilak. She leaned forwards.

Like a torpedo, the shark's head surged out of the water towards her, splashing her with white spray. Light fell backwards, spluttering. Tupilak stood in front of her, offered her a hand to pull her to her feet, then opened his mouth to reveal a silver fish swimming in a pool of water between his teeth. He laughed and swallowed.

'See? In time, the animals of the sea came to know of me. They trusted me to keep their *inua* safe, and so they would offer themselves to me again and again. I became a powerful man – lots of goods to trade, lots of respect. You seem like a good girl. You may never know how tempting power can be. Anyway. The other men became jealous of me. One day when I was fishing in my kayak, they followed me and ambushed me. With their harpoons they speared me and with their axes they chopped me up. Then they dropped the pieces in the ocean. My head they took home to show the others.

'But Setna saw me and took pity. She knew of the respect I showed to her creatures. My head was gone, of course, but she called on the shark that had just eaten my legs, and asked it for a sacrifice. It consented, because no creature denies Setna. Then she called a bear, and asked it for a sacrifice too. The shark and the bear consented, because Setna is their mistress. And they gave up their bodies to her.'

'What happened to the men who killed you?'

'I waited in the sea for their return, for the next time they hunted. Then I killed them. Some I drowned, tearing holes in their kayaks and holding them under with my hands. Some I tore apart with my shark's teeth. All of them died.'

Light felt a little sick. 'Shouldn't you have . . . I don't

 66

know. Turned the other cheek? Didn't Setna mind you taking revenge like that?'

Tupilak laughed. 'Setna is not like your God. She is capricious and cruel. She is also compassionate and kind. But she is not above revenge. And anyway' – he turned his head and opened his wedge-shaped mouth, revealing rows of serrated teeth – 'there is no point in turning my cheek. The other is just as sharp.' He smiled at his own joke. 'I think there is something you don't understand: in the North, our lives are driven by revenge. When we kill a seal or a fish, we must make sure not to waste any of it. Otherwise its spirit will be avenged on us. And we cannot grow food. Only by killing can we live. Do you see? In the North, *life* is revenge.'

'Not for me.'

'Yes, for you. Are you not Inuit?'

'Only half. And I don't believe in revenge.'

Tupilak sighed. 'Let me tell you a story.' He stood up and began pacing up and down the jetty. 'Once when we all lived in the snow and no one lived anywhere else there was an obstinate man who had taken a wife, and he was a cruel man so he beat her. When he wanted to make it an extra special beating he took a stick and hit her with that. One day, when he had been beating her as usual, she ran away. She was pregnant at the time. She ran into the sea and was nearly drowned, and when she woke up again she saw that she was on the bottom of the sea. She built herself a house there and had her child.

'When she saw the child she had given birth to she was horrified: his hair was seaweed, his eyes were pearls and

67

his mouth was a mussel that opened and closed. The child grew up and she loved it as well as she could, until one day it was listening to the children playing on the land above, and it felt lonely and said, "I should like to go up and play with the other children."

'"When you are stronger, then you can go and play," she answered. And so her strange sea-creature of a son began making himself strong, carrying large rocks along the seabed and fighting with sharks.

'One day she saw that he was strong enough. The children above were playing boisterously. "Now I will go with you up to the air," said the woman. "But before you go and play you must visit the house where my husband and family live, for they will want to meet you. When you see them, you must make yourself very frightening indeed, for that is a good game and will make them laugh."

'Her son obeyed her and went to the house where her husband still lived. He made a fierce face and glowered through the door, and everyone inside died of fright. The boy was sad, because he had only wanted to play, but his mother was happy, because the man who had tormented her was dead. She came and caught her son and carried him away to the Far North, where no people lived, and they became *kivigtoks* there, and gave their faith to Frost.'

This was the word Tupilak had used earlier about the men who had attacked the house. From Light's memory of Inuktitut lessons, she thought it meant something like *outcast*. 'That's a horrible story.'

'No. It is simply life in the North. If you wish to save your father, you will need to open your eyes – you will need to hurt those who would hurt you. Frost's people –

they never hesitate. They would kill you with the ease that they would kill a fish. You will need to become like them. You will need to accept that your destiny requires you to kill.'

Light looked into the deep black eyes of the shark-head. 'Never,' she said.

Chapter Seven

Shadow

It was very late at night, and everybody slept.

In the drawing room, planks had been nailed across the broken window to protect against the worst of the wind. Still, cold air stole through the gaps and cracks, prying like frosty fingers into the room. The bodies had disappeared – where they had lain was only a dark and silent staining of the carpet and the air, a scent of violence, dumbly testifying to the death that had happened here.

The hole in the wall where the shotgun blast had thrown the first intruder back had not been patched up – what was the point, after all? It was not open to the elements, or to other intruders. The hole didn't even penetrate to the living room on the other side: the house had been built in the old style, with hollow walls of stone separated by a gap a foot wide, providing both structural soundness and insulation.

Now, while the house slept, a shadow slipped out from the gap between the walls, slinking over the broken

 70

bricks and onto the carpet of the room. The shadow was not attached to anything – it lay flat on the ground, spread out, a black wetsuit waiting to be worn. When it moved it became a circle of darkness, scanning the ground like the beam of a torch that shines with blackness not light.

The shadow was angry. Three hundred years before it had been trapped between the walls of this house like a caged beast. For three hundred years it had walked only in the narrow corridor of the gap, and its mind had become dark with dreams of revenge.

The man who had built Neagh House – Light's ancestor, known to most as Mad Eric – had been an amateur archaeologist, interested above all in the myths of the Greek islands and the Balkans. One of these myths especially intrigued him – the one which said that a new house must be given a soul by walling someone up inside it to die. Or, failing that (because even in 1604 the authorities might have had something to say) you could ask someone to stand in the sun at a certain time of day, then brick up their shadow.

It was believed that anyone allowing their shadow to be imprisoned in this way would die within the year, but this did not concern Mad Eric. It was up to the servant girl to worry about that – and she was unlikely to, since he hadn't told her. The Fairy Queen had been very specific about that, when Mad Eric had spoken to her (indeed, speaking with the fairies was one of the popular inspirations for Mad Eric's nickname). She had provided the girl, too, got her from God knows where and brought her to him, daisies in her hair. Probably snatched at birth, replaced with a fairy changeling. No doubt a mother somewhere played half-heartedly with an unsmiling girl, the blankness of stone in her eyes, unaware that her true daughter had been taken from her.

Sure enough, the girl died within the year, drowned in Lough Neagh (her name was Mary, but in its endless rage the shadow forgot even this, and Mad Eric never knew it in the first place). Her shadow remained, watching over the house from within the walls, willing its captor to die. Sadly, though, Mad Eric lived a long and happy life – that is, until the drought of 1647. When the crops failed and the local farmers began to starve, they went to Mad Eric for help – but he turned them away with nothing more nutritious than a curse and a rather rude gesture.

Within days, he was hanged, drawn and halved in a miniature peasant uprising. Several of the village horses having died of thirst or malnutrition, the men had been unable to muster four in order to carry out the traditional hanging, drawing and quartering, and so had had to settle for pulling from each end, and halving the old git instead. A carthorse and a donkey were procured for the purpose, and these were attached, facing in opposite directions, to the legs and the arms of the solidly-built lord. Unfortunately, the carthorse proved to be significantly stronger, and so to begin with the donkey was simply dragged along the ground backwards, an absurd imbalance which the peasants (once they finished laughing) attempted to remedy by grabbing the donkey and hauling.

In the end, this gruesome tug-o-war was fought between the carthorse on one side, and on the other side a donkey, ten farm labourers and a milkmaid (she was a very *large* milkmaid, who it was said could crush a man's skull in her hand, and milk his brains through his nose). By the time Mad Eric's body finally gave up the struggle and divided itself, spilling his guts on the ground, the fun had gone out of the whole thing and no one even cheered.

Except for the shadow. The shadow cheered and gambolled, and pranced through the hollow walls in delight. Since then it had done whatever it could to take revenge. It whispered through the walls to the sixth lord, telling him his son was an effete parasite who wanted him dead, turning him against his own flesh and blood. Eventually the lord would no longer speak to his prodigal offspring, electing instead to install message tubes throughout the house so that he could torment his son without leaving his room. Whether reading in the drawing room or taking a mug of cocoa in the kitchen, the son would sooner or later hear the *whoosh* of the pneumatic system and a tube would drop from the pipes, bearing a message of madness and bitterness. 'I will never let you inherit, weakling.'

Of course, there was only one possible outcome. One dark night, while thunder crashed outside, the old lord suffered a terrible accident, when a pillow was held with some force over his face, cutting off his breathing. From the walls, the shadow listened and giggled.

But now the shadow was free, and it sensed that its true revenge was near. Earlier that evening, it had listened with interest to Light's conversation with Tupilak. The lady of the house was to go to the Arctic – a place the shadow associated dimly with snow and ice. There, she was to rescue her father. And who knew – maybe the shadow could help her. For a price.

Leaving the drawing room, the shadow slipped silently up the stairs towards Light's room.

Chapter Eight
The offer

Light woke suddenly. The moon was bright, seeping in through her curtains, throwing strange shadows that seemed to move and slide on the wall. From all around her came the creaks and crepitations of an old house settling down, easing its bones of wood and stone into the coolness of the night. Light's imagination raced, populating the house with creeping burglars and monsters with eyes that blinked sideways.

She wondered what had woken her, because normally she was a deep sleeper. It must have been an unfamiliar sound. Tupilak, maybe? She didn't think so. He had gone to his room when they came back from the lough. The last Light had seen of him, he'd been running a bath.

With cold water.

Suddenly a movement in the corner of Light's room derailed her train of thought. She sat bolt upright. Now *that* wasn't her imagination. In the corner of her room, a shadow detached itself from the wall and moved, very

75

deliberately, towards her bed. Light grasped the bed covers and pulled them up to her chin, as if to shield herself. Then she looked down in horror as a hand-shaped patch of darkness crept onto her covers and inched towards her. Scooting as far back in the bed as she could, banging the back of her head against the headboard, she screamed. Suddenly, darkness enveloped her, wrapping itself around her like a cloak, cutting off her breathing.

She stopped screaming.

The darkness lifted, coalescing beside her bed into the ghostly form of a girl, barely a teenager, standing in an attitude of proud defiance. The girl was made entirely of shadows – a shifting grey darkness, with eyes of the blackest night. 'I hope you're not going to scream again,' the girl said. 'It would be a shame to have to kill you already.'

Light stared, terrified. Her teeth chattered. The shadow was giving off waves of cold, so that with it standing beside the bed, the effect was that of being next to an open freezer. 'Wh-wh-what do you want?' she stammered.

The shadow only smiled.

'Am I dreaming?' Light asked.

'Oh, I'm afraid not.'

'Are you a ghost?'

'Of sorts. You could call me a shadow.'

Light used her hands to pull herself even further back, as far away as she could get in the bed, her spine straight against the wooden headboard. She brushed something with her hand, something underneath her pillow, something cold and smooth. Even through the veil of her fear, she saw a way she might be able to get help.

'What are you?' asked Light.

'I am the conscience of your ancestors,' the shadow replied. 'I am the soul that walks the cold corridors of the family's cruel mind, punishing it for its sins.' Light looked blank. The shadow leaned in close and whispered, 'Mad Eric murdered me.'

The dead girl told Light her story: the bricking up of her shadow, the drowning, the three hundred years of solitude.

'That's awful,' said Light, beginning, despite herself, to feel sorry for the girl. 'You poor thing.' The shadow seemed to hesitate, as if not sure how to take this pity from the descendant of her murderer.

'What do you want?' Light asked again, gently this time.

'I want to help you get your father back,' said the shadow.

'Oh,' said Light, playing for time. 'That's nice.' With a sudden movement, she turned and pulled out the message tube she'd found under the pillow, slotting it into the pipe that would whisk it away to Butler's room. It was sucked away into the system. Light knew there was no message inside the tube – but even empty it would wake Butler up.

The shadow hissed and moved forward, understanding that its time with the lady was now limited. 'No,' it said. 'Not nice. There will be a price.'

'A price?' Light trembled. Her brief spurt of action had given her a mental shield – now she felt desperately alone and defenceless against this thing made of shadows, this thing of cold night and infinite darkness.

'You, my lady. *You* are the price. This is the covenant I offer you. I help you to rescue your father, and if we succeed, you replace me in the house, as its shadow – as its soul.' When the shadow spoke, wreaths of its dark mist formed and curled and thinned to let the light through, shifting like motes in the beam of a projector. The detail in the sandy darkness was extraordinary – Light could dis-tinctly see the girl's pretty features, her upturned nose, her bright eyes.

'*Replace* you?' Light asked.

'Yes. You die and haunt this house until you find some-one fool enough to replace you in turn.'

'And you?' Light heard steps coming down the corridor, and saw the shadow turn in alarm towards the source of the sound.

'I achieve peace at last,' the shadow said. She smiled again, a black hole appearing on her face.

'Why would I need your help?' asked Light. 'I could get my father back on my own.'

'I can protect you,' said the shadow.

'Protect me? How?'

The shadow-girl drifted over to Light's dressing table. She began to melt from the top down – a snowman in the sun – until she was nothing but a dark, round pool on the floor. Then she glided to the small stool that sat in front of the table. The four legs of the stool stood in a puddle of blackness. Then, to Light's shock, the stool began to sink, slowly, into the floor. It leaned to the side for a moment – a ship going down – before vanishing into the pool of shadow. A moment later the shadow-girl re-formed, rising up gracefully from the pool.

Light stared. There was no sign of the stool. The pol-ished wooden floor gleamed blankly.

'Oh,' she said.

'Precisely,' said the shadow. 'Think what I could I do to

your enemies.' She paused. 'Your father is close to the shadow-realm, you know,' she added, as if as an afterthought. Light started forwards but the girl waved a calming, nebulous hand. 'He is not dead, fear not. Close, but not yet. He has a message for you. Would you like to hear it?'

Light frowned. Was this a trap?

'Yes,' she said.

'I do not quite understand the meaning of his thought – the only thought that he has, over and over. He is thinking about a journal, I think. But a journal that is also electricity. He says you missed something. Do you understand?'

Light nodded, slowly. Her father's blog. But what had she missed?

The shadow began to fade. 'Retrieve your father and replace me, or lose him and live your life to the end. You have until tomorrow night to decide. And remember – I have already helped you. I do not lie when I say that I will return your father to you.' There was a popping sound and the shadow disappeared.

Light didn't have to wait for long before there was a knock on her door and Butler entered. He sat on the end of the bed. 'I got your message tube, but there was nothing in it. Are you OK?' he asked. 'Nightmare?'

Light nodded. 'Just a bad dream,' she said. 'It's been a long day.'

He straightened up and headed for the door.

'Butler?' said Light.

He turned. 'Yes?'

'I miss him.'

He nodded, not needing to reply, or to ask who she was talking about. 'Now get some sleep, Light,' he said.

Light didn't think she would be sleeping much. There was no time for it. She had to get on the internet, have another look at her dad's last blog entry, find out what the shadow was talking about . . . then there was the trip to plan, because she might not understand half of what was happening, but she knew that she couldn't pass up a chance to get her father back . . .

She was thinking all this as, exhausted, she fell asleep, and Butler let himself gently out of the room.

Chapter Nine

Old journal, new blog

Light sat down at the computer in the library and turned it on. She glanced around, nervously, in case anyone was watching. She'd got up early in order to look at her father's blog in privacy. She didn't feel any great urge to confide in Butler or Tupilak about her visit from the shadow. For the moment, it was her secret.

The library was still and quiet. Tupilak was still in bed – sleeping off his long journey, no doubt. Butler was off somewhere, pottering. It was what he was best at. The last Light had seen of him, he'd been walking across the lawn with a fishing rod.

She was alone.

The desktop screen finally popped into bright life. Light opened the web browser and typed in the URL of her father's blog. She hadn't looked at it for weeks, though she had pored over every detail in the months after his disappearance. She opened the last entry. If he had mentioned something important, left some clue as to his whereabouts, it would most likely be in this last post. At any rate, it was a good place to start. Light read the familiar text.

The Arctic Ecology Blog
Or, the increasingly eccentric musings of a bloke from Northern Ireland going stir crazy on the sea ice.

09:04 EST

Hello Light if you're reading. Still enjoying your summer holidays? Say hi to Butler for me and make sure you don't spoil the hunters' summer too much! Sorry I can't be with you to put up new signs.

Wind abated a lot and good visibility so went out to the ice hole this morning and took some measurements. CO_2 levels seem lower, but will need to get more robust data before I can say anything with more statistical substantiation. Cold's been getting to me: ate a couple of candles this morning. Everyone does it: your body starts craving fat and before you know it those candles look more appetising than a hotdog. Makes you feel a bit dirty, though, especially because these ones are aromatherapy candles (impulse buy in Alaska) and

```
taste like lavender. Ugh.
Snow: heavy.
Weather: Dewy, 998°
```

This time something leaped out at her. She couldn't believe she hadn't noticed it before. *Stupid Light*, she reproached herself.

It was the weather reading: it made no sense at all.

Carefully, she examined it:

```
Weather: Dewy, 998°
```

Dew in the Arctic? She didn't think it was likely. And that temperature was way off. She had assumed – without really thinking about it at all – that it was a typo. But even if it was a mistake, what could her father have been *trying* to say? Even 8° would be unusually hot for the icy landscape in which he lived.

Then it was there, so simple, so obvious, like a flashing neon sign in her mind. This was a message that only she could read, that only she would understand.

Early on in her home-schooling career, her father had taught her the Dewey Decimal system of library classification. He had arranged the library according to its categories, and had shown Light how it worked so that she could always find the book she was looking for. Dewy, 998° must mean *Dewey 998*. All categories in the Dewey system had three numbers that narrowed down the subject.

998 . . .

Well, 900 was history and geography. Light knew that. She wasn't sure about the 98 part. She went over to her father's mahogany desk and picked up the slim Dewey catalogue. She flicked through to history and geography.

960 . . . 970 . . . 990 . . .

And there it was.

998
General History of the Arctic Areas and the Antarctic

Light walked over to the bookshelves, feeling on the verge of something important. The shelves were built into the wall and covered three sides of the room. Light had always loved perusing the titles at her leisure, running her fingers along the cracked, leather spines, inhaling the musty odour that to her smelled like knowledge and adventure and new worlds. Often she would choose a book and take it to one of the comfortable armchairs, then lose herself for a day in its pages, her feet curled under her.

Now, though, she moved quickly.

She came to the right section, but it was too high to reach. She pulled over the wheeled steps and manoeuvred them into place. Then she climbed them and looked at the shelf. A little brass plaque read '998'.

She wasn't sure what she was looking for, but she knew it as soon as she saw it.

It was a small, leather-bound journal, wedged in between two hardback volumes. Unlike any of the other books on the shelf its spine held no title, and no author name. She eased it out and opened it.

On the rear side of the cover was an *ex libris* sticker that identified the owner as Gordon Fitzwilliam – Light's father. Under his name was a short message.

Light,

     If you have found this, then something has happened to me on the ice, and you will almost certainly be in grave danger. Read this journal carefully, because I believe that you are the only one who can save me. Sorry I cannot tell you more. I am still young (though you may not believe it) and there is much I don't know about Inuit myth, but one thing I do know – a hero must learn for themselves how to act. You will have to learn for yourself what you can do, and quickly. I will, however, give you two pieces of advice:

     1) Those who seem to be your enemies may truly be your friends; meanwhile, those who are your friends may turn out to be more than they seem, and more useful for it.

     2) Observe what gives your enemy pleasure. It is usually the key to defeating him.

I love you, pale girl of mine.

Dad.

Light blinked back tears. It was as if her father was in the room, talking to her. She flicked through the book, wondering what was so important about it.

The first and second pages had been pasted in from

another book, from which they appeared to be torn. They were handwritten in a sort of rusty ink which Light suspected – given the spatters and drops that stained the paper – of being blood. Both the handwriting and the words were very old-fashioned – perhaps hundreds of years old.

These pieces of paper, with their wild scrawl, their ink of blood, were not alone on the page. There were also some notes scribbled in the margins, in a much more modern hand.

Her *father's* hand.

Light focused on a single word, a word written by her father in the margin of an old text, a word that made the breath leave her lungs in a long rush.

Frost

Chapter Ten

From the journal of Gordon Fitzwilliam

A yellowing article had been pasted onto the pages of Light's father's journal.

Sir John Franklin

THE BELFAST TIMES

25TH MAY, 1854

THE FATE OF SIR JOHN FRANKLIN AND HIS COMRADES, FINALLY REVEALED

It was nine years ago almost to the day that John Franklin and his crew set sail from Belfast in their ships HMS *Terror* and HMS *Erebus*, bound for the mythical Northwestern Passage in the frozen wastes of the Arctic. But the cries of joy that accompanied their departure have long since turned to sighs of trepidation, as no news was forthcoming of their whereabouts or success in their venture; and for some time since the optimistic spirit that filled the sails of their enterprise has been stilled, while we have languished for year after year in the doldrums of ignorance, and Sir John and his men have sailed into waters not shown on any map.

Now we are privileged to publish to the civilised world for the first time the at length ascertained fate of the noble but ill-starred Franklin and his gallant company. Alas! That fate should have been so sad; and that the problem that has long occupied the thoughts and engaged the energies of the great navigator's countless friends and admirers should be solved by so painful, so distressing a narrative as is contained in the following letter, which only reached us yesterday afternoon. Our own hopes of Sir John's restoration to the world had, we confess, long ceased: but who could have been prepared for such a frightful reality–a miserable and lingering death, from literal starvation–possibly, as Dr Rae conjectures, worse than starvation–on the frozen and desolate shores of the Arctic Ocean?

DR RAE'S LETTER

York Factory, 4th August, 1854, 56° N, 95° W

Dear Sirs–On the 31st March our Spring journey in search of clues to the fate of Franklin's expedition commenced, but in consequence of winds, deep and soft snow, and foggy weather, we made but very little progress. We did not enter Pelly Bay until the 17th. There we found Franklin's ship *Erebus*, which had been frozen in the ice, and which sat in deathlike silence and dread repose, for except ourselves, there were no living souls aboard. The ship was found not to have sustained any very material damage. The ropes were hard and inflexible as cables, and the sails were frozen to such stiffness as to resemble sheets of tin. The paint was discoloured by bilge-water, and the mast and topgallantmast were shattered, but the hull has escaped (apparently) unscathed, and the ship is not hurt in any vital part, only encased in its tomb of ice. For near four years no human foot has trod on the deck of that deserted ship; yet, amid those savage solitudes, where man was none, and might never be, the pilot's wheel made a stern proclamation, for around it were inscribed in letters of brass the immortal words, "England expects that every man will do his duty". I only hope that Sir John was able to fulfil this expectation on him in his final days.

Many days later we met Esquimaux, one of whom, on being asked if he ever saw white people, replied in the negative, but said that a party had perished for want of food some 10 or 12 days walk to the west. The substance of the information, collected from various sources, was as follows:

In the spring four winters past (the spring of 1850) a party of white men, about forty, were seen travelling southwards over the ice, and dragging a boat behind them, by some Esquimaux who were killing seals on the north shore of King William's Island, called Ki-ki-tuk by the Esquimaux. None of the party could speak the native language intelligibly, but by signs the natives were made to understand that their ships or ship had been trapped by the ice and that the "whites" were now going to where they expected to find deer to shoot. From the appearance of the men, all of whom, except one officer ("chief"), looked thin, they were supposed by the Esquimaux to be getting short of provisions, and they purchased a seal from the natives.

At a later date the same season, but previous to the disruption of the ice, the bodies of about 10 white persons were discovered on the continent, and five on an island nearby next to a large stream called Out-koo-hi-ca-lik by the Esquimaux. Some of the bodies had been buried (probably those of the first victims of famine), some were in a tent or tents, others under a boat that had been turned over to form a shelter, and several lay scattered about in different directions. Of those found on the island, one was supposed to have been an officer, as he had a telescope strapped over his shoulder and his double-barrelled gun lay under him.

From the mutilated state of the corpses, it is evident that our miserable countrymen had been driven to the last resource–cannibalism–as a means of prolonging life. The Esquimaux supply a more superstitious explanation, however, saying that the whites had fallen victim to a monster they call Angutagiuppiniq, which name I am given to understand means "man of snow", or an approximation thereof. No doubt Sir John's memory and legacy would be better served by this explanation, which tends more to his honour than the cold facts of the case–

Frost

What happened to the other twenty-five men???

Here the article broke off, Gordon Fitzwilliam having apparently seen no more of interest in it.

But Light stared at the words he had circled, the comments he had written in the margins.

Frost. What happened to the other twenty-five men???

She tried to understand what she was looking at. It seemed that an expedition to the Arctic had failed spectacularly – and that her father suspected Frost might be involved. Could a mythical monster that no one had ever heard of *really* have been responsible for the deaths of fifteen men, and the disappearance of twenty-five?

Chapter Eleven
Decision

Light went to the computer and looked up 'John Franklin'. There were lots of sites dedicated to the expedition. It seemed, as the article said, that Franklin had gone in search of something called the Northwest Passage, never to return. She searched for 'Northwest Passage'. This turned out to be a fabled route through the sea ice of the Arctic from the Atlantic to the Pacific. The idea had been that it would remove the need, when trading with Asia, for sailing round the horn of Africa – a notoriously deadly passage.

As early as 1744, the British government had offered a £20,000 reward to anyone who could find the Northwest Passage. Several explorers had tried, in the eighteenth and nineteenth centuries, motivated by greed – both for the money and for the fame that would surely follow.

Almost everyone who had looked for it during that rush of exploration, including Franklin, had died. Light felt so sorry for these moustachioed gentlemen, utterly unprepared for the extreme conditions of the Arctic. One testimony – from a sailor who had been one of the few to survive a 1785 expedition – seemed to sum up the desperate unreadiness of these early explorers.

The cold was so extreme that no clothes were proof against it. It would so freeze the hair on our eyelids that we could not see.

Tragically, the Northwest Passage *did* actually exist – Light even found a tour company offering cruises through it. But only in the summer, and only if you were lucky, and happened to have a modern, metal ice breaker instead of an old wooden ship with inadequate food supplies.

But Sir John's expedition had been as well equipped as the Victorian era could provide – and the British admiralty, arrogant from their dominance of international trade in the seven seas, believed that was enough. The *Erebus* and the *Terror*, both sailing ships, were also fitted with locomotive engines capable of driving metre-long propellers that could be removed if thick ice threatened to damage them. They each carried 35 tons of flour, 24 tons of meat, 2000 gallons of liquor and a ton of candles. The galley stove incorporated a desalination plant, able to make drinking water from sea water, and the ships were centrally heated by water boilers and a system of copper pipes. The bows were reinforced with iron plates to break through the ice.

None of it had been enough.

Light wondered what her father was trying to tell her. She also wondered whether she should tell Butler and Tupilak about what she had found. The journal could contain valuable clues for finding her father. But it felt wrong. For one thing, Butler and Tupilak were hiding something themselves – she was sure of it. She hadn't been at all convinced by Butler's claim not to know Tupilak. And for another thing, her father had quite clearly and deliberately left a clue that only she could decipher – Butler never used the library, and that meant Light's father didn't want anyone else knowing about the journal.

No, for the moment she would keep what she had found secret.

There were other questions, too. How much did her father know? What did Frost want with him?

And more importantly, what did *her father* want with Frost? As Light glanced through the rest of the book, she saw that it was full of articles, handwritten notes and pages pasted from other sources. There were Inuit legends, stories about the Franklin expedition, even copies of documents that the sailors had written and left with their corpses to be discovered later. Every entry related in some way to the North, or to Frost. Light had a horrible feeling which she only half-articulated to herself in the form of a thought. What if her father hadn't gone to the Arctic for scientific reasons alone? What if he had been *looking* for Frost?

So many questions.

Two things, though, were certain.

First: her father had asked her for help. He had deliberately planted a clue in his blog that would lead her to this journal. For a stranger to tell her she could defeat Frost was one thing. But for her father to leave her a book in which he appeared to have recorded all sorts of stories and articles pointing to Frost's existence – and for him to tell her that she could do something about it – well, that was another thing entirely.

Second: he believed in her.

Light took a deep breath.

She was going to the Arctic.

Chapter Twelve

Footprints in the snow

When Light entered the kitchen she found Tupilak and Butler already there. They had been talking when she came in – she hadn't caught anything but her name – and now they stopped. Butler handed her a cup of tea and a plate of buttered toast.

Tupilak was leaning over the kitchen sink, which appeared to be engrossing him. He lowered his head and tried to fit it in the bowl of the sink, but his head was too big and the sink too small, and he only succeeded in bashing his large snout against the sideboard. 'Dammit,' he said. Light watched in bemusement. Tupilak stood up again, reached into the sink with his hand and flicked out a silver fish, which flew through the air in a graceful arc to land in his open mouth. Water spattered Butler, making him tut. Tupilak grinned and bowed to the four corners of the room, graciously accepting imaginary applause.

'From the lake,' explained Butler. 'I caught them this morning. He says he likes his food alive.'

Light went over to the sink. Two brown trout circled slowly in the water. 'Never a dull moment,' she said. 'Right. Now to be serious,' she continued, her voice taking on a more businesslike tone. Tupilak turned from the sink to look at her. 'It's agenda time,' said Light.

Butler looked at her blankly. With her finger, Light drew an oblong in the air to represent a piece of paper, then plucked an invisible pen from her jeans pocket and pretended to write. She adopted a stiff, formal tone. 'Apologies: none. First item on the agenda: our possible trip to the Arctic. This is in fact the only item on the agenda. Any other business to be discussed later. OK, before we start, does anyone have any updates on last week's agenda items?'

'We didn't have an agenda last week. We didn't have a meeting,' said Butler.

'Shush. Chairwoman speaking here.'

'Oh, for God's sake.'

Tupilak turned to Butler. 'Is she always like this?' he asked.

Butler nodded. 'A lot of the time, yes. You get used to it.'

Light sighed. She made a show of tearing up the agenda and throwing the pieces on the ground. She put the invisible pen behind her ear. 'Fine. But this is important. We need to discuss what's going to happen. First off – why does Setna think that I can defeat Frost?'

'I told you,' said Tupilak. 'I don't know. I'm supposed to take you to the Arctic – that's all Setna told me. For all I know, that's as far into the future as she has seen. She's not omnipotent.'

Light sighed. 'Great. So basically, we're walking into the

 98

unknown, possibly to face a terrifying monster, simply because we think there's a small chance I might get my dad back.'

'Er . . . yes,' said Tupilak.

'Oh,' said Light. 'Well, in that case I'm in.'

Butler stared at her. 'Really?'

'Yes.' She looked at Tupilak. 'But I won't kill anyone. If there's anything I can do to stop Frost, without killing him . . . I'll do it. But I won't take his life, no matter how bad he is.' She could still see, when she closed her eyes, the body thrown back by the shotgun blast, the blood, the gaping hole in the wall.

Tupilak nodded. 'You do not seek revenge. I understand.'

Despite herself – despite her fear and her trepidation – Light felt a frisson of excitement at the idea of travelling to the Far North. It was her mother's country; it was a world of ice and snow that she had only known through stories and books. If it wasn't for her father being missing, and the terror she felt at the idea of Frost – who scared even Tupilak – she would be looking forward to the adventure.

Butler smiled a sad sort of smile. 'I think it's the right decision.' He looked at Tupilak. 'We'll both protect you as best we can.'

'Is there *any* plan at all?' Light asked, turning towards Tupilak. 'When we go to the Arctic, what do we do?'

'We should go to your father's research station and begin looking for clues.'

'Clues. Right. Footprints in the snow. That kind of thing.'

'Yes, that kind of thing.'

'OK,' said Light. 'And how do we get there?'

 99

'I've . . . made some phone calls. I might have found an ice-breaker,' said Butler. 'It's in Belfast. I need to speak to them again but it seems like a done deal. Money can't buy you love, but it can buy a pretty big ship, apparently. Of course, that's if you agree to my spending your inheritance on this trip.'

Light nodded. She didn't know exactly how much money she had inherited from her father, or care, but if it was enough to smooth over little obstacles like the thousands of miles of cold ocean that separated them from her father, then she was glad of it.

'Right then,' said Butler. 'Lots to do. Tupilak – we'll have to stock up on supplies when we get to Nunavut. Warm clothes, rations, gas cookers, rifles. Could you draw up a list? I'll get back on the phone to the shipyard. With any luck, we should be able to leave the day after tomorrow.'

Chapter Thirteen
A new shadow

That night, Light sat on her bed. She turned off her bedside light and called, softly, 'Shadow?'

She had made her decision – she was going to get her father. But she was also terrified that she might fail, terrified that she might never be able to stand up to the deadly and inhuman Frost. She needed help. She also had the tiniest germ of an idea – something she didn't even want to think out loud yet – uncurling at the back of her mind like a fern shoot.

She needed the shadow.

There was a pause in which nothing happened, and Light doubted – for a second – her sanity. Had she imagined the whole thing?

Then from the darkness in the corner of the room a distinct patch of black detached itself, and moved towards her.

'Shadow,' said Light. 'If you take me, will I be a shadow like you?'

'Yes.'

'And will my father be able to see me? If I save him and he comes back to the house, will he see me here, as a shadow?'

'Can you see me?' the shadow asked.

Light nodded.

'Then yes, he will see you. But you will be dead – you will not be able to touch him, and nor will he be able to touch you. And if you show yourself to him you may drive him mad.'

Light considered for a moment. To have her father back, even if he could not see her, even if she could not hug or kiss him – that was worth anything, wasn't it? Because at least she would know that he was safe, that she had rescued him and brought him home. She took a breath.

'Shadow, I have made a decision. You will help me to rescue my father.'

The shadow moved closer. 'That is good,' it said. Light felt a shiver that ran down her spine and tingled through her fingers and toes.

'Now stand up and turn on your light once more.' Light did as she was asked. A little confused, she stood beside the bed. 'See the shadow at your feet?' the voice of the now invisible ghost asked. Light nodded. 'I am going to lie over it, so that I may accompany you on your journey. None will know I am there. In the moonlight I will grow fat and full and in the light of day I will grow thin and long. When you are in candlelight and your shadow creeps along the floor and up the wall to escape the light, so too will I grow long and creep up the wall. Watch.'

Light looked down at her shadow, cast long across the

room by the bedside lamp. Nothing happened. Then it flickered and grew, moving up the wall, and its hand rose to wave at Light. Light looked down at her own hands. They were motionless.

The shadow at her feet – *her* shadow, but not only hers – rippled. 'See?' it said. 'When I said I'd come with you and help you, I really meant it. I'm going to be very close to you from now on. I'm going to *shadow* you.'

Part Two

Ice-Breaker

Chapter Fourteen

The Opening Gambit

Holding the little hand-drawn map the shipping agent had given them, Butler led Light down the quay to where their ship was docked. They had left Belfast proper, and entered instead a strange new town, where boats were buildings and black sea water, foamy with scum, stood in for the street. Everywhere great funnels rose from gleaming metal hulls, and cranes and winches leaned over the water. Shipping containers were stacked brightly on the slippery quay, like giant Lego. Hard-looking men directed the unloading of a gigantic, rusting cargo ship, which in faded letters proclaimed itself the *Pride of Belarus*.

The smell – which combined salt, fish and petrol – was overwhelming.

Light felt uneasy. Low, dark clouds scudded above them, and a couple of times they had to duck to avoid seagulls, which otherwise would have collided with their heads. Sitting on the sides of ships, on piles of rope and on masts were dozens of ravens. Light had also seen them lining the telegraph wires along the road to Belfast.

Silently, the birds watched Light and Butler pass. Tupilak was still in the car boot. They had arranged that he would get out once night had fallen, and join them on board.

The ice-breaker Butler had found had a reinforced, sharpened hull, hot water jets below the water line that could soften the ice and an armoured screw that wouldn't stop if it hit a hard part of the ice shelf. The shipping agent called it a 'sound ship' (Light had made the mistake of calling it a boat, and the shipping agent had frowned).

Light and Butler found their ship at the north end of the commercial docks, sitting squat and heavy in a wide finger of water that extended from the sea into the dock.

Light couldn't help but gasp when she saw the size of it. Seeing it here, floating massively in the water, made the adventure suddenly more real, and gave her a sinking feeling of vertigo. It was at least the length of three football pitches, and towered one hundred metres into the sky. The red and black hull sat low in the water, encrusted with barnacles. On the side was stencilled the name *Opening Gambit*, in peeling white paintwork. The iron of the ship's hull was rusting, causing paint to peel away in blisters.

On the deck, about half way down the length of the ship, a white structure rose five storeys into the air – looking like nothing so much as an office building. On the top floor of this structure, a huge window of glass extended from one side to the other, giving an uninterrupted view of the foredeck. *That must be the bridge,* Light guessed – whoever was navigating would be able to scan the sea in front without having to brave the elements. Behind the white building

108

was a red and grey funnel, its sides blackened by exhaust. And behind that, on the flat rear deck, sat an old twin-prop plane. Light wondered how it was supposed to take off.

As Light and Butler approached, the ship's horn sounded in greeting and Light threw her hands to her ears, shocked by the noise. She'd only once heard a louder sound: on holiday in the Lake District with her father, a fighter jet had gone supersonic over their heads. She'd dived to the ground, terrified by the explosion of sound, and her father had lifted her to her feet again, laughing.

Butler waved to return the greeting, wincing and rubbing his ears as he did so. He and Light stood by the ship, looking up at its great hulking mass, waiting for someone to come down. They had their bags with them – the plan was to head straight off the next day, making good time through the North Channel and then the Atlantic to the Arctic Circle.

Before long, a tall, heavyset man walked down a gangway towards them. He was dressed in a smart blue uniform, complete with epaulettes, but there was a webbing of thin white scars on his face and he walked with a muscular swagger. Light guessed he was the captain of the ship, but he could just as easily have been a pirate. By his side was a thinner, smaller man.

Butler smiled and stepped forwards. 'Captain Blake, I assume?'

Up close, the Captain's scars were shocking – he looked like he'd been thrown through a window.

The Captain nodded to Butler and then drew his finger over his throat, looking at the thin man next to him.

A terrible thought flashed through Light's mind. *Are they planning to slit our throats?* Then the thin man spoke.

'The Captain cannot speak, I am afraid,' he said. The Captain stuck his tongue out and waggled it – or more precisely, he stuck out a scarred stump that couldn't even reach his teeth. Light looked at him with a mixture of relief that he wasn't going to cut her throat, and mild disgust at the missing tongue. Not wanting to offend, she looked instead at the Captain's thin companion. His hair stuck up in tufts like feathers, and it looked to Light like he was evolving into a parrot – one day, perhaps, he'd hop up onto the Captain's shoulder.

Butler looked relieved too. 'Tell him hello, and thank you for taking us on board.'

The Captain made an irritated gesture and the thin man translated.

'The Captain says he can hear perfectly well,' he said.

'Ah, in that case I apologise,' said Butler. He turned to the Captain. 'Thank you for taking us on board. We are in your debt.' It was only a figure of speech – actually they'd paid the crew quite handsomely for their services.

'Shall we go on board?' asked the thin man. 'We will be setting off soon as you requested, but we will have the opportunity to talk more over dinner – and perhaps over a brandy afterwards.' The man winked at Butler. 'The Captain is fond of brandy.' He stage-whispered, 'A little too fond, sometimes.'

The Captain slapped him on the back of his head, quite hard, and grunted. The thin man gave a thin smile. 'He says again, he is not deaf.'

Light and Butler shared a look. This was going to be a strange journey.

Chapter Fifteen

On the Way

Once on board, the thin man who interpreted for the Captain gave Light and Butler a tour of the ship. It turned out he was called Monty, and he was the first mate. Beneath his tufted, feathery hair, his face was quick and kind, with large, expressive eyes. Light found herself liking him immediately.

The gangway from the dock led up to the foredeck – a bare expanse of red metal, slippery already from sea mist, with railings running down either side. A lifeboat was tethered to the railing on the deck side, lying on its side and covered with tightly knotted tarpaulin, to stop the water getting in.

Light went over to the railing and looked down at the water. From the dock, the ship had looked low, though long – now she realised she was very high up. The cold, grey water was at least twenty metres below. Bits of rubbish and dead fish floated on the surface, squabbled over by harshly crying seagulls. A smell of engine oil and fish hung over the ship. At the front – the prow, Light reminded herself – the railing met in a V shape. Light couldn't resist leaning into it and spreading her arms out, recreating the scene from *Titanic*. She called out, '*I'm the King of the castle,*' and then, pointing at the scruffiest of the seagulls hovering in the air over the dock, '*You're the dirty rascal.*'

There was a light cough behind her and Light turned her head, her arms still stretched out in imitation of Kate Winslet's famous pose. When she saw Monty standing behind her, she flushed with embarrassment. 'I was just . . . you know . . .'

'It's OK,' said Monty. He leaned forward conspiratorially. 'Actually, I've done it myself. Between you and me, *Titanic* is one of my favourite films. I always wanted to be an actor, you see. It's just bad luck that I ended up on ships instead.' He tapped the side of his nose and walked off towards the rear of the deck, where Butler was leaning down to inspect a lifeboat.

From the deck, a solid-looking iron door, held together with serious-looking rivets, opened into the white edifice that dominated the ship. Monty turned a wheel-lock and let them in, waving them through the entrance like a proud homeowner.

On the first floor were a library and games room, as well as a canteen and a small, well-stocked bar. Looking at the rows of optics, all held firmly in place to prevent breakages in bad weather, Light supposed that for some passengers on a ship like this, there wasn't much entertainment apart from drinking. On the second floor were two suites. Monty opened one of the doors with a dramatic flourish. 'And this one is yours, Lady Fitzwilliam,' he said.

Light walked into the cabin. The first room was a living room – painted white, it was nevertheless cosy, with a black leather sofa, a writing desk, and a small fridge. Little brass lamps set into the walls cast a golden glow. There was a small, square porthole opening onto the foredeck (well, not actually *opening* – when Light peered through it, she saw that it was bolted firmly to the wall). On either side of the porthole was a pair of blue curtains, bordered with lace.

'I bought the curtains myself,' said Monty. 'Went into Belfast for them.'

'Thank you,' said Light, genuinely touched. 'They're very pretty.'

Adjoining the living room were a small bedroom and a bathroom with a shower. On the bed was a blue and white patchwork bed-set, and beside it was a little bedside table covered with a lace throw. 'Your work too?' Light asked Monty. He nodded, embarrassed, spreading his hands to say, *it was nothing really.* On the wall of the bedroom was an ancient-looking fire extinguisher, and stencilled on it were instructions as well as a boxed-off section reading:

In case of malfunction or emergency, please call the Liverpool Fire Station hotline on 0151 357 4597

Light pointed out the fire extinguisher to Butler. 'I don't think the Liverpool Fire Station would do much good in the Arctic, would they?'

Monty laughed. 'The extinguishers came with the ship when it was first built. Probably don't even work.' He paused. 'Actually, that wasn't very reassuring, was it? Sorry.'

Light raised her eyebrows at Butler, who backed away, making a defensive gesture with his hands. 'It was the only ice-breaker I could find,' he said. 'Give me a break.'

Butler had the opposite suite, which was identical in almost all respects – he didn't have blue curtains, however, and his bed-set was pure hospital white.

Next, Monty took them up to the third floor. 'This is where the crew sleep,' he said. A series of cabins gave off a central corridor. At the end of the corridor was a single door. 'Captain's quarters,' Monty said, pointing at the door. 'That's where you'll be dining tonight.'

Monty showed them his own cabin – Light recognising his design sensibility from the touches of decoration in her own suite. On two of the walls of the small cabin hung attractive watercolour paintings of the English countryside. A shade covered the lamp that was bolted to the wall. On the bed, an Egyptian-cotton bed-set was matched beautifully with brown and beige cushions.

The final floor was the bridge – a huge room filled with communications equipment, with its enormous floor-to-ceiling windows giving an incredible view of the sea. The Captain stood by a large wheel of brass and wood, which looked as if it had been taken from an older ship and bolted on to this sleek, modern bridge. When they entered, he turned and nodded to them. Then he began what looked like an inspection of the equipment, peering at the row of dials and screens that spread across the width of the ship.

Another floor-to-ceiling window at the rear gave a view of the back deck and the little plane that sat there. 'It's a catapult deck,' said Monty. 'Like on warships. The pilot sits in the plane and someone else has to trigger the catapult from the deck. When it works, the plane is accelerated so quickly that when it goes off the end of the ship, it's already moving fast enough to fly.'

'*When* it works?' asked Butler. 'You mean sometimes it doesn't?'

Monty laughed. 'Oh no. I simply meant that it doesn't work at the moment. *Can't* work, really. We don't have a pilot on this voyage, you see. Now, if you'll excuse me, I should see if the Captain needs me.'

'Of course,' said Light. 'We can find our own way back to the suites.'

Monty nodded. 'Thank you.' He walked over to the Captain, and the pair began conferring without speech, their routines so well established, and their connection so great, that Monty seemed able to understand everything the Captain wanted to say, through the merest of gestures.

After dropping off his bag in his suite, Butler came into Light's cabin and sat down on the leather sofa. 'So,' he said. 'What did you think of the Captain?'

'I think he looks like a pirate, with all those scars. I kept thinking he ought to have a parrot on his shoulder.'

'Well, he's got Monty. Those tufts of hair make him look a bit like a parrot.'

'I was thinking exactly the same thing,' Light said, giggling.

Through the metal floor of the suite, a deep rumbling suddenly started. The floor trembled. 'Are those the engines?' asked Light.

'I think so,' said Butler. He looked out of the porthole. 'Yep, definitely.'

Light leaned over his shoulder to look out too. On the deck, crew members scurried around, looking small even from two floors up. They busied themselves with ropes, gesturing to other sailors down on the dock. Harsh white floodlights illuminated their work. Light hadn't expected them to leave so soon. Now, though she could feel no movement, she saw the ship opposite – an oil tanker – begin to slide smoothly backwards. She looked down at the water.

They were setting sail.

'What about Tupilak?' Light asked. 'We haven't called him to say we're on board.'

Butler's eyes widened. 'Oh, no . . .' he said.

At that moment there was a sound from the bathroom. Light and Butler looked at each other. Butler gestured to Light to get behind him, then threw open the bathroom door, his body tensed and ready to fight.

Tupilak was sitting on Light's toilet. He was eating tins of tuna – not eating the tuna *inside*, but putting whole tins in his mouth and chewing, his massive teeth grinding them down with a scraping sound.

Tupilak looked up. 'Sounds like engines. Excellent. I miss the Arctic.' He tapped a pile of tuna tins at his feet. 'The fish here tastes funny.'

 116

Chapter Sixteen

From the journal of Gordon Fitzwilliam

Testimony collected by Gordon Fitzwilliam from a village elder on King William's Island.

Our forefathers have told us much of the coming of earth and men, long, long ago. Those who lived before did not know how to store their knowledge in little black marks, like the tall ones from over the sea, and so they told stories. And from the beginning, their stories were of Tulugaq, the Raven god.

This is one of the first.

When the earth fell from heaven it was always dark and there were no people on it. It was Raven who made the first people, fashioning them from clay, then flapping his wings to breathe life into them.

When he had finished, Woman and Man stood there in the dark.

117

Then Raven scooped up two small pieces of clay and formed them into the shapes of a walrus and a seal. He held them on his palm. When they had dried, he held them up for Man and Woman to see.

'They look very nice,' said Woman and Man.

'Thank you,' said Raven.

Raven made his wings wave back and forth, blowing air on the walrus and the seal, bringing them to life. They grew remarkably in size and started gambolling on the ground, sliding on their smooth skin, chasing one another in circles.

Man looked at the walrus and the seal playing, and he was pleased with them. They were so full of life and energy.

But when Raven saw the way Man was looking at the walrus and the seal with such delight, he scooped them up and put them in the sea so that people would not be able to kill too many of them. When they entered the water they swam strongly away.

Raven made more animals, moved his wings, and brought them to life. Every animal and bird and fish that Raven made, Man viewed with pleasure or hunger. That worried Raven. He thought he'd better create something Man would fear, or else Man might eat or kill everything that moved.

So Raven went to another creek. He took some clay and created a bear and a shark, making them come alive. Quickly, Woman and Man got out of the way of Bear because they understood immediately that the animal was so fierce it would tear them apart and maybe eat them. They ran from Shark because the fish

118

was so slick and fast and sharp it would strip them to ribbons. Raven saw their distress and was glad. He waved his wing and Bear loped off to the forest. He waved his other wing and Shark slid into the sea.

All was well for some time, and Woman and Man made more women and men.

But at this time there was no death on earth, at least from natural causes, and the people began to grow too numerous. They were warm and had plenty to eat, but they were running out of space: children continued to be born but no one died, and that led to wars and fights.

One day, Woman called for Raven. A dark shape appeared in the sky, flapping, and then Raven landed on the ground, a huge black bird. He pushed on his face with his wings and his face became a bird mask that slipped backwards off his head, beak and all. He shrugged off his wings and they fell to the ground as a black cloak and he was only a man, standing before her.

Woman told Raven about the war and the death. She said that people should be able to die naturally, for this would stop them from reproducing too quickly.

Raven told Woman to go away — that he was busy and was not to be disturbed.

But the people continued to multiply and to fight for space in the world, so Woman went to Raven again. Raven went with her to the places where the people lived and saw that what the Woman said was true. He said to the people of earth that if they wanted, they could have Death . There was only one condition: to

119

have Death, they would have to have light as well. Or they could choose to live in darkness, and no one would ever die, except by spear or by water.

'Better to be without day, if thus we may be without Death,' said a younger man.

'No, let us have both light and Death,' said Woman, who was older and wiser.

And when Woman had spoken these words, it was as she had wished.

Light came, and Death.

And with Death came also the sun, moon and stars. For when people die, they go up into the sky and become brightly shining things there.

So it was that Raven brought life to the world – and Death.

Chapter Seventeen
Tulugaq

The Captain's quarters were even bigger than the suites, and instead of white painted walls, they had dark wood panelling. Light, Butler, Monty and the Captain sat at a long table set with fine silverware, in the middle of the living-cum-dining room. Old maritime charts were hung on the walls. Storm lamps burned on low wooden tables, and a tall bookcase set against one wall was well stocked with leather-bound books.

'They're glued down,' said Monty, when he saw Light looking at them.

The meal was surprisingly good – some kind of white fish in a white wine and cream sauce, with prawns. 'Our cook is very talented,' Monty explained. 'We have to pay him a fortune – every time we dock, he threatens to leave for a restaurant on land.'

When the meal was over, Butler had a brandy and, as Monty had hinted, the Captain had several. Light had a cola. Then the Captain stood and brought over a chart from the bookcase, rolled up in a poster tube. He spread it out on the table, moving glasses and plates to make room for it. He sketched a vague circle in the air above the Arctic and raised his eyebrows at Monty. Monty nodded. 'The Captain would like to know where exactly you need to go,' he said.

Butler leaned over the table and studied the map for a moment before tapping it with his finger. 'Here,' he said. 'Several hundred miles north-west of Iqaluit. It's a research station – we're looking for Light's father.'

The Captain pulled a pen from his pocket, scrawled something on a napkin and passed it to Monty, who blanched when he read it. 'I am afraid,' he said, 'the Captain is unwilling to take you to your destination.' While he spoke, the Captain scrutinised the bookcase, fastidiously avoiding Light or Butler with his eyes. Light couldn't be sure, but she thought she saw fear on his face.

'I don't understand,' said Butler. 'We own the vessel. We were given the impression that the crew of our vessel would take us wherever we wanted to go.' He put a very light stress on the words *our vessel*.

'Yes, it is unfortunate,' said Monty. 'But the Captain is quite adamant. He will take you just north of Iqaluit – no further. The rest of the distance you will have to cover on foot, or by sled. The Captain believes it would be danger- ous to go any further.' The Captain nodded vigorously at the bookcase, as if it had just made a particularly salient point in a debate.

'But this is an ice-breaker. It is designed for the Far North.'

'Nevertheless, the Captain will take you no further than . . .' Monty circled his finger pensively over the map –

a plane circling before being given permission to land –
then brought it down firmly. 'Here. This is your destination,
I am afraid – unless you can convince the crew to mutiny,
which I think is unlikely.'

The point he had marked was at least twenty miles from
the research station.

Light touched Butler's arm. 'Leave it,' she said. 'We're not
getting anywhere. We can buy snowmobiles in Iqaluit,
can't we?'

Butler smiled at her. 'Yes, we can.' They took their leave
of the Captain and Monty, both of them wondering just
what it was the Captain was so afraid of. As they left the
room, Monty waved goodbye. The Captain nodded a curt
goodbye to the bookcase.

Back in her cabin, Light got ready for bed. She was just
drifting off when she heard Butler's voice, its tone insistent
and almost angry. Light got out of bed again, slipping her
bare feet into her trainers. The living room was empty. She
tiptoed to the door into the corridor and opened it carefully. From Butler's cabin came his voice and Tupilak's,
raised in dispute. Light crept towards their door and put
her ear against it.

'And you would see the world destroyed again?' Tupilak
was speaking in Inuktitut – a language Light understood
clearly, though his accent was thicker than her father's, and
there were sounds that she had never heard his Irish
mouth produce.

'You know I would not, Tupilak,' said Butler, also speaking in perfect Inuktitut. 'But the girl is so young . . . I'm
afraid for her.'

'You lie. You are afraid only for yourself, as always, Tulugaq.'

There was a sharp intake of breath from Butler, and Light heard a shuffling as the two men apparently walked further away from the door, then continued their conversation in whispers that she couldn't make out.

Light, too, drew in a breath, as she staggered back towards her own door.

Tupilak had called Butler *Tulugaq*.

It meant *Raven*.

Chapter Eighteen
Shetlands

Light sat in the canteen. Or was it called a mess? They were in heavy seas here, and her stomach lurched every time the ship rolled. Tupilak wouldn't come out of the toilet in her suite. He said he was hiding from the crew, but Light suspected he was suffering just as much as her from sea-sickness, even though he wouldn't admit it.

'I thought you were . . . what was it you said? A "*very* good fisherman",' she'd said.

'I am,' Tupilak replied. 'But that's in a kayak. Kayaks don't roll like this.'

On these rough seas everyone – even the normally elegant Butler – walked like crabs, sideways, so as not to fall. Light watched as Butler staggered towards her from the bar, bearing a cup of coffee. He chucked her chin and said, 'Hey, cheer up.'

She grunted, annoyed.

'Ah, I see seasickness has a poor effect on your mood.'

'Sod off, Butler.'

'See?' said Butler. 'Poor mood.'

He stood, clumsily, and began the long crab-walk back to his suite. 'I'll leave you here for a while, see if you feel better with some water inside you. If that doesn't work, you might have to go down to the bottom of the ship, to the engine room. The movement isn't so bad down there.'

Light put her head on the table then instantly regretted it. The crew had soaked the tablecloths on the long tables with water – they said it made it easier for the plates and glasses to stick to it – and now her face was damp to add to her misery.

On the table in front of her, Light's glass of water tipped alarmingly. Inside, the water hung at a sharp angle, echoing the angle of the sea she could see out of the portholes. There was a water jug further down the table and it was doing the same thing. Only the little vases full of artificial flowers were different – their fake water, complete with bubbles, was made of some kind of jelly.

Light couldn't take her eyes off her water glass. It was as if all the water in the world – though separated into sea and water glasses and rivers – wanted only to be together, and still thought with one mind. It made Light uncomfortable, seeing her water follow the sea's level so faithfully – it made her think of when you cut a piece off the end of a worm and it wriggles off. She pushed the glass away in disgust.

Monty sat down next to her. 'I always feel the same thing,' he said. 'Like the water wants to be out there, in the sea. Or like it's calling the sea to come in here. Not a nice feeling.'

Light looked at him and smiled. He'd put his finger on it exactly.

126

'I have a spare hour,' said the first mate. 'If you like, I'll take you outside. We're about to pass the Shetlands – perhaps we'll see them from the deck. And the air might do your seasickness some good.'

Light thought about it. Maybe it *would* be nice to get some fresh air . . .

They negotiated the rocking corridors, then Monty took Light out onto the rear deck. To get to the rails overlooking the back of the ship, they had to skirt around the little Cessna plane, stepping over the thick cables that formed its catapult.

Monty touched Light on the arm and led her to the back railing of the ship. Beneath them, Light could see the churning white foam thrown up by the ship's propellers, frothing violently like an underwater explosion. A trail of white followed the ship, stretching straight out to the horizon. Gulls wheeled overhead, screaming, dive-bombing the fish thrown up by the ship's passage. Salt water hung in the air, making Light's clothes and hair damp. She breathed in the enormous smell of the sea.

'Over there,' said Monty, pointing to the right. Was that the port side? Light hadn't worked it out yet. She followed Monty's finger and saw a land mass rising from the sea, a mile or so away. Black mountains rose from the water, capped with white snow and wreathed in mist. They looked too big and too threatening to belong to the British Isles.

'Those are the Shetlands?' Light asked. 'Really?'

'Yes,' Monty smiled. 'Wild-looking, aren't they?'

The ship's course brought them closer and closer to the massive, craggy cliffs of the islands. 'Ah, now *this* is what

I brought you out for,' Monty said. He looked down at the sea directly below the ship. Light followed his eyes and gasped. Skimming along the water beside and behind the ship were dozens of little birds with brightly-coloured beaks and fat black and white bodies.

'Are those penguins?' Light asked. 'They're beautiful.'

Monty tutted. 'Puffins,' he corrected. 'Penguins live in the Antarctic.'

Light leaned on the rail – cold and slippery to her touch – and watched the cute birds as they bounced on the waves, sometimes plunging into the water and slipping through it like torpedoes, before bursting through the surface again into the air. Their red and yellow beaks and their shadowed eyes gave them a pensive, wry expression.

Light watched until the puffins began to fall away, and the black rocks of the Shetlands slowly disappeared from view.

Light was still thinking about those black islands when she got back to her bedroom and tried to read, ignoring the sickness in her stomach. It was difficult to concentrate – whenever she started to get into the story, she was distracted by a dark movement in the corner of her vision. She sat up, and saw that the shadow of her body cast by the lamp was rocking from side to side on the bed, its arms raised as if to clutch its head.

'Shadow?' asked Light. 'Are you all right?'

There was a groan. 'No, not really.'

'What's wrong?'

'The motion . . . the constant motion. It is giving me an ague.'

Light raised her eyebrows. 'You mean, you're seasick? But you're a ghost. Or a shadow, or whatever you are. You can't get seasick.'

'It would seem that I can.'

'But you don't have a stomach.'

'Don't say that word.'

'What word? Stomach?'

The shadow groaned again. 'I'm going down to the engine room like your Butler suggested,' it said. 'But don't think I am leaving you. I'll always be nearby – and don't get yourself killed without me.'

Then the shadow shimmered and shook. A dark patch moved away from Light, down the bed, and disappeared under the door of the cabin.

Light peered out of the door. Butler was nowhere to be seen. The shadow had gone.

She reached under her mattress and took out her father's journal.

Chapter Nineteen

From the journal of Gordon Fitzwilliam

Testimony given to Lieutenant Schwatka, 1879.

Puhtoorak told that the next time he saw a white man it was a dead one in a large ship about eight miles off Grant Point. The body was in a bunk inside the ship in the back part. The ship had four big sticks, one pointing out and the other three stabbing up. On the mainland, near Smith Point and Grant Point on the Adelaide peninsula, an Esquimaux party which he accompanied saw the tracks of white men and judged they were hunting for deer. At this time the tracks indicated there were four white men but afterwards the tracks showed only three. He saw the ship in the spring before the spring snow falls and the tracks in the fresh spring snow when the young reindeer come of the same year. He never saw the white men. He thinks that the white men lived in this ship until the fall and then moved onto the mainland.

Puhtoorak told how the Esquimaux, not understanding how to get into the ship, cut through one side. When summer came and the ice melted the ship righted herself but the hole in her side being below the water line she sank as the water poured in. After the ship sank, they found a small boat on the mainland. When he went on board the ship he saw a pile of dirt on one side of the cabin door showing that some white man had recently swept out the cabin. He found on board the ship four red tin cans filled with meat. The natives went all through the ship and found also many empty casks. They found iron chains and anchors on deck, and spoons, knives, forks, tin plates, china plates, etc.

When the ship finally sank her masts stuck out of the water and many things floated on shore which the natives picked up. There was a compass which Puhtoorak showed to me, and which I recognised as belonging to the party. It was a beautiful object of brass and wood, and on the reverse was engraved a dove with an olive branch in its bill and surrounded by a scroll and on the scroll the motto *Spero Meliora*, this being a favourite dictum of Franklin's and the motto of his expedition.

With a gasp, Light put down the book. She went to her bag and rooted through it till she found the compass her father had given her. She turned it over in her hands.

131

On the back was the familiar dove, and the motto.

Spero Meliora

Her father's interest in the Franklin case was not new – he had given her a compass from one of the ships. That meant he must have been collecting information about the expedition for years . . .

Light opened the journal once more.

Testimony given to Charles Francis Hall on Baffin Island, 1855.

Tetqataq and Ukuararssuk tell that they were with Mangaq on the west shore of Ki-ki-tuk (King William's Island) with their families sealing, and this a long time ago. They were getting ready to move – it was in the morning & the sun was high – when Tetqataq saw something in the distance on the smooth ice, something that looked white; he thought it was a bear. As soon as Tetqataq saw this something white, he told his companions of it, and they all waited, hoping it was a bear. As they watched, the white object grew larger, for it was moving towards them. At length they began to see many black objects along with what they had first espied as white in the distance. These black objects were men, dressed in clothes, and the white object was according to them a species of monster that Tetqataq called Angutagiuppiniq, which I translate as 'man of ice', or 'man of snow'. Tetqataq and Ukuararssuk were much afeared by this apparition and buried themselves in the snow so as not to be seen. At length it – and the white men with it – disappeared from view. Neither ever saw it again,

I asked them what had frightened them so but they only kept repeating that word, Angutagiuppiniq, which I never heard before in all my years in this country, though the Inuits are a superstitious people and have many legends and monsters. Tetqataq pointed to the north, and all at once dropped his head sideways into his hand, at the same time making a kind of combination of whirring, buzzing, & wind blowing noise. I took this as a pantomimic representation of a person being crushed in the ice. Repeatedly he mummed for me the shivering of a very cold person. Ordinarily I am able to collect these testimonies with a dispassionate spirit, but these mimes of his struck in me a sort of childish fear, and I was glad when that evening I could return to the warm hearth of my cabin by the river I-ka-lik.

Testimony given to Charles Francis Hall by Eveeshuk, 1869.

Q. Did you ever go to the place where the boat with many dead Kabloonas was found by the Inuits?
    Ans. Yes, I have been there.
Q. Where is the place?
    I now show her Rae's chart; she puts her finger on the w. side of the Inlet west of Pt. Richardson & says that was the place where the boat was found.

Q. Did you see any bones of the white men there?

She did – the land low & muddy there – the seawater close to. Saw pieces of the boat after the Inuits had broken it up.

Q. Can bones – skeleton bones – be seen there now when snow and ice are gone?

Ans. She thinks not, for it is so muddy there & the mud so soft that they have all sunk down into it. She continues – One man's body when found by the Inuits had the flesh all on & not mutilated except the hands sawed off at the wrists – the rest a great many had their flesh cut off as if someone or other had cut it off to eat.

Light flung the book away.

She was astonished by the power of the old stories in her father's journal to frighten her. All of this had happened a hundred and fifty years ago – yet it felt immediate, and terrifying. Every element of the story both repelled and fascinated her: the ghost ship trapped in the ice, the mutilated corpses, the Inuit reports of a creature of white. What had her father got himself into?

She put down the journal and lay down.

Sleep was a long time coming.

Chapter Twenty
Taking the wheel

On the day that they passed from the North Channel into the Atlantic, the Captain sent Light a message via Monty, asking her to join him at the bridge. He wondered if she would like to take the wheel of the ship for a moment. Butler was busying himself in the ship's library, reading about the Arctic. Light offered to take him along, but he waved her away, engrossed in an old leather-bound tome.

Light ascended the stairs to the bridge with some trepidation – Monty was busy, and she was a little worried about spending time alone with the Captain. Would he be able to communicate? As it turned out, she needn't have worried. The Captain proved himself a courteous and informative host, showing Light the various screens – GPS, underwater sonar, radar – and explaining with gestures what they were for. He spread out charts on the navigation table, tracing with a pencil the ship's course: up the North Channel to the Atlantic, then curving west to find the entrance to the Baffin Sea, before following that channel up to the Arctic, by way of Nunavut. After showing Light all the equipment on the bridge, the captain beckoned her over to the map table, gesturing at a laptop that sat open on the charts. He turned the laptop so she could see the screen, and the breath caught in her chest.

```
The Arctic Ecology Blog
Or, the increasingly eccentric musings of
a bloke from Northern Ireland going stir
crazy on the sea ice.


12:50 EST

Heavy seas in the Atlantic but I've finally
reached Iqaluit in Nunavut. Strange to
leave America and Canada behind and enter
the Inuit nation — it's as if the rules
change when you come into this white land,
as if the technology and predictability of
North America give way to something older.
One expects to meet talking bears at any
time, patchwork creatures, caribou gods. As
always when I come here I feel I have
entered a different world — bubble-shaped
buildings designed to withstand the snow,
signs and shopfronts in Inuktitut.
Wonderful place. We'll be staying here a
couple of days to take on supplies. As I'm
going on the ice soon, I need some new
things. Snow shoes, maybe a snowmobile,
warmer clothes. I can get to the research
```

station without them – but I'd be pretty
much stuck there once I arrived.

Light looked up at the Captain. He smiled and pointed at
one of the charts, his large finger pressing down next to
the word 'Iqaluit'. Then he mimed the turning of a watch.
'Tomorrow?' Light asked. The Captain nodded, beaming.
He touched the top of the laptop screen then picked up a
pen and wrote on the corner of the chart.

Met him once. Good man.

Light felt a pang in her heart and then the hot welling of
tears in the corner of her eyes.
'How . . . how did you know?' she asked.
He wrote quickly again.

*Can't buy a ship without giving your name. Told
me you were looking for your father. Put two and
two together.*

Light smiled at the Captain and nodded her thanks. He
smiled back, returning to the wheel. Light's heart beat rapidly in her chest. At times the adventure of the trip had
taken over and she had forgotten her true mission, the real
point of the journey. But always the memory of her father
would resurface when she least expected it – a whale
breaking the water to breathe. Seeing his blog brought
back the reality of what she was doing, reminded her of
the seriousness of her intent. She would get her father
back, wherever he was.

137

The Captain pointed at the ship's enormous wheel, and then at her.

Do you want to take the wheel?

Nervous, Light placed her hands on the wooden struts. The Captain pointed to the left and made a turning motion with her hand. Light turned the wheel to the left, until the Captain raised his palm in a *stop* signal.

At first, Light couldn't see anything happening. Then, watching the foredeck carefully, she saw that it was swinging, very slowly, towards the right. She felt a rush of pride – *she'd* done that, *she'd* moved the massive ship. The feeling was intoxicating. Spontaneously, she hugged the Captain. He grinned and laughed – and Light was startled to hear that his laugh sounded perfectly normal, kind and deep. She supposed a tongue wasn't necessary for laughing.

Light leaned on the wheel and watched the sea before them, lit by shafts of afternoon sunlight. There were no other ships – indeed, Light had been struck on this journey by how immense the oceans really were. Apart from the occasional oil liner or fishing boat, the sea stretched empty for miles on each side. It was amazing that there were such lonely places left on this earth.

The Captain tapped Light on the shoulder, interrupting her reverie. She looked where he pointed and laughed with surprise. Leaping from the water by the ship's prow was a school of dolphins, gleaming silkily in the sunshine, shimmering it seemed, then falling back into the water. 'Can I—'

The Captain nodded and shooed her away with a faux-impatient gesture. Grinning, she ran down the stairs to the front deck, and watched the dolphins playing in the ship's wake, leaping and spinning, until the stars began to come out.

Light was endlessly surprised by how many more stars she could see, now that they were so far from any man-made light. The sky was alive with them, thousands and thousands, a dusting of diamond light between the big stars she had seen before. The dome shape of the sky was revealed, and for a moment Light imagined that the ship was covered by a great black bowl, and the stars were little holes in it.

Light spun, her head tilted back, staring at them, until her neck hurt and her stomach turned.

Then the fog light came on.

And off.

On.

Off.

On.

Off.

A message from Butler.

-.. — . / ..-. — -. / -... . -.. / .-.. .. —. .... -

Time for bed, Light.

Chapter Twenty-one

Moon Town

The next day Light climbed down the ship's ladder. They had reached the inlet that led to Iqaluit, and the Captain had spotted a kind of road sign driven into the snow on the bank. It was too dark to read it, though, and Light had volunteered to take a closer look. After all, this was her expedition, and she owned the boat. The sailors knew that Butler was only a proxy, the one who held the purse-strings. Light was the heir. The *lady*.

To have sent someone else in her place would have struck the crew as evidence of weakness, as strong and unmistakeable as the loud, flashing *blip* that marks a whale or a sub on the sonar screen.

Light pushed off the ladder and jumped the final metre to the ground. She gasped. From above, the snow had looked soft and loose, like a great white duvet in the half-light, but now she made a mental note: *snow is hard enough to hurt if you land on it from a height.*

Light's breath made mist before her.

140

She stood up, steadying herself by holding on to the ladder screwed into the side of the ship. Barnacles clung to the iron bars, and they scraped her hand as she pulled herself up. She barely noticed the pain, concentrating instead on not falling into the thin, dark strip of water between the ice and the ship – she knew that this far north she would die of cold before she had a chance to drown. She hugged herself – despite the thick goosedown jacket she was wearing, and the mittens that protected her fingers, she could feel the intense cold insinuating itself into gaps in her clothing and between layers, freezing her skin.

Her teeth chattered a cymbal accompaniment to the rapid beat of her heart.

Light trudged towards the blurry sign. Under her feet the snow was crunchy on top like a meringue, but softer underneath, and she supposed that it must have melted slightly before the darkness sucked any warmth out of it, and it became cold and black with grief for the short hours of sunlight. Light shivered, with the cold but also with the knowledge that this landscape would kill her if given the chance. *Landscape?* she thought. *There's no land here. Snowscape, maybe.*

The sign had been hammered deep into the ice. Light walked right up to it.

> # IQALUIT
> ### Population 2495.
> ## 10 Miles.
> ### Un-passable except by ice-breaker
> ### between November and March.

 141

Light felt strange to be nearing a town where her father had been only months before. She had read his description of it, and now she would see it through his eyes as well as her own. She missed him, wanted him back. Where *was* he? For the thousandth time she asked herself what had happened. Was he being held somewhere by Frost? She pictured a castle of ice, turrets gleaming in the northern lights.

Light climbed back up the ladder, and a couple of hours later the ship arrived in Iqaluit. Few other ships were docked there – it was November, and already the inlet was closed off by the ice to ordinary ships.

At this time of the year, the sun only shone for twenty minutes of every day, creeping along the horizon like a peeping Tom. Light had barely noticed it before it dropped liquidly below the horizon.

The few ships that *were* at dock were covered with a thick layer of soft snow, as was every car, truck and house that they passed on the way into town. Light looked around, fascinated. The snow was beautiful – covering the familiar shapes of cars and power lines with its glinting whiteness, it turned the mundane details of the town into a strange and mysterious scene, imbued with fairy-tale power.

There was something pure about the snow, something pristine.

Something holy.

But there was also something sinister about it: as much as it brought an eerie beauty to the things it covered, it also erased every aspect of individuality, hiding the features of homes and vehicles under an annihilating whiteness.

The centre of town was a surprise. Light had been expecting – well, she wasn't sure what she had been expecting, but it probably involved igloos and fur caps. What she saw, though, was a sci-fi city crossed with a Wild-West border town. Men walked around in winter gear – salopettes, down-lined jackets and boots – and drove snow-mobiles or quad bikes. Some of them had rifles slung over their shoulders. There were low-lying huts running down small alleys at the side of the street, finished in corrugated iron and with satellite dishes on the roofs. Everywhere lay mechanical detritus – broken-down cars in driveways, buried quad bikes, telegraph poles keeled over by the snow. This sad flotsam littered the streets like the aftermath of a shipwreck on the shore, as if the town had run aground on cold and ice and had gone down, shattered.

The larger buildings were low-slung, bubbly things, some like UFOs and some like Lego bricks. All of them bulged outwards to let snow or water run off. The windows were few, and very small. The walls were made of plastic, and as a result each building was brightly-coloured: red, green, blue and orange. They stood on concrete stilts, above the ground, trying to conserve as much heat as possible.

It was like a frontier town in a war with the cold.

As Light walked around, with Butler, she saw a handful of scraggly trees, clinging on to life. They were stripped entirely of leaves by the scrubbing wind, their branches pushing jaggedly into the air, looking for all the world like roots, drinking the sky. The impression of an upside-down world was heightened by the raised footprints in the snow all around them. Butler explained how these came about: when a person walked, he compressed the snow beneath his feet, making it dense and hard. Then when a strong wind blew, it scraped away the top layer of snow on the street, leaving these upside-down footprints standing in relief against the ground.

Light felt that his explanation lacked imagination. To her it seemed that the earth was hollow, and there were people living on the inside surface, walking around like mirror-images of the people on the outside, leaving their upside-down footprints in the snow.

After what Light had seen in the last few days, her interpretation did not seem unreasonable.

Light could see evidence of fear everywhere in this small Northern town. As she stood on Iqaluit's main street, she saw a group of distraught-looking people huddled around a space which looked like it should be filled by a person. One of the women in the huddle began to cry. Another began gesticulating wildly, as if she wanted to throw her arms off her body and across the street. A man gesticulated back at her.

Light turned to Butler, who was watching the mourning group with open curiosity. She asked him quietly, 'Should we find someone to talk to?'

He nodded. 'Someone young.'

'Young?'

'Yes. The adults will not talk to us. They will worry that if they talk about the people who have disappeared, they will scare off visitors and explorers. Then people would stop coming here to stock up on their way into the Arctic Circle. Maybe Airbus would find somewhere else to cold-test their planes. The young are not concerned with such things.'

'OK.' Light switched from a half-whisper to full voice, loud enough for the other men to hear. 'We've got two hours in Iqaluit,' she said. 'And I'd like to get as many supplies as possible. Butler and I are going to find someone who might be able to give us directions. The rest of you, head off to get supplies. We want a couple of snowmobiles, if you can find them, some jerry cans of petrol, candles and a small, folding spade. Also tinned food. And powerful torches – it's going to be dark most of the time up there.'

Monty smiled. 'If you have the money, we'll get the snowmobiles. This is a frontier town: it's open for business.'

Light handed over a wad of dollars, then steered Butler away from the others. They entered one of the alleyways between corrugated-iron dwellings, and walked briskly away.

The first child they stopped only looked at them, wild-eyed, and then ran. Either she had been told not to talk to strangers, Light supposed, or she was simple. The second one – a boy, this time – let them ask about the monster but then only smiled, and gibbered something in a language that wasn't English *or* Inuktitut.

But as they doubled back to the main street, a boy of about twelve or thirteen stepped out in front of them, smiling widely. He was wearing a Green Bay Packers cap and a Manchester United sweatshirt, which didn't look nearly warm enough. Light went for her money but he frowned.

'I'm not a beggar,' he said.

Butler leaned down. Bent over at the waist, his body

folded to bring his face down to the boy's level, he looked like a wading bird dipping its head to fish. 'How do you do, boy who is not a beggar?' he asked.

'I'm fine, thank you,' the boy answered politely. 'And you – bird man and snow-white girl. You wish to know about the *isserkat*?'

'No, not cats,' said Light. 'The monster that takes people away. That's what we want to know about.'

'That's what I said,' the boy replied. 'The *isserkat*. That is what the old people call your monster.'

Light didn't know the word, but Butler must. She frowned at him. He seemed to be pretending, for the moment, to be a mere visitor to this land. Light wondered why.

Butler didn't look at her. He straightened up. 'What do you know about this monster?' he asked the boy. 'We will pay for good information. We also wish to know about a man who passed through here. A white man. He went on to a research station about a hundred miles north, and then he disappeared.'

The boy frowned. 'A lot of white men come through here. Are we supposed to keep track of them all, in case they go missing? We are not babysitters.'

Light drew in a sharp breath, and the boy's eyes shot wide open. Light noticed that his eyes were beautiful, big and brown and honest like a seal's.

'Oh, no . . . this man, he's a relative of yours, isn't he?'

'My father.'

He pursed his lips. 'I'm sorry. I didn't mean . . . well, I'm sorry. Anyway, I'm afraid I can't help you with the man. But the monster, yes. Perhaps.'

'What do you know about it?' asked Butler.

'People say that the monster is an *isserkat*. The word means "inlander",' said the boy. 'People from myth who live in the Arctic Circle. They are big and mean. Like trolls. Some of the old people call them *tukimut uisorersartu*, because they say that their eyes blink sideways.'

Light started, looking at the boy with surprise. She remembered the men who had attacked the house, and the way they had blinked like cats.

The boy didn't notice, but carried on his explanation instead, demonstrating the sideways movement of the eyelids by bringing his hands together as if to pray, then moving them slowly apart and together again.

'But others say that the monster is not an *isserkat*. They say that it is a *kivigtok*.' Light knew *that* word. Tupilak had described her attackers as *kivigtok*, and had told her a story about a *kivigtok* boy. With pearls for eyes and seaweed for hair. A boy who had frightened his father to death.

The boy in the baseball cap went on. 'A *kivigtok* is a man who has run away from other men, because his family don't want him or because he has done something very bad. *Kivigtok* is dangerous. He can speak to all the animals, and he is quick and agile like a fox. Maybe your monster is a *kivigtok*. Yes.'

But he didn't look convinced.

'And what do *you* think?' Light asked.

The boy brightened. 'Me, I think the monster is not a person or an inlander. I think it is something else. You know that the ice caps are melting, yes? And the polar bears are dying out. They can't swim far enough between sheets of ice, and so they die. When you leave the town, you may see one, feeding on the tip. That is what they do now – they come further out from the North, and eat our trash. Me, I think Nanook is angry and he has sent his soldiers to attack us.'

'And who is Nanook?'

'Nanook? He is the king of the bears.'

Back at the ship, as she inspected the two snowmobiles that had been found for her (one was a little old, and worn, but the other was new and looked streamlined and fast) Light found herself thinking about the boy and his stories of inlanders and bears. Of course, she knew that he was wrong about Nanook – she'd seen the attackers herself, and they were definitely men, even if very strange ones. They were definitely *kivigtok*. She also knew that the king of bears had nothing to do with her father's disappearance.

It was Frost.

Inconveniently, given that she was supposed to be inventorying the new equipment, she kept finding herself thinking about the boy's smile. She was embarrassed to admit this even to herself – but she thought he was rather handsome.

She made herself stop thinking about him and turned her attention back to the snowmobiles, though in truth she didn't really know what she was looking for. No one had ever taught her much about snowmobiles, and she hoped Butler or Tupilak knew more about these things. Anyway, it wasn't like she would ever see that boy again.

*

On an electrical wire that ran along the port side, a large seagull watched the odd little girl below, whose hair and skin were so white. This seagull had lived within reach of Iqaluit for all its short life, and its brain was roughly the size of a walnut. Even so, it was a wise bird, and unlike the humans who lived here it was aware that this was a magical place, which existed in not one but two worlds – the light world, which lasted half the year, and the dark world, which reigned for the rest.

Soon, the town was going to enter the second world – the world of darkness – where it would remain for six months or more. The great red ball of light was dropping slowly, far away. As it fell, its weight dragged down the levers of the sky to unfurl a great tent of darkness, large enough to cover the town and everything around, as far as the seagull could see. The seagull wondered why this girl who seemed so confident was not frightened of the long dark, and the days when the sun would not even rise.

It tossed its head and cried, loudly, already forgetting what it had been thinking about. Below, a movement caught its eye. There was someone else watching the girl: a young boy in a green cap peering out of one of the ship's portholes.

As they did many times a day, the thoughts of the seagull turned suddenly to food, and it forgot what it had been doing.

It unfolded its wings and flew away.

Chapter Twenty-two
Graves

Light and Butler stood on the bridge, looking out through the vast windows streaked with wetness. Two days earlier, they'd left Iqaluit with their snowmobiles and their supplies. And unknown to them, a stowaway.

The sea they were passing through was beautiful – which is to say, it was completely flat. So far they had had to endure some pretty severe waves, and Light had been sick every time. On some days the sea had looked to Light like a big open mouth, a gaping maw filled with white-capped waves like little teeth.

They were far to the north now, west of Greenland and well on their way into the Arctic Circle. The sea was covered in a thin rime of ice. Behind them, a grey path revealed their course. A few miles behind, the cold stitched it back into blackness, concealing their tracks. It was nearly fully dark now, at all times of day – a kind of permanent dusk. Winter didn't come slowly here. Back at Lough Neagh it was a gradual countdown, a video of spring shown in reverse – leaves browned and fell from trees, birds disappeared.

Winter here came sudden as a storm, blacking out the world.

They were sailing northwards through the thin passage of Baffin Bay. On either side, where the sea ended and the land began – and it wasn't always easy to see where that was – stretched a disorientating, vast tundra of snowy wilderness. The snow wasn't white, though, and Light suspected it wouldn't have been even if there were more light. Instead it was the greyish colour of white clothes too often washed, dull and lustreless, while wrinkles in the fabric threw up icy waves that imitated the sea at its roughest.

On the port side, an iceberg drifted lazily past, brushing through the thin, spotty surface ice as if it wasn't there. This one was big, a building-high white wall like a slice of Christmas cake with sugar icing. Light could see its smooth sides and its cool blue interior, so perfect in its clarity it was like a hymn to the colour blue. She couldn't get over the icebergs – they were beyond comprehension, with their perfect blue cores and their towering heights.

Twice already they had seen whales. The first time, Light had only just got there in time to see a spray of water, and a big black tail disappearing into the sea. The next time she had watched a mother and its calf as they cruised sedately alongside, just under the ice when it became thicker, rolling occasionally to show their barnacled flanks.

Once, they had even seen a polar bear, sitting quite calmly at the foot of a cliff on the eastern side, washing its fur.

Now they watched a small island as it drew near. It was grey and rocky, partly covered in snow.

The Captain tapped Light on the shoulder, and handed her a note.

That's it. Beechey Island.

Light shivered, and not only from the cold that radiated from the floor-to-ceiling window.

Beechey Island was where the graves were.

In those graves rested, forever entombed in the ice, five of Sir John Franklin's crew – the ones who had been found scattered on the snow, or under an upturned boat, on an island far to the north – as well as one rescuer. They had been waiting, still perfectly preserved, where the Inuits interviewed by Dr Rae said they were.

Months after Dr Rae's report, a British rescue ship had found these corpses and brought them back here – where a sort of base-camp for the expedition had been erected – then interred them with the rites and respect they deserved.

Buried alongside them was one of the rescue-ship sailors, who perished from the cold while digging the graves.

Nor was he the only one to die. The rescue ship, too, had been poorly provisioned and it had been trapped by the ice on the way back to Iqaluit. It was never seen again – presumed pulverised and sunk.

In the end a second rescue ship had been dispatched, following much the same route Light had taken to get to this point. She had read about it in her father's journal.

When they spotted the toothed shapes rising from the island – the first sign that anyone alive had seen of Franklin's expedition for five years – a junior sailor had shouted out, 'Graves, Captain Penny, Graves! Sir John's winter quarters!'

Winter quarters – and eternal quarters.

The Zodiac bounced over the waves, breaking through the thin, grey rime of ice. Light and Butler clung to the back, as Monty piloted them towards the island.

'I've never been in one of these!' he shouted, not very reassuringly. But he traced a confident course through the ice, gunning the outboard motor when they hit stretches of clear water.

Light had thought Iqaluit had been cold but she realised now that some warmth, some ambient heat, must have seeped from its houses and cars into the surrounding air.

Here, just breathing brought on a splitting headache, buried deep in her sinuses. The air as she breathed it in tugged at the hairs in her nostrils, moisture instantly adhering to them as ice. In her lungs, too, the air solidified, and she repeatedly coughed up crystals.

Light was glad when the inflatable boat bounced onto the gently sloping land of Beechey Island and stopped, slowing the air that met her mouth and nose.

The cold was slightly easier to bear when stationary.

Butler stood and jumped down onto the rocky shore. There was no earth here – only black stones and the ever-present snow, which sat, sinister and silent, in the cracks, as if plastering over the imperfections of the world.

'The graves should be on the west side of the island,'

153

he said, heading towards the right. Light and Monty followed.

Pretty soon – the island was very small – they came to a desolate spot where five white stones rose from the snow, sharpening to points at the top.

They looked like teeth.

Light, Butler and Monty tramped up the slope to the graves. Now they could see that each one bore a rectangular, black plaque. Inscriptions identified five of the men as members of Sir John Franklin's crew, dead in 1848 – a Royal Marine, a stoker, an able seaman and two officers, one of them presumed to be Sir John Franklin himself.

The sixth grave, belonging to the rescuer, was unmarked.

They turned from the graves and walked over to the wreck of Northumberland House – wooden beams sticking out of the snowy ground like the spars of a sunken ship from the sea floor. This had been Sir John's depot, built as a supply cache should he ever return and need more provisions. Now Light and Butler sifted through a mess of useless, exhausted objects. Rusting barrel hoops, piles of ruined gunpowder, unopened tins of food. A large plaque noted that it was by these graves that the only documentary evidence of Franklin's failure had been found – a logbook note in which his succeeding captains recorded his death and the loss of the ships, and the intentions of the crew to walk southwards in search of help.

Near the house stood a modest monument that brought a lump to Light's throat. Someone had pressed tins into the soft gravel of the ground, forming a cross.

Chapter Twenty-three

Last reports

The document pasted to the page of her father's journal was a facsimile – or was it real? Light wouldn't put it past her father to acquire the original – of an official ship's log from Franklin's expedition. A note from Light's father explained that it was torn by Franklin from a book of such logs, designed to be put into bottles and dropped into the sea, as a measure of the currents – for the Franklin expedition had sailed into uncharted waters, and the currents there were not mapped or charted. Instructions at the bottom of the note told anyone finding it to note the time and place of discovery.

In this case, the time of discovery was five years after the expedition set sail from Belfast; and the place of discovery was on the corpse of an officer presumed to be Captain John Franklin.

It was the last record of what had happened to the Franklin expedition, and it was found with the corpses of five men on King William's Island, close to an upturned boat, exactly where the Inuits had said they would be.

These same men were now buried on Beechey Island, the only traces ever found, apart from a ghost ship, of the Franklin expedition.

The document was pre-prepared with a number of blank sections in which to record important information. These had been filled in by Sir John Franklin himself, in a confident, healthy hand.

Franklin's report:

H.M.S Erebus *and* Terror
28th of May 1847
(Wintered in the ice at) Lat. 70°.5 N Long. 98°.23 W
Wintered in 1846 at Beechey Island in Lat. 74°.43 N Long. 91°.39 W after having ascended Wellington Channel Lat 77 and returned by the west side of Cornwallis Island.
Sir John Franklin commanding the expedition.
All well.

WHOEVER finds this paper is requested to forward it to the Secretary of the Admiralty, London, with a note of the time and place at which it was found: or, if more convenient, to deliver it for that purpose to the British Consul at the nearest port.

Around this, in more hasty writing, was inscribed a more chilling note:

25th April 1848. H.M Ships **Terror** *and* **Erebus** *were deserted on the 22nd April, 5 leagues NNW of this, having been beset by ice since 12th Sept 1846. Sir John Franklin died on 11th June 1847 and the total loss by deaths in the Expedition has been to date 9 officers & 15 men. The officers and crew consisting of 105 souls under the command of Capt Crozier landed here in Lat 69° 37' 42" Long 98° 41' . . . Start on tomorrow 26th for Back's Fish River.*
Captains James Fitzjames and FRM Crozie

Under both, on the pages of the journal itself, was a note from Light's father.

Extraordinary that these men — the only corpses ever found — were lying dead near a boat full of heavy provisions. Tins of food, axes, guns. The message in the margin was left with these dead men, so that anyone finding the corpses would know where Fitzjames and Crozie had taken the remaining crew.

FIRST QUESTION: How did they drag the boat five leagues from the ships? It would have been terribly heavy; not easy for starving, cold men to pull. And how did they think they were going to make it to Back's Fish River? That's 1200 MILES from King William's Island.

ANSWER: With the exception of Franklin and the other 23 who died — probably of exposure — they must have been in good health, and well-fed. No one in any less than rude health would contemplate a 1200-mile walk through the Arctic tundra, or talk about it with such calm matter-of-factness.

SECOND QUESTION: If they were strong, and they intended to walk to Fish River, why didn't they make it? Only five bodies were ever recovered, and the document only mentions 24 deaths. But that leaves more than a hundred crew members, and over a hundred men do not simply disappear into thin air – especially in the permafrost. If they die, they are preserved forever, for later explorers to find.

SO WHAT HAPPENED TO THE OTHER 105 MEN?

ANSWER: Frost.

Chapter Twenty-four
Training

Light was sick of survival training.

But Butler insisted on picking it up every time they were alone in Light's cabin at the end of the day.

'You never know,' he said. 'You might end up on the ice on your own. And if you do, I want you to be prepared.'

The lessons covered everything: melting water to drink, burrowing into the snow to conserve heat, orienteering. Light had learned some fascinating things: apparently, if you walked in the snow without setting your heading by the stars, you always pulled a little towards your stronger hand. Not by much, but if you were right handed, you could expect to describe a mile-wide, clockwise circle instead of moving in a straight line. There was more, but Light struggled to assimilate it all.

Sometimes there was a change of teacher. Tupilak handed her an apple one evening and told her to smash it with her bare hands. She picked it up and squeezed, hard, for a long time. Nothing happened. Tupilak took the apple back and threw it at the wall, where it broke into pieces. 'You have to think laterally if you're going to survive out there, Light,' he said. 'The solution to a problem is not always the most obvious one.'

What Light *was* starting to appreciate was just how hostile this environment was. It didn't want you there – it wanted you *dead*. And before it made you dead, it would make you mad. Butler had told her about snowblindness, about disorientation, and about the strange feeling of dislocation you got when living in such a blank place – the way that people lost on the ice tend to hallucinate to fill in detail, their minds incapable of dealing with the flat, grey nothingness.

Light shivered whenever she looked out of the portholes or the huge bridge window onto the tundra.

And not just with cold.

Right now she stood with Butler and Monty at the bridge, looking through the vast window to the open sea. Light gazed out at the scene outside: grey and black ice, illuminated by the blue glow of the ship's lights. Far off to the north, they could see the aurora, lighting up the black sky with green and red swathes, like silk banners. The Captain had told them (through Monty) that the lights would get even more impressive the further north they travelled.

Monty swept his hand to cover the sight in front of them. 'It's so . . . natural, isn't it? There are no streetlights. No other ships. No engines. Nothing. It's more natural than natural. It's *super*-natural.'

'I don't think that word means what you think it means,' Light said. 'Supernatural means . . . I don't know. Magical. More than real. Superpowers and stuff.'

Monty looked at her with the expression of a maths professor allowing a sales assistant to explain a percentage discount. 'I *know* what it means,' he said.

Light entered her cabin and promptly screamed. She was used to finding Tupilak in odd places, but this was different.

It wasn't an odd place.

And it wasn't Tupilak.

Sitting on her bed and beaming at her was the boy she and Butler had met in Iqaluit, his Green Bay Packers hat still firmly on his head.

'I'm sorry,' he said, smiling the same wide smile as before. 'I didn't mean to startle you.'

'What are you *doing* here?' she asked. 'What are you doing on the boat? On *my* boat?'

The boy looked surprised. 'The ship is yours? I thought it belonged to the tall man who was with you.'

'Butler? No. He's my—' She didn't think 'employee' was the right word. 'He's my friend.'

The boy's smile grew even wider – it looked like it might run out of room on his face. 'How lucky you are, to have such a friend!' he said. 'So tall and so strong!'

'Um. Yes. I suppose so. But you haven't told me what you're doing here, or what your name is or . . . well, anything.' Light was a fairly good judge of character and liked to think of herself as brave, but she wondered whether the boy was here to harm her – whether he was a spy of Frost's, or something. She backed subtly towards the door.

The boy stood and held out his hand. 'I am Arnauyq. It means, "boy who looks like a woman". When I was young I had a girlish face, apparently. My mother had a strange sense of humour.' He grinned, as if it didn't bother him much. 'You can call me Arnie, though. Everyone does.' Light stayed at the door, still not sure whether to trust the boy – she waved a greeting and he dropped his hand.

'I'm Light,' she said. 'My mother had a sense of humour too, I guess.' She pointed at her white hair and pale skin.

Arnie laughed. 'Parents can be so cruel.'

'You haven't told me what you're doing on my boat.'

'I'm running away,' the boy said.

'Running away from what?'

'From Iqaluit.' He paused. 'They don't like me much there.'

Light thought this was strange – how could the whole town of Iqaluit not like this boy, who smiled so sweetly? She felt a sense of unease, and hoped Tupilak was listening through the toilet door. '*Who* doesn't like you?' she asked.

'The people. They are starting to think I might have something to do with the disappearances.'

'*You?* What could you have to do with it?'

'I am an *anghiak*.'

'You're a what?'

'An *anghiak*. An abortion.'

Light frowned. 'But you're alive.'

'Ah,' he replied. 'Well, that's the problem. Some people in Iqaluit still believe the old stories. Old people mostly. They believe that if a woman aborts a child before it's born, that child will be an *anghiak* and it will haunt its relatives ever after, bringing bad luck on the family. Me, when

162

I came out of my mother I was dead, and it took the nurse several minutes to bring me to life. For this reason, I was called an *anghiak* by the old folks, and they told my mother she should give me away, to a Canadian family who would not know how unlucky I was.'

Light touched his arm, feeling sorry for him. 'That's horrible.'

'Yes. But no one listened to the old folks at that time. My mother kept me and we were happy until last year, when she died.' He paused, knowing that Light was about to speak, and wanting to cut her off. 'It's OK. She died peacefully.' He sounded wistful. 'Then the people started to go missing, and the old folks started to talk again. They said that it was *ilisinek* – witchcraft – and that I was a witch as well as an *anghiak*. That is why when you asked me about the monster I was happy to answer you. You were lucky to find me – no one else would have spoken to you about it. They all listen to the old folks now, and the old folks say that the monster is the doing of a witch like me, or an evil *angakut*.'

'An *angakut*?' Light asked. She knew what the word meant, but didn't feel ready to let the boy know that.

'A shaman. A witch-doctor. One who can see and travel beyond this world, and commune with the spirits. The old folk think that an *angakut* could have brought this monster on us, perhaps by conjuring up a *tupilak*.'

Light's attention had been drifting and now it snapped back into place, like an elastic band you've been absent-mindedly stretching. 'A *tupilak*?'

'Yes,' Arnie replied. 'It is a monster made from different animals, all stitched together. In the old days, the *angakut* would call down the *inua* of a dead person – that's like a soul – and then put it into this patchwork animal. Then he could command the *tupilak* to kill his enemies.'

Light frowned. Tupilak had said that his kind had a bad reputation, but the way Arnie said the word *tupilak* reminded her of the way people in the West said 'vampire'.

A *tupilak* was a monster, in these parts.

Arnie noticed her expression. 'But I don't believe it. A *tupilak* is a stupid thing, which can only understand the simplest of instructions. There is a story about an *angakut* who was hiding in a hole in the snow, making a *tupilak*. He had a great rivalry with another *angakut* and he wished to kill him using the monster. But the man he had quarrelled with happened to be walking by, and he saw his enemy down in the hole. Even though they were enemies, it would have been impolite not to say hello, so he called down into the hole. That made the man in the hole lose concentration, just as he was saying to the *tupilak*, "you must kill and eat the first man you see". He had meant to move around as he reached the end of the spell, so that he was standing behind and could not be seen, but he was distracted by his rival and stayed right where he was. The *tupilak*, which had the head of a bear and the claws of a wolf, fell on him and consumed him.'

'What a horrible story,' Light said. 'What's the moral sup-posed to be?'

'The moral?'

'Yes. You know, what does it mean? What does it say about how you should behave, or whatever?'

Arnie looked confused. 'I don't think our stories work like that. "Don't get distracted when you're making a monster out of a bunch of dangerous animals", maybe?'

Light slotted the clip into place, spun on the spot and fired. Even with earmuffs on, the report was deafening. She felt as if she had stood in a church bell while someone hit it with a mallet.

Her shoulder – which had been wrenched backwards by the colossal force of the shot – ached terribly.

But the life-jacket was untouched – she'd missed.

The pistol was a 9-millimetre Israeli Army-issue Desert Eagle: if you hit something, you would know about it.

'Again,' said Tupilak. 'If a bear sneaks up on you, you will not have time for a second shot. Remember that they move silently.'

Light hissed with frustration and raised the gun.

'No,' Tupilak said, putting a hand on her arm. 'Steady the gun with your left hand. You're not in a film – the recoil from the gun will jerk your arm back if you fire with only one hand, and your shot will go wide. Remember, I can't always be there to protect you.'

They were standing at the bow of the ship. The engines had been stilled for the night and Tupilak had taken the opportunity to climb down onto the ice and set up a target there: a bag of potatoes dressed in a life-jacket. The crew were all inside, watching the latest Tom Cruise film on black-market Chinese VCD. Tupilak and Light were shielded from view by the lifeboats that ran down one side of the ship, but if anyone came out Tupilak would have plenty of time to shimmy down the side of the ship and hide in its shadow. His rear bear claws gave him uncanny purchase on the cold steel of the hull.

Light put her earmuffs back on, cradled the handle of the gun in her left hand and fired. This time the life-jacket was knocked backwards, turning slightly, and she felt a thrill of triumph. Tupilak nodded his approval. Light looked at him and took off the earmuffs.

'You're here to *protect* me?' she asked. 'I thought you just had to get me here because Setna said so.'

Light could swear that a flush of red seeped into Tupilak's shark-head. 'Perhaps the decision to protect you is my own. But you can be assured that I will die before allowing any harm to come to you.'

Light was touched, and embarrassed. She didn't know what to say.

Just then Arnie stepped out of the door onto the deck and waved to Light. Tupilak spun and took the gun from Light's hand in one fluid motion, pointing it at the boy. 'Who are you?' he hissed. 'I haven't seen you before.'

Arnie put his hands in the air, trembling. The blood drained from his face. 'It's OK,' said Light to both of them. 'He's my friend. He stowed away in Iqaluit.'

'Ah,' said Tupilak, starting to relax. He lowered the gun and Arnie's shoulders slumped a little with relief. 'Running away from home I can understand. Come, boy.'

Arnie walked over to them tentatively. He looked down at Tupilak's feet, then back up at his head. 'You're a *tupilak*,' he said, his voice full of wonder. He stared at the shark's head and bear's legs for a moment, shaking his head slightly, as if to allow the idea to settle. Then he looked at Light, with mild accusation. 'I feel a bit stupid for telling you that story when you were already friends with a real live *tupilak.*'

Light nodded. '*Unnukkut*, Arnauyq. Sorry for not telling you. I didn't know where to start.'

'You speak Inuktitut?'

Light nodded again. '*Aap.*'

Arnie slowly approached. When he was close enough, Tupilak held out his hand to take Arnie's. 'My name is Tupilak,' he said.

'Well, that's easy to remember,' replied Arnie. 'I'm Arnauyq. Arnie for short.' He held out a still-slightly-trembling hand. 'Can I . . .?'

Tupilak nodded and Arnie touched the skin of his head. 'Oh,' he said. 'It's smooth.' He turned to Light. 'But tell me, why do you have a *tupilak* on your boat?'

'He's going to help me get my father back. And defeat Frost.'

'Frost?'

'The monster who took my father. The monster who has been making people disappear.'

'But when you were in Iqaluit you asked me what the monster was,' said Arnie, confused.

'Yes, sorry. We already knew. We just wanted to know what people were saying about it.'

'Right . . .' Arnie looked wounded for a moment, and then the expression faded, like he couldn't be bothered to keep it up. 'Why did this monster – Frost, you called it? – take your father?'

'I don't know. Dad used to come to the Arctic a lot, doing scientific research. We think he must have run afoul of Frost somehow.'

Arnie nodded, slowly, as if weighing up whether to be angry or not. 'Well, you've made my life a lot more exciting so I can't blame you too much for lying to me, I suppose.'

Tupilak led Light and Arnie to their cabin. 'We'd better clear this with Butler,' he said. When they entered the cabin Butler was standing over some charts. He looked up, recognised Arnie from Iqaluit and frowned at Light.

'Don't look at me,' Light said. 'He stowed away.'

When Butler had shaken Arnie's hand and welcomed him aboard – on the understanding that he would be dropped off again in Iqaluit on the way back, and would have to go back to school, all of which Arnie nodded at solemnly – Arnie turned to Light. 'And him?' he whispered. 'What is he? An *angakut*? A *tupilak* in disguise? A god?'

'No,' said Light. 'He's just Butler.'

Even as she said it, she didn't really believe it.

Chapter Twenty-five

Attacked at sea

Light looked at the clock in her cabin. Eight o'clock. She didn't want to be late for the farewell dinner – the Captain was practically the ambassador to Earth of capable efficiency, and he didn't like it when schedules weren't adhered to. But there was time to check her pack. Dinner wasn't till eight-fifteen.

Axe, pot for melting water, a metal cup, dry socks, unsalted biscuits, beef jerky, matches, an emergency flare gun, a sewing kit. The 9-millimetre semi-automatic pistol, for shooting polar bears – or monsters. The ammunition was in a separate, waterproof container.

She waited for the ship to pitch the right way, then used the momentum to launch herself onto her feet. She didn't understand how the sea could be like this when what they were traversing was basically ice, not water, but still it continued. She struggled to get both legs into her smart trousers, falling a couple of times when the boat listed.

Butler had made her buy a 'nice outfit' in Belfast in case

they dined with the Captain, and though it turned out that dining with the Captain usually meant wolfing something down in the canteen, or a casual meal like the one they had eaten on the first night, Butler's wish had eventually come true: there was to be a proper feast in the Captain's quarters tonight, because tomorrow she and Butler would leave the ship on their snowmobiles to scout out her father's research station. They had agreed that the ship would wait for them three days – in theory, the station was only a few hours drive across the ice – and they didn't have enough supplies for a longer trip. They weren't sure yet what they were going to do about Tupilak, but it would probably mean meeting up with him out of sight of the ship. He had already told them he wouldn't get on a snow-mobile, but had assured them he could move quickly over the ice.

Or under it, if required.

Light pulled on her brand-new blouse and knocked on the toilet door. It swung open, revealing Tupilak, crouched over the toilet bowl.

'I'm off then, Tupilak,' she said. 'Get better soon.'

He looked up and groaned. There was a strong smell of fishy vomit.

Tupilak held his hands up in front of his face, making a box in the air, then pressed his finger down as if taking a picture with an imaginary camera.

'What are you doing?' asked Light.

'Taking a mental picture of you in your smart clothes,' said Tupilak. 'In case I never see such a wonder of civilisation again. Who knows, maybe one day I can tell your kids about it.'

'Oh, very funny,' said Light, who always felt more comfortable in jeans. She thought of something that *was* funny. 'You know, you look kind of green around the gills.'

Tupilak didn't laugh, but pulled himself away from the toilet with an effort and lashed his head around, snapping his jaws shut as his mouth passed her stomach. She looked down, shocked. Had he *bitten* her? He sat back on the floor, grinning. A piece of paper was lodged in one of his teeth, hanging from a thin plastic cord.

'You left the label on,' he said.

Light ran down the corridor. OK, she didn't *run*, exactly. She scuttled, trying not to fall over as the ship lurched. She climbed the single flight of stairs, crab-walked down another corridor, then almost fell into the Captain's quarters, and looked around confusedly to see that only the Captain and Monty were there.

Light had expected Butler to get there before her, and now she felt shy and awkward. Nervously she backed out of the cabin. 'I'll just . . . go and see if Butler's ready.' She walked quickly down the corridor.

Back in Butler's cabin, she watched him doing up his bow tie. Butler insisted on a smart appearance at all times, which Light just couldn't understand. Comfort was much more important to her.

Light was trying to put her finger on an odd sensation. It had started when she was walking down the corridor, and she still felt it now. It nagged at the back of her mind, like the feeling you get when you forget something.

Then she got it – and as soon as she realised what was wrong, she couldn't believe she had missed it.

'*Butler*.' Her voice was urgent. '*Butler*.'

He turned around.

'The ship isn't moving.'

Butler frowned and moved quickly to look out of the port-hole. He beckoned Light over and pointed outside. Where before there had been a thin covering of ice on the sea, which the ice-breaker had easily cut through, now there was a wall of ice five metres high, pressed against the hull of the ship. It was as if the ice had suddenly laid siege to the ship.

Snow whirled in the air, describing spiralling eddies and curls. The glass of the porthole was beginning to frost up. 'I don't like this,' said Butler.

Something moved close to the ship, black against the swirling whiteness, and Light saw that it was one of the sailors – he held something long and thin in his hands, and Light supposed that the Captain had stopped so that the men could fish.

There was a flicker in the air near the sailor's silhouette. A tall creature – too gangly to be elegant, and obviously strong – stalked towards the sailor. The way it walked reminded Light of the men who had attacked her at Neagh House. This one was wearing some kind of grey fur cloak. It was human in shape, but at the same time it was the least human thing Light had ever seen. It looked like a monster dressed up in a human suit.

It was hard to see the creature fully in the grey semi-darkness, but there was an impression of long, sharp teeth. Light felt a horrible feeling in her stomach – the visceral feeling of inevitable, unstoppable horror. She screamed a warning through the thick glass of the porthole, and dimly heard Butler beside her, shouting too.

As the thing neared the sailor – who started to run, desperately – Light saw that it was trailing something behind it, something like a balloon. The balloon was man-shaped and man-sized, bulbous, and the tall creature was dragging it in the air behind him by some kind of cord. When the creature raised his arm, Light realised that the cord was attached to a short, business-like spear, and he was about to throw it.

She watched, horrified and impotent.

Then the spear was arcing towards the sailor, and she could only gasp quietly as it plunged into his back, dragging the man-balloon with it.

The sailor slumped to the ground, as if an expert butcher had filleted all the bones out of him in one deft stroke. Now the balloon-man was floating above the sailor's body, tethered to it by the cord. The tall creature who had thrown the spear stood and watched.

It was when the sucking, slurping noise began, and the balloon-man started to sink lower in the air with extra weight, that Light saw it was *alive* – alive and feeding.

Light felt the dizzy lightness of incipient panic and to get a grip on herself she counted, grasping the edge of the porthole hard and feeling her palms indented by the large rivets. *One elephant, two elephant, three elephant.* This was the way her father counted, and for Light, time had always been measured in elephants.

Then, on the sixth elephant, the tall, fast thing picked up the sailor and slung him over his shoulder. The balloon-man bobbed along, still plugged into the sailor's back by the cord and the spear at the end of it. The thing with the sharp teeth stretched its shoulders, then started to run north, towards the Arctic Circle. In seconds it was gone.

173

Light thought: *Frost*.

Then she thought: what does he want now?

At that precise moment, a deafening klaxon sounded, and carried on sounding – a rolling, wave-like siren. Light remembered ferry crossings to England and to France with her dad, and how the captain would come on the tannoy before the ship departed to tell everyone what to do if they heard an alarm. You were always supposed to report to your nearest muster station, which was marked by a big picture of a stick-figure family, huddling close. The association was so strong that even now, standing in Butler's cabin, Light could picture a muster station vividly, its green and white colouring symbolising safety to her scared mind.

But there were no muster stations on the ship.

Light looked around wildly. Tupilak might know what to do.

A sailor ran past the open door, shouting, 'Panic stations!'

Light wondered absently what a panic station would look like.

That was when another sailor – Light thought it might have been the chef – fell past the porthole outside, screaming and trailing blood like the tail of a kite. Light followed the body with her eyes. The man lay unmoving on the ice, the snow angel shape around him made not by sweeping arms and legs but by a spreading stain of blood.

Butler grabbed Light and they ran out into the corridor, then up the stairs to the Captain's cabin. The ship didn't have a large crew, but it seemed like everyone on board was running up and down the stairs.

On the floor outside the Captain's cabin lay the ship's

doctor, a man Light had only met once before, when they'd first come on board and been introduced to the crew. IIis head and one arm were missing. Light fought the urge to vomit.

The Captain – which is to say Monty – was shouting at another sailor. 'I said, when did you last see him?'

'J-j-just now sir, when I came in to tell you. He was lying here just like this.'

The Captain jerked his head at Monty, grunting, and Monty translated. 'He says, when did you last see him vertical and symmetrical, and, you know, *with all his blood* inside *his body?*' Monty spoke with the paradoxically drawn out syllables of someone who is trying to overcome their impatience.

The sailor at the receiving end, a short red-haired man who didn't look designed to deal with danger, shook. 'I don't know, sir. I don't know.'

Light and Butler turned away from this scene when a piercing scream came from the corridor they had just run down. They saw the sailor who'd been calling out 'panic stations' running towards them. Behind him was a tall man with rangy, loose limbs and a lolloping, wolf-like gait. He was covering ground much more easily than his prey, and Light gasped when she saw that he was dragging another floating man behind him – a grotesque parody of one of those birthday balloon animals, leering a sharp-toothed grin and flapping his arms as if swimming in the air.

The lower of the two monstrous men raised his spear and Light was shocked to realise that it wasn't cord attaching it to the floating man – it was *entrails*. She was immobile with terror, and couldn't even move when the spear flew by her face, singing a zip-like hum in the air.

The creature on foot ran past, whooping, and disappeared down the corridor. Light's legs unlocked and she turned to see whether Butler had been hit.

He hadn't. The spear had struck the metal wall and bounced off. The floating man, unanchored now, was bumping against the ceiling and gnashing his teeth.

Butler seized Light by the arm. '*Frost*,' he said. The Captain gasped and Light whipped her head around to see an expression of shock, fear and – yes – recognition on his face.

He knows who Frost is, she thought.

The Captain recovered quickly, though. He grabbed Butler and gestured at the corridor, then at the porthole which was visible through the open door of the cabin.

The message was clear: *get outside.*

The thing was, Light didn't think it was safe outside either.

But the Captain was the focus everyone needed to get out of their dream-like state of shock and move. As all the crew knew, he was a hard man to knock down. Occasionally, they would all acknowledge, he betrayed a certain ugly cruelty, showing itself through his normally composed face like a businessman's long-regretted tattoo, exposed by the movement of a loose suit.

But if you wanted strong leadership you had to put up with these things. Now the Captain ran, and his crew followed him.

They came to the flight of stairs that led down to the deck.

And they stopped dead.

176

Standing on the stairs and growling down at them was a polar bear, so tall that Light would only reach its waist. Its huge, clawed paws were as big as dish plates, and Light knew that it could rip her head off her shoulders. The bear roared, its lungs so powerful that a breeze washed over her, smelling strongly of rotten meat. It stood on its haunches, waving its paws in the air threateningly. Light felt her knees shake with fear.

Butler pushed her aside. 'Go back to the other stairs,' he said. 'All of you. I'll deal with this.' From his pocket he pulled out his 9-millimetre pistol.

Light started to say no but Butler grabbed her arms. '*Go,*' he said. 'If you can, try to get to the plane. I'll meet you there.'

'You can fly?'

'Yes.' And it was truer than Light could possibly know. 'We just need someone to trigger the catapult.' He paused. 'Someone who would have to stay behind. The trigger is on the ship.'

There was silence for a moment.

Then the Captain pointed to himself.

'But you'll be left here,' said Light, staring at him. 'You'll die.'

He made a few signs to Monty. 'With my ship. As is only right,' Monty translated.

Butler nodded gravely, and waved them away. 'Go now. Leave me.'

The bear roared again, but didn't move from the top of the stairs.

Light looked at Butler with rising panic. 'But what if you don't come?'

'Then you'll be in very grave trouble.'

The Captain picked Light up before she could protest and pulled her down the corridor, away from Butler. Monty ran alongside them, with a sailor whose name Light didn't know.

Behind them, and unseen by any of them, Butler put the gun back in his pocket. It was just for show, after all.

Down in the bowels of the ship, a dark shadow – one which bore no relation to the interplay of light and surfaces where it lay – peeled away from the wall and slunk slowly along the floor. There were intruders on board who would threaten Light's life, and the shadow could not allow that. Oh no, it could not allow that at all. Because if anyone was going to threaten Light's life, it would be her.

As soon as Butler was out of sight the Captain stopped and pulled Light into the doorway of a cabin, looking at her with accusatory eyes. 'What?' Light asked. 'Shouldn't we be running?' The Captain waved at Monty.

'Your companion said that Frost was attacking. Is that true?' the thin interpreter asked, hurriedly.

'I think so. I'm sorry – this is all my fault. But . . .' Light looked at both of them. 'You know who Frost is, don't you?'

'Oh, yes,' said Monty. 'Frost took the Captain's tongue.'

'He *what?*'

'Took the Captain's tongue. We were far north – this is why the Captain did not want to take you to your research station. We had some cargo on board that . . . well, let's just say that we should not have had it. A local vessel warned

178

us that an American Navy ice-breaker was heading towards us, and the Captain decided to jettison our cargo – it was heavy and sank without a trace. That evening, after the Americans had finished their inspection, a man entered the Captain's cabin. We were eating dinner.' Monty looked stricken. 'The man wore a cloak and had a face all of ice, with only holes for eyes. He introduced himself as Frost. He told us we had defiled his kingdom and then he . . .'

'And then he what?' Light prompted, gently.

'And then he picked up the Captain like he was . . . like he was a *doll* and he said, "You are not fit to lick my boots but you will do it anyway," and he threw the Captain to the ground. The Captain . . . he is not a coward, you understand. But he believed that we would die if he did not submit. So he licked Frost's foot, which he later told me was a block of ice, as if carved from crystal. His tongue became stuck there – you understand? Like a child's tongue on a lamp post.'

Light shivered. She could picture it very well.

'Then Frost picked up the Captain once more and threw him onto the table, and blood was spraying from his mouth. The rest I think you can imagine. Frost said, "I am a secret and you will not speak of me." Then he looked at the Captain and laughed. "Even if you could."'

'Oh God,' said Light. 'I'm so sorry. And now I've brought him to you again. It's me he wants, you know. He took my father and now . . .'

The Captain tapped Light on the shoulder and smiled, and Monty said, 'The Captain would like to thank you for this opportunity to erase the stain of his earlier cowardice. He would like to thank you for this opportunity to *fight*.

179

Right at this moment, though,' Monty added, peering into the corridor, 'I suggest we run.'

As soon as they stepped out, Light heard a high whistling sound and Monty clutched his heart. He staggered a couple of paces then fell to his knees, blood already forming a pool around him.

The Captain moved quickly, ducking low and sweeping down the corridor to where a thin man stood, blinking rapidly with eyelids that moved the wrong way. Before Light had even understood what was happening, the Captain had slammed into the man, his right arm rigidly horizontal and crushing the attacker's oesophagus even as it knocked him to the ground. The Captain stooped, picked up the man and smashed his head into the wall like a battering ram. The body slumped to the ground as the Captain returned to Light and Monty, tears in his eyes. He knelt over his friend, his translator and his confidant.

The Captain made a low keening sound in the back of his throat.

Monty spoke wheezily, translating even in his dying moments. 'The Captain says, "Don't die, my friend." I fear . . . that is one order . . . I cannot obey.' He looked at Light. 'Look after each other.'

Then his eyes rolled back like slatted blinds being drawn.

The Captain made a choking sound. He gently closed Monty's eyelids, then stood up straight and pointed down the corridor.

He and Light ran.

Halfway up the stairs on the other side of the ship, the Captain turned suddenly and stared at Light. She pushed him, saying 'Come on!' and then realised why he had stopped.

Her first, selfish thought was: *my God, who will trigger the catapult?*

It was followed by a wave of shame.

Sticking out of of the Captain's shoulder was the shaft of a spear, bubbling over with blood. Uncoiling from the spear was a length of gut, and at the end of that was a monstrous floating man.

The Captain fell back heavily, slumping against the wall.

Light shrank back into the stairwell. Above, the floating balloon thing was feeding on its victim with sick little *slurp* sounds, and she could see the Captain's face going white already, like an ice lolly when you sucked on it. She couldn't see the man who'd thrown the spear. Had he gone, leaving the balloon-man to feast on the Captain?

Wherever he was, she couldn't leave the Captain to die.

She turned and ran back down the stairs, then followed the corridor to her cabin. She grabbed her survival pack and threw it over one shoulder, then ran over to the wardrobe. She pulled out her warm parka from Iqaluit – the one with the fur lining – then grabbed the fire extinguisher from the wall.

She was about to leave when she remembered her father's journal. She reached under the mattress and pulled it out, stuffed it into the bag.

Then she ran.

The parasite was still there, floating above the now ashen Captain, sucking greedily. Light slammed the flat bottom of the heavy fire extinguisher against the cord of

 181

entrails that linked them, putting all her force into the blow. The cord of flesh severed with a spray of blood.

The balloon-man shrieked and lunged towards Light, drifting down the stairs. Aiming the nozzle at its face, Light pulled the trigger. A jet of white foam shot out, knocking the creature a few feet back. For a second or two, Light thought the fire extinguisher might save her – the balloon-man was separated from his victim now, floating free, and the foam had covered its eyes. The Captain looked awful – like a mummy covered in chalk – but already he was stirring and groaning, as if awaking from deep sleep.

But then the balloon-monster shook its head, clearing the foam from its eyes and face. It reached out a hand and took hold of the steel banister that ran down the stairs, helping the crew to keep steady feet even in wet weather.

It began pulling itself down, grinning at Light. The remnants of foam on its chin made it look like it was drooling.

Arnauyq had picked up the first weapon to hand – another fire extinguisher. He ran down the corridor, and collided with a fearful monster.

He screamed.

Tupilak screamed back automatically, and then the two of them clutched at each other, giggling madly with shock.

Tupilak led Arnie to the stairs at the bow of the ship, where Light had left Butler and the polar bear. They saw no one.

The unlikely pair burst onto the deck, shouting a war cry. One of the spear-men turned quickly but it was too late – Arnie hit him with a dense spray of foam and then

Tupilak was running towards him, his head lowered to the side like a rugby player, the jaws wide open. The impact was so quick, and his teeth so sharp, that the attacker's lower half was left standing on the deck for several moments, swaying gently in the cold breeze. Tupilak spat out the torso and head.

'Don't spray foam on my food, boy,' he said.

Arnie threw the fire extinguisher away. It was heavy, and he had an even better weapon now: Tupilak. Together they crept down the deck, back towards the bridge. That was the soul of the ship, its nerve centre, and so it seemed logical that whoever was coordinating this attack would head there too – if only to stop the crew from calling for help.

They stepped out from the shelter of a lifeboat, into an exposed section of deck, and two shapes barrelled into Tupilak, dragging him towards the side of the ship and the low rail.

The great shark's head tried to twist around to snap at the enemy, but the men were big and strong, and they were moving fast in a kamikaze attack that showed no hesitation at all. So fast did they move that Arnie barely had time to process what he was seeing as his unusual new friend was carried over the rail and into the sea. Falling, Tupilak had time to scream, and then there was a muffled thud followed immediately by a splash as the three heavy bodies hit the black ice and smashed through it into the sea. Arnie did a U-turn and huddled by the lifeboat. It seemed like these men were willing to die to take the shark-man out, and that wasn't good. Not good at all.

*

183

Light threw her fire extinguisher aside and knelt behind the Captain. She unzipped her bag and took out the flare gun – there was no time to load the pistol.

With one hand she pulled back on the Captain's shoulder – he grunted – while with the other she drew the flare gun level. She fired and the gun kicked her arm backwards. The flare hit the floating man in his hollow stomach, burning bright red. He was engulfed quickly by the flames, causing him to sink to the deck as whatever gases kept him afloat burned away. Then, as the fire ate through his skin, the form of his body collapsed, leaving only a burning heap on the ground, like a bonfire burning out.

Light turned to the Captain. He was looking at her through half-open eyes, smiling faintly. He made a weary gesture.

Pull the spear out.

Quickly, she tore one of the sleeves off her thermal vest. Then, with a deep breath, she pulled hard on the spear. It came out with a sucking *pop*, followed by a sluggish trickle of dark blood.

Light gagged.

Steeling herself, she lashed the sleeve tightly around the wound, bandaging it as best she could. The Captain beckoned her close and, with monumental effort, breathed a phrase that was all vowels. 'Ge away . . . say yourell . . . ah'oh'ay . . .'

Get away. Save yourself. I'll be OK.

The worst thing was, she knew he was right. She couldn't stay here with him. She had to find Butler, get to the bridge. See if she could get an SOS out.

184

If she survived – *then* she would send help for the Captain.

If she stayed, she would only be able to hold his hand as they both died.

It hurt to leave him, though. Light threw the flare gun aside – she didn't have any more flares – and pulled the 9-millimetre from the pack. She loaded the gun with a clip from the bottom of the bag, thumbed off the safety and took a deep breath to steady herself. Then she pressed the gun into the Captain's hands. He tried to give it back but she shook her head.

'I'll send help,' she said.

She ran down the stairs and past the still smouldering heap. She was on the deck now, and she ducked as she ran, feeling exposed. It didn't help much: she barrelled into one of the spear-men almost immediately, making them both cry out.

But it did help a bit: because she was ducked down low, she hit him where it hurt most, and now he was bending over, coughing.

She had to think fast.

It was the same strategy she'd used on a village bully once, stunning him into humiliated silence. She hoped it would work again. Grabbing the man by the hair at the back of his head, she pulled in close and kissed him full on the lips. She felt his pulse quicken under his fur clothes. As she pulled away, she could still feel his heart-beat despite the distance between them: slowing and growing fainter in a long diminuendo, like something dying.

Light pulled the gun out, levelled it and pulled the

 185

trigger, not allowing herself time to think. The bullet went wide. The man grinned at her and lunged forwards.

There was a sound of wings and a dozen or more crows flew past Light's head, their feathers touching her skin, filling her vision with black movement. They dive-bombed the man, pecking at his eyes, clinging on to his skin with their claws. They screeched as they attacked.

Light moved, silently thanking the birds. She had seen crows occasionally in the Arctic – they were so improbable and black against the snow, they were like a miracle. God only knew how they survived.

But she was glad that they did.

Light ran, only half thinking about the crows that had saved her back at Neagh House, only half questioning their meaning, and the way that they seemed to protect her.

The stairs to the bridge were only metres to her left. Someone grabbed her from behind and she squealed, turning round and lashing out with her fist.

'Ow!'

Arnie was standing behind her, clutching his ear. He grimaced, and then smiled at her. But behind the smile was a twinge of pain.

'What's wrong?' asked Light.

'Tupilak,' he said. 'They got him. He fell into the sea.'

Light gasped. She'd left Butler and the Captain – who could both be dead for all she knew – and now Tupilak was gone too. With a conscious effort, she pushed this worry to the back of her mind. There was nothing she could do now except try to survive. And at least Tupilak could breathe under the water – which was perhaps more than their unknown enemy could do.

'Come on,' she said. 'Let's get to the bridge. We might be able to radio someone. The Captain is badly wounded. We need help quickly.'

She knew Butler wanted her to go for the plane, to save herself and forget the Captain – but Butler wasn't here and there was no way Light was going to let a wounded man die.

They ran for the shelter of the door, looking back as they heard an ululating war cry, like something from an old cowboy film. One of the tall spear-men was standing on the deck by the plane, looking straight at them, raising his spear to throw it. It was a dark night, and the spear-man was illuminated starkly against the blackness of the sky by the yellow glow of the ship's fog lamps. Behind him, a balloon-man drifted in the air.

As he drew his spear back, Light and Arnie started to back away.

'*That* is an *isserkat*,' Arnie hissed.

Then a black shape appeared in the air above the deck, swooping down on the man. Light squinted . . . the thing swooping down looked like a bird, a blackbird, but the scale was all wrong. Its wingspan was wider than a man and its head was the size of a football.

'What the . . .' said Arnie.

The enormous black bird dropped fast towards the attackers. It cried out, a harsh caw like a crow's, and then slammed into the balloon-man with an audible *puff* like a punctured lilo, before grabbing the lower man and pulling him up into the air.

The giant bird climbed quickly, spiralling, then banked sharply and dropped its cargo. The man fell on the hard

 187

deck with a crunching sound. Above him, the balloon-man floated lopsidedly for a moment, his papery body torn in several places, and then sank to the deck.

The giant bird spiralled and then flew off into the star-spangled night.

Light stared after it, one word going round and round in her head:

Tulugaq.

The Raven god.

She pulled at Arnie's arm. 'Let's go,' she shouted. They turned and ran, leaping the steps up to the bridge two at a time.

Behind Light, Arnie was breathing heavily. There were four flights of steps to the deck, and the climb was strenuous enough at normal speed. At a run, it put a huge strain on Light's lungs.

On the second flight of stairs, from the suites to the crew's cabins, an *isserkat* stepped out from the shadows, grinning. It lowered its spear. Light stumbled and nearly fell down the steps. She clutched on to Arnauyq. Then one of the shadows moved, and resolved itself into the dark, flowing shape of a girl. The shadow-girl raised her hands and blackness streamed from her fingers.

The darkness flowed around the *isserkat*, concealing him in a cloak of black fog. Then it dissipated, as suddenly as it had appeared, and the *isserkat* was no longer there. Light heard an echoing giggle. 'Go,' said the shadow, in a tone full of amusement. 'You live to die another day. At *my* hands, not his.'

They burst through the door to the bridge and stopped instantly. On the other side of the room was a sailor Light vaguely recognised, holding a gun. To their right, by the huge window, was another sailor.

But this one was dressed in the crimson uniform of a British Royal Marine, tattered and faded with age.

Light had seen that very uniform before.

In a maritime museum.

The ancient sailor turned to Light and smiled. He tipped his cap, revealing a skeletal face, the flesh hanging off it in black, frostbitten flaps. Only his eyes – bright and wide – had been untouched by the years.

He blinked, his eyelids closing sideways like the men who had attacked Light at home. His fingers were bone, washed white by the snow and the salt air. He grinned. 'A pleasure, young miss. Lamplighter Jones at your service.'

'Oh, God,' said Light.

'What . . . is . . . that?' asked Arnie, trembling.

'It's one of the men from Franklin's expedition.'

The sailor gave a bow. 'Never quite returned home,' he said. 'The cold got into my bones and wouldn't let go. What I wouldn't do for some warm clothes . . . some hot food.' He shambled forwards, bony fingers clutching at the air. 'The heat of living meat in my mouth and belly.' He opened his mouth wide.

'No you don't!' the sailor from the ice-breaker shouted, and fired a succession of shots. The first smashed into the window, making it shiver, spreading a web of cracks and letting in a sudden, thin rush of cold air. The second ploughed into the communications equipment, next to the wheel and the power lever.

The third took the Victorian sailor's face off, spinning him like a top. He crashed to the ground.

189

The man stared at the gun, then at what he'd done, emitted a little sob and ran down the opposite stairs to the deck. He was to die within minutes.

Light went cautiously to the sailor's body and kicked it.

The sailor sat up. 'Come here, my pretty,' he said, through his ruined face. 'It's an age since I had a good meal. I'm perishing hungry . . .'

Blackness pooled around his body as he sat up, portions of his rotting uniform falling from him like confetti.

Then Light's shadow opened into nothingness and with a sucking sound the sailor fell through the floor.

'What was *that*?' said Arnie.

'I don't know,' lied Light.

She felt a rush of revulsion. She felt . . . *violated*. As if these things had no business existing, and their presence on a ship – or in the drawing room of a house – was simply unacceptable to a human being.

She ran to the control panel and checked the radio. The bullet had torn through the twisted cable for the HF mike, cutting it off. They could hear through the speakers, but couldn't say anything. It was useless. She slammed her hand on the window in frustration, forgetting that the spider-web bullet hole to her right had already weakened the glass. The window shattered outwards, sending glass spiralling down three storeys onto the deck.

Light sank to the floor. She was going to have to head for the plane, but she didn't know if she could go through with it.

She was drawing herself to her feet wearily, when Arnie gave a yelp of triumph. He was holding a hammer and pointing at the panel. 'I smashed into the panel to find a live wire.' He held up a wire wrapped in red and yellow plastic. At the frayed end, there was a ponytail of metal strands, in which blue flashes of electricity pulsed. He held the wire to the exposed mike cable.

Nothing happened.

'You think nothing's happening,' he said, seeing Light's expression. 'But I think if we flick to an open channel, anyone receiving will hear white noise when we touch the wires together. We can't speak, but we *can* send an SOS.' He touched the wires together – three short touches, three long, three short.

A jumbled message came through the speakers in reply. Light couldn't make it out. She grabbed the live wire from Arnauyq, keeping her hand well away from the sparking end. 'Watch the door,' she ordered.

She pushed the wires together rhythmically, to make a fast Morse signal.

-.-. —.- -.-. —.- -.-. —. - -.. . — .—. . -. .. -. —. —. .-
— -.... .. - .-. ... - .—— .—— .—

CQ CQ CQ DE OPENING GAMBIT RST 111
Calling anyone, this is Opening Gambit, you are RST 111 (poor readability, poor signal, poor tone)

Her father had taught her the Q-codes and abbreviations used by the British and other navies. They were an extra level on top of Morse code, making it quicker and more efficient. She'd never thought it would come in useful – mostly, it was used by ham radio geeks. But Light was starting to think that any knowledge comes in useful at some point in your life.

The speakers flared again, but instead of jumbled speech, she heard the channel open and close rhythmically. It was a clever way of getting around a poor signal: turning the mike on and off to create Morse code. Light felt a surge of happiness: whoever she was speaking to, they were clever.

Arnauyq was looking at her in frank amazement. She pursed her lips, concentrating. The crackle of the radio as it came on and off again resolved itself into a standard greeting.

— .—. . -. .. -. —. —. .- — -... .. - -.. . .... — ...
..-. — —. .- -. - -.— -.- -.

OPENING GAMBIT DE HMS FOGARTY KN
Calling OPENING GAMBIT, this is HMS FOGARTY, back-to-you

Light touched the wires together with quick, practised gestures.

—. .- -.. .-. — — ..- .-. .-. ... - ..... —. .—.
-. — .— ..... .-. —... —.. ....- —.. -. — .-. .
.... —... ....- — — — .— . ... - —. .—. .. ...
.-.. .. —. .... - ... — ... ... — ... ... — ...

GA DR OM UR RST 599 NOW HR = 77 48 NORTH 74 00 WEST OP IS LIGHT; SOS SOS SOS.
Good day old man, Light here, reading you well. Location 77º 48′ North, 74º 0′ West. SOS SOS SOS.

The crackle and hiss of the speakers filled the bridge with a reply.

```
- .... -. -.-.   .-.-. -   .-. .-. .--. -.. -... ?   --- -- .-.. ..
```
```
--. .... - ..-.- .... ..... ......   --.. -   .--.- .... ..-.-. -. . .-
```
```
. - ..... .. -.-. .--.- --.-   .-.- . - --.- -..-. ... ..-.--
```
```
... --.- -.-. -. -... ..... .--. -.-- .- -. ... -. --- . - --... ...
```
```
..--- .--.- .-. ..- .-.- . - .-. --- .- -   . ... .... .--- -.-.
```
```
- .... -. -.   . ..   ..-.- --   -.. .. .... .--. .-.-. .-.-.- .---- ....
```
```
-.-- ... .- ...- .-.- ...-. .... ..-.. -... -. . --- -- .---- .--- ..--
```
```
-.-. . ..--..
```

THNX FB RPRT DR OM LIGHT UR 558 = QTH
UNDER THE ICE, WE
ARE BN SUB, 76 34 NORTH 72 23 WEST = NAME IS
JOHN + S1 DE S2 KN . WHY SOS? SRS? NOT JOKE?
Thanks for the nice report dear old man Light. I
read you 558. I am under the ice at 76º 34′ North,
72º 23′ West. We are a British Navy submarine. My
name is John. Why SOS? Serious? Not a joke?

Light began touching the wires again.

Arnauyq hissed at Light, interrupting. 'What's going
on?'

'It's a British Navy sub. Let me concentrate. I'll translate
as I do it.'

She tapped the wires together, feeling the old fluency
return. It was time to switch to ordinary code. She gave
Arnauyq a running translation.

```
— . / .- .-. / ..- -. -.. . .-. / .- - - .- -.-. -.-
```
We are under attack.

```
— .... — / .. .... / .- - - .- -. -.-. -. .. - . -. . — . / -.- .— — .. - .—..
```

193

Who is attacking you?

..- -. -.- -. — .— -. .-.- / .—. . — .—. .-.. / .— ..
- .... / .... .—. . .- .-. ... .-.- / - .... . -.— / .... .- ...- .
/ -.... . . .-. ... / .— .. - .... / - .... . — .-.-.-

Unknown. People with spears. They have bears with
them.

Arnie interrupted again. 'They have *bears?*'

'Yes. I left Butler fighting one.'

Light choked back tears. She wished she could check
out the foredeck stairs, and see if there was a dead bear
there. Or a dead Butler.

The radio flared into life again.

...- . .-. -.— / ..-. ..- -. -. -.— / ... - — .—. / .— .-
... - .. -. —. / — ..- -. / - .. — . .-.-.-

Very funny. Stop wasting our time.

Light swore with frustration. She felt like she might cry.
Tupilak had disappeared. Butler had gone after a polar
bear with nothing but a pistol. And she still needed to get
Arnie off this ship, and get help for the Captain.

If she had possessed the luxury of time to think, Light
might have been surprised at her selflessness in danger –
the idea of saving herself never even occurred to her.

She moved her hands in a blur, one last time. It was all
she could do: she had to hope it would be enough.

- .... -. — - .- .— — -.- . .—. .-.. . -
... .-.. —. ..- ... .— . .... .- ...- . ...- .

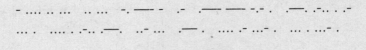

194

.-. .- .-. .-.. -. .. .- -.. .- -. -.. .- -..... . -.-. .- —— . . .- .. -.

.. ..- . .-. . .-.. .— —— .— .- -. -.. . -.. .-.-.

....- .. ... —— -. .- .... —— ..- - .... -.. . .-. -.-.

... - .- .. .-. ... .-.- .... ..- .-. .-. -. -.— .-.-.

This is not a joke please help us we have several
dead and the captain is severely wounded. He is on
the south deck stairs. Hurry.

There was a bigger problem, too. One she hadn't quite
allowed herself to think about.

'There's no way off the ship,' she said. 'Butler's disappeared. He's the only one who can fly.'

'Um . . .' said Arnie.

'What?'

'I can kind of fly a plane.'

'You can *fly?*'

'My dad, he did flights for Airbus – cold weather testing
out of Iqaluit. And we'd often fly to his cabin, go fishing,
you know. He taught me.'

Light hugged Arnie and saw him smile widely. 'What
are we doing here, then?' she asked. 'The rear deck may
be clear. We'll go back for the Captain then take the
plane.'

The two of them headed to the door opposite where
they'd come in, where the sailor had gone down, and then
Light stopped in the middle of the floor.

'What is it?' asked Arnie.

'Clothes,' said Light. 'I've got my fur coat, but look at
you. You'll freeze.' Arnie was dressed in his usual football
shirt and cap. 'You'd better take the clothes from that dead
isserkat.'

195

Arnie stared at the dead body on the ground. 'You've got to be kidding.'

'He's wearing fur. It'll keep you warm.'

Shaking his head, Arnie went to the corpse and started gingerly removing the fur cloak, his shoulders hunched with disgust. Eventually he got it off and put it on, pulling a face when he saw the blood that stained the front.

'Beautiful,' said Light, in a Californian drawl. 'Blood stains are so hot right now.'

Just then, a crackle came through the radio speakers.

The voice that followed was much clearer than the fuzz they had heard earlier – it was as if the speaker was in the room.

'Light? I don't know where I am . . . you have to help me . . . come outside . . .'

Light knew that voice.

It was her father's.

Chapter Twenty-six

Night flight

'It's a trap,' said Arnie.

'I know it's a trap,' said Light. 'But we're still going out-side. That's where the plane is.'

They ran down the four flights of stairs to the rear deck, then stepped out into the cold darkness, under the indif-ferent light of the stars.

There was no one to be seen.

'Perhaps they're all dead,' said Arnauyq.

'Great, thanks for that,' Light replied. She was worried about Butler. Very worried. Where *was* he?

Miraculously, the plane was still there and seemed undamaged. Arnie opened the cockpit door and jumped in, his hands immediately flying over the instruments. 'Ugh,' he said. 'There's a dead guy in here. One of ours, I think. He still has a pistol in his hand.' There was a pause. 'Ah,' said Arnie, with the tone that precedes very bad news.

'What?'

'We need oil, or the plane won't start. They can't keep it

197

on the plane because it freezes. It'll be in the bridge, I think.'

Oh no.

Light looked back at the bridge. Suddenly it seemed a long way away.

She held out her hand. 'Gun.'

Arnie looked from her to the dead sailor, and the gun in his hand. 'You can't be—'

'Quickly,' Light said. 'I'll get the oil, then we'll start the engine and go for the Captain. But I want a gun.'

Arnie reached into the plane. 'Oh, gross, his fingers are frozen onto it.'

There was a horrible snapping sound and Arnie handed Light the gun.

Light ran, hearing Arnie call out behind her, 'The safety!'

She looked down at the pistol in her hand, saw a small button on the side and slid it downwards. A red window appeared – the gun was armed.

Now she was only five metres from the door but she felt like it was more.

She skidded through and ran up the stairs.

Inside, the cold had spread quickly – too quickly. There was no window, of course, and Arctic air was blowing in, but that didn't explain how everything had frosted up. The air hurt Light's throat and lungs as it entered. What if the oil had frozen? She scanned the room, flinching at a sudden movement from the left until she realised it was wind coming through the window, stirring papers on the console.

Light felt under the nav table. *Please be there, please be there.* Every instinct was screaming at her to get out, to run, and she had to fight hard to overcome the urge. She felt exposed, vulnerable, but she reminded herself that she would feel much worse if the plane wouldn't work because it didn't have oil. She groped with her fingers in the narrow space under the nav table.

The jerry can was there, and it sloshed when she grabbed it.

She pulled it out and turned to head for the door.

Light ran for the door and scrambled, slipping and sliding, down the stairs. The frost was following her – she could see it dusting the stairs and banister as she ran, moving like something alive.

What if this was Frost? What if he had found her?

She hit the door to the outside with her shoulder, pushing it open and falling through. The jerry can cracked when it hit the ground and she swore. She checked the crack quickly – it wasn't huge but she'd have to be quick – and then ran towards the plane.

Oil dripped in a line behind her.

She pulled herself into the plane and handed Arnie the oil can. 'Fill it up quickly,' she said.

Arnie took the can, then froze. 'Oh, no,' he said.

'What?' asked Light, her voice cracking.

'We still need someone to trigger the catapult. Someone who doesn't mind staying behind.' Arnie turned and pointed – a large metal lever was set into the deck floor, near the door to the bridge.

Just then the door banged open again, a hard ring of metal on metal.

The Captain stepped out onto the deck, one hand clutching his bleeding chest, the other holding the door handle. He took a step forwards, saluted Light weakly, and stumbled to his knees.

'Captain!' Light shouted. 'Come on! Get to the plane!'

He pushed himself up onto his feet again, his movements heavy and awkward. Blood dripped on the deck.

Then a figure stepped out of the door behind him.

The Captain turned, startled, and lost his footing. He crashed to the floor, gasping.

It wasn't one of the spear-men or the bears – or one of the English sailors. No, Light could tell by the way it moved that this was something much more dangerous. She felt her insides turn to mush, as if she'd heard a wolf's howl while out camping, or seen the silhouette of a shark while swimming in the sea. The figure was wearing a high, deep hood and a kind of monk's robe. The hood was so big that when it moved its head, the fabric didn't stir.

Inside was only darkness.

The thing stepped towards the Captain, who was struggling to get to his feet.

'Light.'

The word rang like crystal in the cold air. The hooded figure's voice was curiously artificial, like that of an automaton, as if the syllables and consonants had come off a production line in some factory, and were merely being *assembled* by the creature's mouth.

Light recognised that voice.

It was the same as the one that had come from the hawk, before it was killed by the black birds on the front lawn of Neagh House.

Frost.

The face was still invisible within the shadow of the

200

cloak. The creature stood very still, but Light got an impression of energy being held back, or just temporarily in check – the moment when a ball thrown high in the air hangs, immobile, before falling back to earth.

Light could only stare as the thing pulled its hood back and off, revealing a skull of pure ice. She was looking at a walking ice sculpture – the light passed straight through it. There were eyes, of a sort – holes in the head that ran from front and back, and through which Light could see the structure of the bridge. She could see through the rest of the head, too, but the view was blurred and less distinct, like looking through a thick window. Cold came from the figure in waves.

Light looked into those eyes and knew that she was lost.

Frost spoke again. 'I have come for you, Light. Like I came for your father. Come to me.'

Light pinched her arm and the spell was broken. In the corner of her eye, she could make out Arnie, checking controls and switching on lights. The Captain was inching himself towards them, dragging himself over the metal of the deck.

They might all stand a chance of getting away, if she could hold Frost for a while.

'No. Give me back my father.' Light was surprised by how loud her voice sounded. She needed to keep Frost talking. Meanwhile, she was fumbling in her bag, trying to get hold of her matches. She didn't know if engine oil burned, but she was sure as hell going to find out.

'Ah, Light, you disappoint me,' said Frost. 'You're really not in a strong negotiating position, you know.'

As if to prove his point, the plane's engine sputtered into life and then died again. Arnauyq cursed.

 201

Light tried to stall for time. 'It would be easier to negotiate if I knew what you wanted.'

'What I want is simple,' said the seductive voice. 'I want every person on earth to be dead.'

Light stared, shaken.

Frost continued. 'You are intruding on my territory. You have annexed a piece of the Arctic precisely the size of this ship we are standing on, and I consider that incursion an act of war . . . I would very much like it if you would step over to the rail now and throw yourself into the sea.'

'Well I wouldn't like it!' said Light. 'I'd die.'

Frost waved a dismissive hand. 'Such a selfish generation. Only consider – I would be watching, and I would find it very entertaining. Your cries, your struggling, your feeble hands clutching at the cold water as you drowned. And this will happen whether you choose or not. I am giving you the chance to decide your own destiny – to give yourself willingly to the icy water.'

Light felt herself drawn to the idea. To throw herself into the sea, to end it all now, so simply . . . it was a seductive offer . . .

From behind Light, Arnie shouted, 'Don't listen to him, Light!'

Frost hissed. 'Oh, but you *should* listen, Light. You should listen very carefully.'

Suddenly he turned his head to where the Captain was inching forwards along the deck. He made a *tut-tut* sound.

'Trying to leave?' he said, quietly. 'Just when we're all getting to know each other?'

He glided towards the Captain.

And that was when the Captain drew the gun Light had given him from his jacket, and fircd it at Frost.

For a moment, all was still as the echoes of the detonation rolled slowly out into the Arctic darkness.

The bullet bored into the ice of Frost's head. But Frost just shook himself, like a wet dog, and the bullet fell to the ground.

The Captain swore but didn't move. Instead, he tensed and stood up straight.

'Ah,' said Frost. 'A noble stand. How boring.' From the folds of his cloak he produced an ancient-looking revolver, chased with silver filigree. He fired at the Captain's feet, causing the wounded man to jump, his fingers white against his shirt-sleeve bandage as he tried to hold in his lifeblood.

'You do know,' said Frost to the Captain, 'that you will fail, don't you? You will die and I will take Light anyway.' He laughed.

The Captain, swaying as he stood between Frost and Light, began to cry. Light saw the tears glisten on his cheeks, brilliant in the starlight.

Suddenly, Frost leaned forwards like a cat sniffing at prey. His face of clear ice split into an enormous smile of pleasure.

And Light remembered what her father had written in the front of the journal.

Observe what gives your enemy pleasure. It is usually the key to defeating him.

Frost leaned forwards and touched the Captain's cheek with his forefinger. A tear froze there, like a diamond. He

 203

looked at it for a moment, with something like wonder, then let it drop. It made a faint *ping* when it hit the deck.

Tears, thought Light. *He likes tears.*

Then Frost began to caper and sing, his voice gravelly and booming, the sound of rocks rolling and rattling in a glacier crevasse. His gaze was fixed still on the Captain's tears. At the same time, he fired several more shots at the man's feet, making him dance like a marionette, his steps uncertain, his breath rasping.

The words Frost sang were crazy, incongruous, and sung in a heavily cadenced skipping-rope rhythm. It took Light several moments to understand them:

> *I'm a little Dutch girl*
> *Dressed in blue.*
> *These are the things I like to do:*
> *Salute to the captain,*
> *Curtsey to the queen,*
> *Turn my back*
> *On a British submarine.*

On 'salute to the captain' he gave an elaborate, scrolling salute in the direction of the bridge. On 'British submarine' he stopped and laughed, reloading his revolver with eerie grace and speed. 'Of course, you didn't turn your back on the British submarine, did you?' he called out to Light. '*They* turned their backs on you!'

Light, who had been scared before, now felt a new core of frozen fear inside her, like the hard bit inside some food that hasn't defrosted for long enough.

If Frost knew she'd failed to get help from the *HMS*

204

Fogarty, that must mean he'd been watching her try . . . the thought of it was horrible – the idea that he'd been *observing* her, as she called for assistance . . .

She clutched the frame of the plane's cabin door.

Frost raised his gun and started singing again, all his attention on the Captain, who was wavering now on his feet, exhausted and overcome. Tears ran freely down his cheeks as he sank, finally to his knees.

> *I'm a little Dutch girl*
> *Dressed in blue.*
> *Here are the things I like to do:*
> *Salute to the captain,*
> *Curtsey to the queen,*
> *Turn my back*
> *On a British submarine.*
> *I can do the tap dance,*
> *I can do the splits,*
> *I can do the holka polka*
> *Just like this.*

Light realised with horror that Frost was mad – completely, irrevocably mad.

Then she heard the Captain laugh, the sound liquid as it left his tongueless mouth.

Light gaped at the kneeling man, his blood forming a puddle around him, and feared that Frost's enchantment was working: the ridiculous playground rhyme had snapped his mind. But then the Captain mimed the act of lighting a match.

The oil. He had smelled it.

Light fumbled with the box, tried a match, but it went out. Cursing, she went to grab another, but only knocked the box and upended the matches onto the plane floor . . .

She was about to bend down to pick them up when the Captain raised his pistol, turned it and pointed it at his own head.

'No!' she screamed.

Frost roared with anger and raised his own gun.

There was a loud bang that resounded through the night air, and set the cold metal of the deck to shivering, tinnily.

Frost had fired first.

The Captain jerked backwards, his body lifted into the air by the force of the shot, and landed heavily on the deck.

Lying on the deck, the Captain had something like an epiphany. It was not the life of the sea he had been looking for, he now realised, all those years before when he set out as a sailor. Instead he had been looking for something to love, something to protect. And now he had seen the light and in her he had found something worth protecting.

This was something to die for.

A bear stepped out from behind Frost, walked over to the Captain on its four huge, ambling paws, and ripped his left arm off neatly at the shoulder with its jaws – probably thinking that he was already dead.

Easy meat.

The Captain grinned and shot the bear in the face. His lifeblood was spilling away; his purpose and power remained. Another revelation shot through his mind, sun slanting through clouds: *It is a wave it is* light *it is the sun it is rainbows, rainbows*, he thought. *It is all sacred all of it and I am the wave I am the sun I am the wind I am . . .*

Light, tears running down her face, finally managed to light one of the matches and dropped it on the deck in front of her. With a slow *whump* like the sound of cushions being plumped, the oil that had dripped from the cracked jerry can caught fire. Flames rose instantly to the height of a man, racing towards the door to the bridge, writing a blazing line on the deck.

Light pulled herself into the plane, holding on to the doorframe. She could no longer see the Captain's body, obscured as it was by the curtain of flame. The knowledge that he had given his life to try to save her burned in her throat.

The knowledge that his sacrifice would be for nothing was worse – these flames would die, and they would still be stuck, unable to trigger the plane's mechanism.

Frost too could see the inevitability of the situation.

'I see that we have arrived at an impasse, my dear Light. I cannot cross the flames, for then I would melt. But you can't fly away, either, without someone to trigger the plane for you. And so we remain here, caught in a trap from which neither can escape.'

He drew in breath.

'However,' he continued, drawing out the syllables, 'the quandary is only temporary. These flames will die down quickly, you see, and then I will be able to come to you. And you – oh, yes, you will still be unable to fly.'

Light stared at the gun in her hand as if it could help her. The flames were already weakening and falling, the severe

cold of the air killing them. They had minutes, if not seconds to live.

She looked through the plane's open door, saw the
flames drop to a flicker and Frost and his disciples step forwards. She saw a spear raised and thrown, and ducked
back inside as it whistled past.

Then the Captain moved, and Light gasped. He was still
alive, and Frost hadn't noticed – he was too busy looking
at Light.

They could still save the Captain.

Light grabbed the side of the door and started to move,
wanting to get to the Captain, wanting to rescue him. But
Arnie pulled her back into the plane. 'No,' he said. 'There
is nothing you can do.'

Light struggled against him, vision blurred by tears, but
fell still when she saw the Captain wave her back with his
one remaining hand.

Then the old man, who had given his tongue, his
blood and his arm to Frost, and who had treated Light so
kindly, pulled himself up on one elbow and grabbed the
lever.

Seeing it, Arnie swore, turning the key in the ignition.
'Start, start, start . . .' he muttered.

Light wedged herself back into the plane's netted cargo,
preparing for the jolt of the forward force . . .

The world seemed to turn very slowly for a moment on
its axis . . .

And the Captain threw his body weight on to the lever.
Bang.

The plane was thrown forwards with sudden and shocking force, and Light clung to the side of the door as they

rocketed away from the bridge, towards the rear deck and the twenty-metre drop to the cold sea.

'Come on . . .' Arnie said, as the plane dropped off the back of the ship, air whistling through the cabin. Light felt her stomach dropping in her body, the downward motion of the plane giving her a rush of fairground excitement, even as she understood that she was probably about to die. She thought, *if my father is dead then I will meet him now.*

A strange emotion rose within her, one that only those who have faced death can understand – the tug created when your mind gets ready to leave the world, while at the same time desperately clinging on to it.

The engine spluttered into life and the butterflies in Light's stomach were replaced by a muscle-wrenching force as the plane suddenly changed direction. 'Oh, yes!' Arnie shouted, raising his fist in the air. 'It's not the scrap-yard for you yet.' The plane caught on the air, hung for a moment like a yo-yo at the bottom of its run, then started to move upwards.

Light closed her eyes and sank back into Arnie with relief. So it was something of a disappointment when he snapped upright. 'Look!' he shouted. She peered out and saw what had scared him: the back of the plane was on fire.

Flames licked at the fuselage and threatened to engulf the tail. The plane was moving quicker now, but the fast-moving cold air was not putting the flames out, only fanning them brighter.

On the deck of the ship hundreds of metres below and behind them, Frost reached into his cloak and took out his weather bag. If he could not capture the girl, he would destroy her.

With his other hand he reached down casually, plunged his fingers into the Captain's chest and pulled out his heart. What came out was not gory flesh; it was instead a glass-like, glittering simulacrum, frosted pink with frozen blood – a grotesque and beautiful parody of a cut-crystal paper-weight. Neither did the wound in the Captain's chest bleed: it had been cauterised by the same fingers that made it, and now it was only a frosty hole. Frost's cold raced through the Captain's body like cracks through a window, and when it reached his face it froze his tears, making them glittering jewels against his skin.

The bloodflow to his brain cut off, the Captain died. (*Rainbow rainbow I am a rainbow*)

Frost dropped the heart on the deck where it made a delicate smashing sound, a tinkling like a broken wine glass. He opened his weather bag, muttering the spell that would send a storm after the plane.

There was a tremendous crash and the plane shook. A succession of loud volleys, like gun-shots, rattled the fuselage. 'What the—' said Arnauyq.

Light looked out and saw great hailstones the size of fists falling all around them. The plane was caught in some kind of freak ice storm – one that had come from nowhere and that only seemed to be affecting the immediate vicinity of the plane. Behind them and in front of them, the air was calm, the snow beneath glittering softly in the starlight. Around the plane though, large hailstones fell in a flurry of snow.

Arnauyq gripped the controls and fought to keep the plane aloft.

Light risked another look and saw that the plane was no longer burning – the snow must have put it out. She felt exhilarated. Frost must have created this storm magically – the way it was falling only around the plane made that clear – but he hadn't realised they were on fire. The very thing he had sent to destroy them was going to save them!

Light felt a moment of pure happiness, a thrill of survival. But it was followed instantly by guilt. The Captain was dead. Butler and Tupilak were left behind, perhaps dead too . . .

She hadn't wanted to cry in front of Frost, not after she had seen the way he smiled at the Captain's tears, as if enraptured.

But now she began to sob.

A hailstone struck her forehead and her head smacked painfully against the corner of the plane's open doorway. She felt hot blood trickling down her face. Arnie gasped when she fell back into the cabin, tears welling up in her eyes.

'I can't keep us up,' he called out. 'We're going down. Best I can do is to try and crash-land on the ice.'

Arnie held Light and she put her arms around him too, as the plane fell fast towards the hard surface of the ice cap.

Chapter Twenty-seven

Rescue

Butler flapped his wings to descend from the sky, landed crouching on the deck behind the shelter of a lifeboat. He started inching his way towards Frost. The ice-monster was pacing the deck angrily, not paying attention to his surroundings. There was a smashing sound as he stepped on the Captain's heart, crushing it completely. Butler grimaced. He had liked the Captain.

So had Light.

A crow landed suddenly on his shoulder and Butler turned his face towards it.

'What is it?' he whispered.

'My lord,' the crow said, in a raspy, aspirated voice. 'We followed the girl's plane but were driven back by a storm. Many of us were killed by hailstones. I myself have broken a wing.' The crow lifted its right wing, showing how it was tattered and bent.

Butler grimaced. 'Let us hope the plane's wings remain unbroken,' he said, and curled his arm up to place a hand

 212

on the bird's broken wing. He muttered something and his hand glowed red then returned to its normal colour, like a poker heated and then cooled. The bird twitched, then folded out its wing – mended and straight.

'Thank you, my lord.'

'It is nothing. Go – and thank the others. I would not have you die at Frost's hand. His men are too many – our chances are not good.'

'You direct my life, my lord, but you do not direct my death. If I wish to die by your side, then die I will.' The crow puffed up its chest, not moving from Butler's shoulder.

'Very well. Let's go.' Butler began inching his way forward again.

That was when the unlikely saviours appeared, their sleek black machine rising through the thin ice like a special effect, a preposterous *deus ex machina* that just happened to be true.

The first sailors to step out onto the deck of the submarine *HMS Fogarty* were armed with British Navy-issue assault rifles and they opened fire on Frost's men without a moment's hesitation. After the strange distress call, they had initially dismissed the appeal as a prank, but had found themselves unable to remain blasé. If there was someone in trouble then let it not be said that the British Navy had turned their backs. And besides, they had heard strange stories from the Inuits in Nunavut – stories that the distress call brought uncomfortably to mind.

They were only thrown for a moment by the fact that some of the pirates appeared to be dressed in old-fashioned naval uniforms. Then their training kicked in, and their guns kicked as they fired.

213

From Butler's right an *isserkat*'s body jerked sideways, dragged into his frame of view by the force of the bullets, prancing like a marionette as it fell backwards and then lay still on the deck. Butler breathed in sharply while instinctively changing back into his human shape. The intruder must have been waiting on the other side of the lifeboat for him to make his move, and he hadn't had any idea.

Still standing by the door to the bridge, Frost whirled around just as the bullets struck him, making a glassily-metallic *ping* sound like crystal glasses being struck together in celebration. The bullets couldn't harm him, Butler knew, but he was thrown backwards, screaming. A hail of bullets hit the side of the lifeboat and Butler crouched lower, covering his ears.

When he looked up again, Frost was gone.

There was some resistance, but spears are no match for assault rifles, and those *isserkait* who had managed to arm themselves with more modern weapons lacked the training dispensed by the British Navy, and soon were captured or killed. One *isserkat* had got hold of a gun, and he was the last to die – he had had the sense to get up high, and was able to hold off the rescuers from the safety of the bridge until the smoke grenades sailed through the wide open windows and the sailors followed them, their guns blazing.

Tupilak dragged himself up the ladder a few minutes later – after struggling hard to break through the ice, which had frozen over again almost as soon as his body smashed through it. The sailors turned their guns on him, screaming, but Butler rushed forwards and waved his arms for them to stop.

'He's with me,' he said. 'One of the good guys.'

The sailors lowered their guns – but only a little.

Butler looked at them all with his clear, oh-so-convincing eyes. 'These men attacked us. My friend Tupilak helped to defend the ship. He is a little different from you, but I hope you won't hold it against him. You're better brought up than that.'

Some of the sailors began to nod, seeing the sense of what the black-suited man said. He seemed honest. Reliable. And it was true: they *had* been brought up well.

The British submarine captain took a step forwards. He too was armed, and Butler eyed his gun warily. 'His head . . .' the man said, looking slightly confused. 'It looks . . . well, like a shark.'

'Of course not,' said Butler. 'He is only a little out of proportion.'

The captain nodded, sagely. 'A little out of proportion. Yes. Best not to mention it, really. Might make him uncomfortable. I was brought up better than that.'

Butler nodded, smiling, and held the captain's gaze with those shining eyes.

'Thank you, Captain, for coming to help us.'

The captain smiled. 'Our pleasure, sir. We are the Royal Navy. We do not shirk our duty.'

'No,' said Butler, 'I don't suppose you do.'

The captain put down his gun and shook Butler and Tupilak by the hand. Then he invited them to spend the night on the submarine, under the safety of the ice. They gladly accepted. They knew that the Navy would have radar, heat-sensing equipment – a whole battery of high-tech tools that could help them to locate the plane, and with it Light.

They were climbing down the ladder when a figure hailed them from the ice. *Frost.* He was standing a hundred metres away, his dark cloak flapping in the wind. In the dark, it was impossible to make out his features, but Butler and Tupilak knew Frost of old.

'Hello!' he called. 'If it isn't my old friends, the patchwork man and the penguin-suited factotum! I am so glad you have found a safe, warm berth for the night. I am sad, though, that your surrogate daughter – the lovely Light – can't share your warmth. Oh, yes, she is swaddled in colder blankets than you can imagine, my dear old friends. Water fills her mouth, not whisky, and her body is wrapped only in seaweed. Fish and plankton feed on her eyes.'

Butler's grip tightened on the cold steel of the ladder's rung. 'You lie!' he shouted.

'Ah, but no,' said Frost, his mellifluous voice carrying seemingly without effort. 'I am afraid to say that you are mistaken. I killed her myself you see, and for that I say *mea culpa.* The fault is entirely mine. What I will not say, of course, is that I'm *sorry.* To gaze on your tears . . .'

Sure enough, hot tears were coursing down Butler's face. He felt like someone watching the earth unmoor itself and go careening across the galaxy, leaving him behind on a cold, small lump of ice.

'. . . is sweet reward enough for me. Oh, yes, I see your tears, though I am far enough away. And I relish them, my old friends. It is a process that never fails to give me pleasure; a magical process, if you will. I have only to open my weather bag, call up a storm of snow and ice, and someone dies. Then – wonder of wonders – their death brings forth tears of sadness from their loved ones – water springing forth from their bodies. It is something I will never tire of.'

Frost turned, swinging his cloak, and began walking away into the dark wilderness of ice. Turning his head over his shoulder he called out, 'Enjoy your nightcap, gentlemen.'

And then he was gone.

Chapter Twenty-eight

From the journal of Gordon Fitzwilliam

Once, many years ago, ice covered all the land. Everywhere, people struggled to survive in a world of endless winter.

The Cold saw this, and was glad.

But people are clever, and they always find a way to survive. They discovered fire, furs, the warming properties of caves and tents.

The Cold saw this and was angry.

All at once, the ice melted – though the sun still was faint and distant. It was almost as if the Cold had deliberately loosed its hold on the ice. Quickly, the land was overrun by water and people began to drown.

Soon there was only one settlement left on all of earth. Everyone with supernatural powers had already tried to save it – everybody, that is, except for Tulugaq. Tulugaq was the raven and had many magics at his disposal, but he

218

wouldn't use them because he did not believe in his ability to succeed. He loved to make things out of clay, but was afraid to stand up against the Cold, because he feared that his magic could only create, not fight.

But the situation looked hopeless so the people begged Tulugaq to help.

Finally, the Raven god could bear no longer to see people dying and floating on the endless sea, bloated with the gases of decomposition. He had always had a weak stomach for violence and death.

Tulugaq made a ball of clay. Using all his power, he spoke a spell and flapped his black wings. The ball of clay spun, expanded, and grew to cover the entire earth, forcing the water to recede.

The last settlement of man was saved.

Tulugaq, however, never recovered from his cowardice, and the shame it provoked. He thought always of the people who had died — who might have lived if he had acted sooner. The consequences of his doubts were grave: for ever after, his descendants — the crows and magpies and ravens — were destined to be shiftless and lazy.

Tulugaq swore he would never again abandon the people of earth.

Part Three

The Ice

Chapter Twenty-nine

Alone

A lump of ice the size of a basketball hit the left wing of the plane and tore it off in a single violent stroke, spinning the plane in the air. Light and Arnie screamed, hurtling downwards.

When they struck the ice cap, the usual coordinates of her existence lost any meaning for Light. Up and down deserted her – as did left and right, inside and outside. There was only whiteness and movement.

Light could hear Arnie screaming and hoped vaguely that he would be OK. Snow came through the open door in a great violent drift, choking her. There was a jolt and she was thrown against the roof – or was it the floor? – and then there was nothing, blackness taking the place of the whiteness of the snow.

Light rose slowly back to consciousness, like a diver coming up gradually from the depths to avoid the bends.

223

She opened her eyes. Ice stretched out in front of her, soaked pink with blood.

Arnie!

She called out his name, over and over, beginning to panic. He couldn't be dead he couldn't he couldn't . . .

'Light!'

She turned her head – wincing at a deep ache in her neck – and saw Arnie huddled on the other side of the cabin. There were several small cuts on his face, but he was smiling weakly. Light tried to move and found that she was stuck. 'Arnie!' she said. 'I'm paralysed!'

'I don't think you are,' he answered. 'I think you're just caught in the netting.' Webbed plastic netting had been stretched across the cabin to keep the cargo from sliding around when the plane banked and turned. Light craned her neck as far back as she could and saw that her body was wrapped in this netting, as if cocooned by a spider.

'Well don't just stand there then,' she said. 'Make yourself useful and cut me free. There's a knife in my pack.' She gestured with her chin at the bag lying next to her under the webbing, its strap still around her shoulder.

Arnie shuffled across the cabin, groped through the webbing, found the knife in the bag and used it to cut Light free. As the webbing came free, Light felt herself sliding forwards – she clung to the doorframe. Slowly, her bearings sank in. The plane was at an angle.

Light braced herself against the doorframe and peered out. The plane was at the bottom of a steep snow slope, which it had apparently slid down like a toboggan. She supposed they had been lucky: if they had struck the facing slope head on, the plane would have concertinaed from the impact, with her and Arnie inside . . .

A huge, round moon glowed above her, painting the ice with pale light. Light stepped out gingerly onto the snow. She reached into the cabin and grabbed Arnauyq's elbow as he got out, helping him to balance.

They stood gazing at the moon. The snow underfoot glittered prettily in the moonlight, as if jealous of the attention being paid to the moon. A ridiculous number of stars gleamed in the sky above them. Arnauyq pointed at them. 'They say that once, the world was always dark and there was no death. Then when death came to the world it brought light with it, because when people die they go up to heaven, and become shining stars there.'

'I know,' said Light. She had heard the story from her father. She hesitated. 'Do you suppose the Captain is up there?'

'Maybe,' said Arnie.

Light looked up at the stars, trying to tell whether there was a new one – but it was impossible; there were so many and her eyes were so tired. She shivered. The thought that the stars might be the souls of people, looking down on them, was not entirely pleasant.

'Back there on the ship,' said Arnie. 'That was . . .' He trailed off, gesturing vaguely to convey the madness of the battle.

'Yeah,' said Light. 'It was.' She thought of the attackers – the *kivigtok* – and their strange floating helpers. As the two of them crunched up the snow slope to check out the surrounding landscape, she asked Arnie, 'You talked about the tall men with the sideways eyelids. But do you know what those balloon-men were?'

Arnie shivered and hugged himself. He looked around, as if to make sure that no one was listening.

'*Hollow people*,' he whispered. He sped up.

Light hurried to keep up with him, slipping on the hard-packed snow. 'And they are . . .?' she prompted.

'When people die they become stars, to shine in the night sky for the benefit of the living,' said Arnie.

'Yes. We just covered that.'

'But before that, they are taken to the moon spirit, *taqqiup inua*, who is also called Malina. And before they are taken to Malina, they must face the terror of *Aukjuk*.'

'Aukjuk? What's that? Some kind of monster?'

Arnie sounded a little embarrassed. 'Um . . . an old woman.'

'Right. Scary.'

'It *is*. You see, Aukjuk's job is to try to make you laugh. She capers and dances and falls over. But if you laugh . . . Well, she wins.'

'She wins?'

'She eats out your entrails with a spoon.'

Light stumbled on a lump of ice. '*What?*

'She eats your insides, and then Malina sends you back to earth. Back home, I heard the elders speak of a man named Kanak who died suddenly and was taken by Death's dog sled to the moon. When Kanak got there and faced Aukjuk, she did a humorous dance for him, licking her own back and contorting herself in many funny positions. But Kanak did not laugh. Then Aukjuk cursed and began to walk away and Kanak felt a sense of triumph.

'But as the old woman walked she tripped, or pretended to trip, and the dish fell down on her foot. She cried out in pain and Kanak burst into uncontrollable laughter. Smirking, Aukjuk came back to him and slit his belly open, pulling out his stomach. This she arranged on a silver dish and then wolfed down, licking the juices from her chin with her long tongue. Kanak was shocked but not hurt, though he was so light now that he floated up to the ceiling and bumped against it. Soon the man from the dog sled came back, shook his head more with resignation than pity, and with the aid of a ladder got Kanak down and strapped him onto the sled. He brought him home, and after that, Kanak's wife had to keep him tied to the end of their bed, so he would not float away into space.'

Light frowned. 'And the balloon-men . . . they've all had their entrails eaten and been sent back to earth?'

'I know. It sounds ridiculous. But we did just see a man made of ice.'

'True.' Light thought of the way the balloon men sucked the blood from their victims. 'Why do they eat people?' she asked.

Arnie thought for a moment. 'I think Aukjuk takes their souls, and they feed to fill the hole inside them.'

It wasn't a nice thought, and they continued to walk through the grey snow in silence. Soon they reached the peak of a snowdrift, and the vast emptiness of the Arctic was laid out around them.

They stood in blankness.

Apart from ice mountains on the far north horizon, and the black sea twenty metres to the west, there were no landmarks at all in this vast, blank country. Light felt strangely disorientated. She had never had a very clear mental picture of the Arctic, and now she found that the place itself was similarly vague. Antarctica had always seemed clear to her: a country of penguins and explorers, pinned firmly to the bottom of the globe in her bedroom by a thin metal pole. It was fixed, it was definite.

If she had ever pictured the North, though, it was only as a cold and enormous emptiness.

'We don't have a sled, and I don't know how to build an igloo,' said Arnie. 'All we have is your pack, and what's in it. What have you got?'

Light sighed. 'A torch. A GPS. A little gas heater, and some beef jerky. That's about it. I used the distress flare to kill one of the balloon-men.'

'Great,' said Arnie, sarcastically. 'I mean, it's not like we're in distress, or anything.'

'He *was* trying to kill the Captain.'

'The Captain who we left behind to die? That Captain?'

Light glared at him, ready to retort.

But arguing wasn't going to solve anything.

'We're going to have to bury ourselves in the snow and keep close to preserve warmth,' she said. She took the GPS system from her pack and turned it on. After a few moments, the system made an electronic *ding* and an arrow icon appeared, hovering over a blank space, devoid of any labels.

The Arctic.

Light scrolled through a few of the options. 'Ah. We do have one more thing,' she said.

'And what's that?'

'A heading. Dad's research station is thirty miles north-east of here.'

Chapter Thirty

On the ice cap

They were living in an erasable world. They left tracks –
footprints in the snow – which went back forever. It was
incredible, to turn around and see so clearly your trajectory, to be able to identify in the impressions of your feet
the way you'd come, and the way you were going. Light
felt like she was making something happen whenever she
saw her footprints stretching out behind her, like she was
making a new story appear on a fierce white page.

And then a flurry would come along, or a storm, and the
tracks would be gone. Time and time again, the elements
erased any trace of the pair, shaking a vast etch-a-sketch
machine that returned the world to untouched whiteness
and made them feel that they were being given an
unfriendly message. When they breathed, it was like
breathing needles. The cold stabbed at their lungs with
every breath.

Then there were the gaps. Up to now they'd been able
to jump across the cracks in the ice, clearing the water

easily. But soon, they both knew (though both said nothing about it) they would have to swim. They were walking on an ocean – a thin crust of ice separated them from watery deaths. Light felt like one of those insects that you see walking on the water in ponds: as far as that insect is concerned, it is on a solid footing, on *terra firma*. But really it is walking on surface tension, impossibly thin.

Snow whirled around them. The white-out had descended half an hour ago, reducing their world to a cloak of white. They sat down – it was impossible to proceed, not knowing if you were going to fall into the cold, cold sea.

Light sat in the encompassing whiteness and felt a tear roll from her eye, then freeze on her cheek. She was desperately afraid. Here on the ice cap she felt like a flea on the back of a polar bear, and at any moment the bear could choose to scratch . . .

To distract herself, she turned to Arnie. 'We're like the white girl and the Inuit in that story,' she said. 'The ones that got lost in the Arctic and died.'

'What story?'

'The one I'm about to make up. *Once upon a time . . .*'

'Great,' said Arnie. 'Way to cheer me up.'

In a white-out the line between the sky and the ground is blurred and elided – all is one and all is white. Not being able to see accentuated Light's hunger, reminding her forcefully that she had only eaten beef jerky for the last couple of days, and even then in tiny, rationed amounts. For water they had been melting ice in a metal cup, using a small gas burner. Light's training had kept them alive this far – moving only for short periods, eating frequently, keeping their bodies close for warmth. But it wouldn't take them much further.

Both of them were learning that there were lots of types of snow: dry, soft flakes like those in a snow globe; wet snow that turns to ice; flurries of snow swept up by the wind; and of course blizzards, in which the ground and the sky become the red and white on a barber's pole, whirling around in such a blur that you can't tell the difference any more. Then there was the worst snow of all: hard grains like sugar which added bite to the wind, scouring your face and leaving you red and sore.

Some time later – Light's watch said it was only a few minutes, but neither of them believed it – the blizzard died down and they were able to start moving again. They picked their way north-east, keeping an eye out for deep cracks in the ice that might have been covered over cosmetically by the new snow.

In truth, they weren't sure what these cracks might look like, but they avoided places where the snow was grey, figuring that where the ice was thinnest the black of the sea must show through.

Light took the GPS from her bag and turned it on. She looked at the screen for several long moments, not believing what she was seeing.

'Uh, Arnie,' she said. 'We have a bit of a problem.'

He stopped. 'What? What's going on?' She showed him the screen. 'Oh,' he said.

According to the GPS, they hadn't moved in the last few hours. Light's father's research station was still ten miles away. Light shook the thing. But the coordinates stayed stubbornly the same. 'Broken,' she said. 'Must be the cold.' She threw the expensive gadget away. They would have to follow the stars now. In theory, the research station was north-north-east, so they could simply follow the North Star, bearing just a little to the right.

But if they misjudged by only a degree or two, they could walk straight past the research station. Light swore.

'If we're talking problems, then I have another one,' Arnie said. He nudged Light and pointed west. She turned, squinted and saw what he was pointing at.

About ten metres away, a dark shadow was moving along the ground. Light looked up, but couldn't see a bird.

This shadow wasn't attached to anything.

As Light watched, though, the shadow seemed to realise also it was being watched and came to a halt, turning into a dark patch on the ground like any other. Light squinted again.

'It's been following us,' said Arnie.

Chapter Thirty-one

Snow Crows

Butler slammed his palm into the dented side of the plane. *Gone.* They were gone, into the emptiness.

Tupilak came round the plane's half-submerged nose. 'No tracks. The snow has covered them.'

Butler struck the plane again. 'Oh, Light,' he said. 'If you'd just stayed where you were . . .'

Tupilak lifted a hand to his eyes and scanned the horizon. Some hundred metres away was the glossy black hump of the British submarine, rising from the water like a whale's back.

Apart from that the landscape was empty.

'Can't you . . . I don't know . . . find them, somehow? Use your powers?' asked Tupilak.

Butler shook his head. 'I make things. I don't *find* them.'

Tupilak shrugged. 'Then make something to find them.'

Butler opened his mouth to speak, then stopped. He looked thoughtfully at the shark-man. Then he cracked his finger joints, stretched his arms, and whispered words that twisted in Tupilak's guts. He bent down and scooped up some snow.

The tattoos on Butler's forearms melted, ran down to his hands, and soaked into the snow, blackening it. Then the dark snow shivered, trembled, and grew wings.

Butler threw his hands up.

Crows burst from them like inverse fireworks, draining the light from the stars. Cawing, the birds wheeled away in all directions, dwindling over the waste of snow to points of darkness. Soon only three were visible to Butler and Tupilak, hopeful suspension dots on the blank page of the ice cap

. . .

and then even they were gone.

Chapter Thirty-two

Ghost story

Light woke slowly.

She couldn't feel her body and she could see only whiteness.

Confused, she sat up – it seemed harder than usual, as if a weight were pressing on her. Reaching with slow, clumsy hands, she felt for her stomach and legs. There was something odd about the sensation, a resistance . . .

Then she understood. Her fingers were groping through snow, her eyes were blinded by it.

A drift of it had come down in the night, burying them.

Panic seized her, making her body shake and her mind babble to itself madly. She scrabbled at the soft whiteness, trying to find the surface. She'd gone to sleep on her back, so . . .

What if I turned over in the night, and now I'm burying myself deeper?

But a moment later she broke through the snow, and

saw again the dark gleam of the sky. She pulled herself free of the drift and began to dig for Arnie.

An hour or so later, Arnie took another sip of cold water from the tin cup. He and Light were huddled in a snowdrift of their own making, keeping close together for warmth, still shivering from their time under the snow.

But the cold was not the worst of it. The worst thing – which neither of them had dared yet to mention – was how easy it had almost been. How uncomplainingly their bodies had sunk into numbness and repose, as the Arctic snow stitched a funeral shroud of whiteness to cover them. If Light had not woken when she did, they might have passed from their shallow sleep into a more permanent rest.

At least their bellies were full. The previous day – or at least, the previous waking stretch – they had come out of their burrow to find a seal carcass laid out neatly beside them, not yet frozen but already cold. Light had thought it must be a trap – or maybe bait designed to lure a polar bear into attacking them – but Arnie had pointed out the way the seal had been carefully bled and gutted, so as to smell as little as possible and not attract bears. Unfortunately, it hadn't been cooked. Light had almost gagged when the raw meat slid down her throat, but some survival instinct had overridden her disgust.

Next to the seal were two leather necklaces with strange packages hanging from them. '*Ini'Go tied*,' said Arnie, wonderingly. 'Who could have left those there?'

He looped one of them around his neck.

'What are they?' asked Light.

'Protective amulets. They're made from seal blubber wrapped in wolf's fur, and they'll protect us to some extent against any evil.'

Light had tied her own amulet around her neck. She wondered if this was the shadow's doing – helping her, as it had promised.

Now, cold but no longer hungry, Light looked up at the Northern Lights. This place stirred a strange mixture of emotions in her: fear over their lack of food and shelter; the black-humoured camaraderie of survival with Arnie; the strange feeling of sadness that fills your chest when you look at a beautiful, empty landscape.

Above her, the garishly beautiful colours of the Northern Lights swam in the sky, as messy and uncoordinated as a child's finger-painting. The bright colours of the sky seemed to mock the stiff old snow, with its deathly pale palette of white, black and blue – the colours of a drowned man's face.

'I saw the shadow again yesterday,' said Arnie, suddenly. 'In fact, not just one but two, following us.'

Light looked up, stunned. '*Two?*' she asked.

'Yes,' said Arnauyq. 'Why?'

'Oh, nothing,' said Light, unsettled. *Two shadows?* One of them must be her shadow from Neagh House. But what was the other one? She cupped her hands together and breathed into them, trying to warm her fingers. Breath didn't mist here; it formed instantly into solid shards in the air, which shimmered and then fell to the ground.

Arnie looked at her, seeing her fear. He smiled comfortingly and leaned back against the hard-packed snow. 'I think the shadows are good luck, you know. Perhaps they even left these amulets.' He paused. 'The old folk talk about a race of shadow people. They call them *tarrayarsuit*. There's a song, but I don't know if I could—'

Light snorted. 'Are you shy about singing to me?' she asked.

'Yes,' said Arnauyq, simply. 'Singing is a very personal thing. You wouldn't sing in front of just anyone, would you?'

'Actually I probably would. Irish blood and all that.'

'Oh,' said Arnauyq. 'For us, singing is important. We say that when you sing, you let out your *inua*. Your soul goes into the song. "*Everything in me is song.*" That's what the elders say.'

Light nodded. 'I like that.' She moved closer to him, sharing his warmth.

Arnie too edged closer. He started to sing.

Light took a sharp breath. Arnauyq's voice was clear and melodious, seeming to hang on the cold air like the Northern Lights that shimmered in the sky above them.

There is a tribe of invisible men
Who move among us like shadows – have you seen
  them?
You can see their tracks in the snow
And even their igloos,
But never the invisible men themselves.
They cannot be seen except when they die
For then they become visible.

It once happened that a human woman
Married one of the invisible men.
He was a good husband in every way,
But the wife could not bear the thought
That she did not know what the man she married
   looked like.
One day when they were both at home
She was so overcome with curiosity to see him
That she stabbed with a knife where she knew he was
   sitting.
And her desire was fulfilled:
Before her eyes a handsome young man fell to the
   floor.
But he was cold and dead, and too late
She realised what she had done,
And sobbed her heart out.

When the invisible men heard about this murder
They came out of their igloos to take revenge.
Their bows were seen moving through the air
And the bow strings stretching as they aimed their
   arrows.
The humans stood there helplessly
For they had no idea what to do or how to fight
Because they could not see their assailants.
But the invisible men had a code of honour
That forbade them to attack opponents
Who could not defend themselves,
So they did not let their arrows fly,
And nothing happened; there was no battle after all
And everyone went back to their ordinary lives.

When the song ended, Light sat there for a while, still as the ice around them. 'That was . . . wow. That was beautiful,' she said. 'Your singing, that is. The story was just really, really sad.' Light huddled closer still. 'How do you know all these things, anyway?'

'You know I told you on the ship that no one listened to the old folk?' replied Arnauyq. 'Well *I* did. I liked to sit with them whenever I wasn't at school, learning the old stories. Until they started accusing me of witchcraft, that is.'

Light sighed and sat still for what felt like a long time, listening to Arnauyq's heartbeat. 'How horrible for those shadow people,' she said, so as to hear something other than the boy's heart. 'To be unable to defend themselves because of their honour. Do you think the shadows following us are these invisible men?'

'I don't know,' replied Arnauyq. 'But if they are, we should remember that the *tarrayarsuit* are not dangerous. It is said that they were made by Tulugaq before he made people – a kind of trial run, I guess – and they serve him still.'

Light blinked. *Tulugaq.*

For a while now she had nurtured a suspicion – a ridiculous suspicion, really – but now she took it out again and turned it over in her mind, as if it were a curious object.

She thought Butler might *be* Tulugaq.

Once Arnauyq was asleep, Light hissed, '*Shadow.* Come out where I can see you.'

The familiar patch of darkness moved towards her over the snow.

'What is it, mi'lady?' the shadow asked with a touch of sarcasm.

'There's another shadow following us,' said Light. 'Maybe more than one. Do you know what it is?'

'No,' said the shadow. 'I don't know.'

'I thought you were going to help me,' Light said. 'You're not being helpful.'

'I am so,' said the shadow truculently. 'Didn't you get the seal?'

'That was you? Thank you,' said Light, sincerely. 'How did you know how to skin it so well?'

'I was a country serving maid. I know how to prepare a dead thing.' The tone was mildly threatening.

Light shuddered at the thought of the poor seal, suddenly set upon by a thing of pure darkness. 'And thank you for the amulets, too,' she said.

'Amulets?' asked the shadow.

'Ah,' said Light. 'That must have been the other shadow. You really don't know what it is?'

'Not *it*,' the shadow said. '*Them*. And no, I don't know what they are. All I can tell you is they are not ghosts. They are definitely alive.'

Chapter Thirty-three

Rescue, redux

On a winter's day when you don't have to go to school, snow is a beautiful thing: white and other-worldly, it falls gently to the ground in unique, fragile flakes, covering the earth in a softening layer that can make even the ugliest of landscapes breathtaking. In the Arctic, though, the beauty of snow is underpinned by deadly danger – in the same way that a beautiful bunch of flowers becomes something more terrible and more devastating when you see it propped against a lamp post at the side of a busy road, with a note pinned to it.

They had been forced to stop once again by a white-out, and they were both close to giving up. Light and Arnauyq held each other in the falling snow. Though neither of them mentioned it, they both believed they would soon die. They could not see – they could not walk. They could only sit as the snow fell around them, softly burying them by degrees.

Light's limbs became heavy – foreign objects weighing

down her body, pulling her into the snow. She closed her eyes. This would be an easy death, blanketed by snow, so soft, so light. 'Arnie,' she said, quietly. He didn't reply. She half opened her eyes and saw that he was lying beside her unconscious, his face serene. She put her arms around him and was about to close her eyes when she saw something move – an anomaly in the darkness around them. 'Shadow?' she whispered.

'Do you wish me to take you now?' asked the shadow, as it formed itself into the shape of a girl that hung in the air. 'Are you ready to take my place at Neagh House? What a shame, when you have come so far.'

'No,' said Light, surprising herself. 'But my bargain stands. When I have rescued my father, then I will come with you. But I need your help.'

'Very well,' said the shadow, nodding. 'What would you have me do?'

'Can you look around? See if there's anyone near here who could help us?' It was a vain hope, Light knew, but it was their only chance. The shadow fell to the snow like rain and was gone. Light didn't know how long it was before it returned, but she was forced to open her eyes – an effort, now – when the girl's voice said:

'There is a house of ice nearby.'

Light wondered what that could mean – a house of ice. An igloo? Or Frost's lair?

She decided it was worth the risk.

'How near?' she asked.

'A hundred paces, no more.'

Light rolled to the side and managed to get her knees under her. Then she fumbled with her pack, unable for a few frantic minutes to get the zip undone. Finally she did it and pulled out the torch. She slumped against Arnauyq's body and began flashing the torch on and off,

. . . – – – . . .

sending the weak beam of the SOS over and over again into the thickly falling snow. 'Thank you, shadow,' she said, even as her thumb weakened on the torch's button, 'Thank you.' She did not know how many times she sent her message of distress before the cold and her own weakness claimed her and all was black.

Light woke in a dome of ice.

An igloo.

She stood, looking around. It was warm in here, even though the walls were made of ice. Light looked at the walls, lined where ice bricks had been piled on top of one another, marvelling at the thieves' conspiracy that kept the slippery bricks of ice together. In the corner was a pile of dogs, all curled up together and moving with their breath as if one creature. Hanging in the air just below the roof was a constellation of stars, turning in the lamplight. They were three-dimensional, like tiny diamonds, glittering brightly.

Light caught her breath when she saw that nothing was supporting them – they were simply hanging in the air, as if by magic.

There was also a glowing ball about the size of an orange, floating in the air above the middle of the room. Light stepped closer and saw that it was a tiny replica of the moon, complete with dark seas and indentations – only a sliver of the ball was lit, glowing brightly, looking like a single segment of an orange. The rest of the ball – more than three-quarters of it – was dark.

'It follows the real moon,' said the reedy voice of an old man. Light, startled, turned to his voice. 'Right now the moon is waning, and so is my magic moon. Soon it will be only a ball of darkness. Not the most efficient of light sources, but it gives me pleasure. And the stars shine always, of course.'

Sitting by a small fire in the centre of the room was a wizened old man with a shock of pure white hair and a lined, friendly face. He gazed up at her and waved her towards the fire. Light thought, *Arnie!* and looked anxiously around her and there he was, beside her, just waking up and smiling at her as if this were the most natural thing in the world.

'My name is Taliriqtug,' said the old man, 'though I have borne different names in my life. You may call me Tal. I am an *angakut.*' He looked at Light. 'Do you know what that means?'

Light stood, unsteadily, and moved towards the fire. 'A witch doctor,' she replied. 'A shaman.'

'That is exactly right,' Tal said. 'I am a shaman. Do you see this white hair? I won it from an Arctic fox. Before that I was completely bald – like an egg. For all the months of that winter I was happy as a seal in the green sea, for all admired my new hair, which was thick and white like the fox's. But then summer came and I realised that the fox had outfoxed me after all: he gave me only his winter fur and it did not turn brown in summer. So from then on my hair has been completely white.'

'It happens to the best of us,' said Light, pointing at her own white hair.

Arnie and Tal laughed and in that moment a bond was made, invisible but powerful as all the best things are.

'I am an *angakut*,' Tal continued. 'And there is much I know. For instance, I know that I must help you in your quest to find your father. Your friend told me all about it.'

Light felt a surge of hope, then slumped with disappointment. 'I'm sorry,' she said. 'We have nothing to pay you with.'

Tal smiled. 'There is no payment for an *angakut*,' he said. 'We merely suggest that an . . . exchange be made. People who make no exchange are apt to find that their charms for safe sailing desert them, leaving them to capsize in their kayak and drift to Setna's realm below the sea, feeding the fishes with their flesh and littering the sand of the sea-bottom with their bones.'

'We don't have anything to exchange, either,' said Arnie, his face bleak with thwarted hope.

'Of course you do. You have your company, and that's good enough for me.' Tal took a small pot from over the fire and ladled something hot and liquid into three bowls. He passed two of them to Light and Arnauyq, then reached behind him and passed around slices of something white which looked like streaky bacon without the meat part. 'Blubber,' he explained when he saw Light peering at the thing in her hand uncertainly.

Light was dubious but she ate it anyway, starving as she was. It was horrible – more because of the texture than the taste – but the stew was delicious.

She didn't ask what was in it.

 246

'I didn't know anyone still lived in igloos,' said Arnie. 'Wouldn't you like a TV? A cooker? All the, you know, conveniences of the modern world?'

'I don't live in the modern world,' said Taliriqtug. 'I live in a landscape of my own mind, which my heart has stolen from my childhood.'

'Uh . . . right,' said Light.

After eating Light leaned back on the fur rug that was stretched out on top of some kind of tarpaulin on the ground. Her fingers itched. After being outside for so long, the heat in here was somewhat painful. But the simple, smelly fur was so soft and welcoming, and it seemed to Light like a mad luxury, like a drink made from pearls.

For a while, Tal and Arnie spoke in fast Inuktitut, Arnauyq gesturing animatedly as he explained their adventures. He held his hands out and made a rising whining noise, miming the flight of an aircraft. Light smiled to herself. She was a little tired to follow the Inuktitut, especially so heavily accented, but every so often she caught an English word in their speech, like the flash of a goldfish's tail as it swishes past in a murky pond. She closed her eyes. When she opened them again, Tal was looking at her with a kindly expression, his conversation with Arnie obviously over. Around his neck, she noticed, was a shining steel dog tag on a leather thong of some kind. She gestured to it with her eyes and asked him, sleepily, 'Were you in the army?' Tal's eyes widened and Light realised that she had spoken in Inuktitut.

'You speak our language?' Tal asked.

'Yes.'

Tal nodded slowly. 'A white girl who speaks Inuit, a

plane crash, and a search for a missing father . . . I thought I had seen all there was to see on this ice cap.'

Light smiled and snuggled back into the rug.

'To answer your question,' Tal continued, 'I was not in the army. This is my E-number, or was anyway. The Canadians gave them to us in the Twenties. Came to my village and counted us all, then announced that we were to be given new names. Our own names were too confusing, they said. We didn't use Christian names and surnames like you do, so we were given numbers. I was the thirty-seventh person they counted that day so I became E-37. They engraved it on my tag.' He lifted the dog tag. 'Of course, we didn't know what the numbers meant, really, but we liked the tags. So we rubbed them smooth and wore them anyway.'

Light was shocked. She sat up, perfectly awake now. 'Numbers? For *people*?' She thought of what she had learned from Butler about the Nazis, and how they branded numbers on the arms of Jews in the concentration camp. It was strange to think of the Canadians doing something similar.

'Oh, yes,' the *angakut* replied. 'The *qallunaat*, the Westerners, always have some new plan to make our names easier to understand. Nowadays they just give us your Western surnames. What's your name, boy?' he asked Arnie.

'Arnauyq Smith,' he said.

Taliriqtug nodded. 'You see?'

Light leaned over the fire to get a closer look at the dog tag. 'E-numbers mean something different in Europe,' she said. 'They're artificial flavourings.'

'Doesn't sound different to me,' said Tal.

Light smiled.

'And now,' he continued, 'I think it's time you two got some sleep. Would you like a song? There's nothing like a song to rock you to sleep, even if you're not a baby any more. For us old Inuit, there's nothing more important than song. Because—'

'Everything in you is song,' said Light, remembering what Arnie had said,

Taliriqtug beamed. 'Exactly right.' He went over to a corner and brought back two fur sleeping bags. Once Light and Arnauyq were snuggled inside them, he sat again by the fire and looked into it, breathing deeply. Then he began to sing, in the strangely contrasting language of the North, all guttural Ks and Gs anchoring wavering, lifting vowels, which seemed to rise up and down above the hard consonants like a boat riding the waves above the rocky ocean floor below.

takujumagaluam Ut qangalannuarm ik im ma
  qingaruktillunga saktumik sangaram
  inakpuqqama
innuillamut
sam ungagu
Unaaya . . .
takujumagaluam Ut uksu lingm ik p ifiksailiriju m
  ik tuakjuk qangani takujumagaluam Ut
  qangalan
uarm ik p ifiksailirijum ik Unaaya . . .

Many of the words were old and strange, but Light was surprised to find that she understood perfectly.

 249

Eager to see caribou shedding old fur,
I moved to higher ground, and faced the hunting
grounds,
The old hunting places of winter.
Eagerly, I looked for something with fat,
A seal, on the thick ice, waiting . . .

There was more, but Light didn't hear it. She was already asleep.

Chapter Thirty-four

A spirit journey

When Light woke up Tal had gone and the fire had burned down to embers. Arnie was fast asleep beside her. She decided to leave him to sleep. In their corner, the dogs stirred but didn't move. Light hadn't seen them awake yet. Perhaps they slept all the time to preserve warmth.

Outside, the air had cleared and the light from the stars illuminated the snow brightly, so that the landscape was lit from both sides, by starlight and its reflection. It was as if the snow was distilling the essence of the starlight, and glittering with it.

Fifteen or so metres away was a strange white figure, hunched over. It looked like a yeti. Light took a step towards it and it waved at her. It was only when she walked further forwards that she realised it wasn't waving *at* her but waving her back.

She stopped.

'Damn it,' said the creature which was not a yeti but Tal, standing up and shaking the snow from its fur clothes.

'Sorry, Tal,' said Light. 'What are you doing?'

'I *was* attempting to fish through the ice,' said Tal. 'Now I'm scaring the fish away with my voice.'

Light sat down by the hole in the ice. 'Let's fish together then,' she said. 'I'll be quiet.'

And she was. Within half an hour, Tal had lined up three fat salmon on the snow.

When he and Light stood their bones creaked, and they carried the fish back to the igloo. Tal prepared them as Arnie, now awake, looked on. Tal plunged a knife into the head of one of the fish, broke it in two and removed two black things which looked like small stones. He set them down beside the fire. 'Do you know where those stones come from, Arnie?' he asked.

Arnie shook his head.

'In the beginning of the world, the salmon was a light fish and used to float on the surface of the water. That made people very happy, because they could catch the salmon very easily, and have a feast every day. But when Tulugaq the Raven saw that the salmon was being caught too frequently, he put these two stones inside its head, so that it would sink under the water and evade capture.'

Tulugaq again. Light wondered if these people had stories about anyone else. She changed the subject.

'Your song last night was beautiful,' she said. 'I felt like I knew you afterwards.'

'It is as the old folk say,' said Tal, who didn't seem to place himself in this category. 'Songs are only the soul, sung out with the breath. A song is beyond the control of its singer: the singer is moved just like an iceberg on the current. That is why Tulugaq gave us songs, so that we could share our souls with one another.'

Light gave up and sulked in the corner, thinking about Butler. Was it possible that he really *was* Tulugaq, the Raven? And if he was, why hadn't he told her?

When they'd eaten – the salmon was delicious and even managed to raise a smile from Light – Taliriqtug went over to his things and brought back a leather thong like a sling. Then he picked up one of the stones from the salmon's head. He handed the two objects to Light.

'What are these for?' she asked.

'I am going to perform a *qilaniq*,' replied Tal. He demonstrated how to put the small stone inside the thong and then hang it from her fingers. 'Do you have anything belonging to your father?' he asked. Light took the gold ring from her left hand and handed it to him. He added it to the pouch of the thong, with the stone. Then he laid himself down on the ground. 'I am going to try to call a dead spirit, an *apiqsaq*, down into that stone, so that I can ask it about your father. When the *apiqsaq* comes you will feel it – the stone will become much heavier and it will be hard to hold it. But you must not let it fall. If the stone breaks with the spirit inside it, the spirit will be destroyed.'

Light couldn't imagine the stone getting heavier. At the moment it was so light that it felt like she was only holding leather straps. The ring was probably heavier than the stone.

Tal began chanting. '*Apiqsauvutit, apiqsaqarlanga*, you are the *apiqsaq*. Let me have an *apiqsaq*.' He repeated this several times. Light listened sceptically.

Nothing happened.

Tal carried on chanting. '*Apiqsauvutit, apiqsaqarlanga*, you are the *apiqsaq*. Let me have an *apiqsaq*.'

Then, to Light's amazement, the thong started getting heavier, weighing down on her hand. Was she just imagining it? She didn't think so. Soon she was bracing her hand with her other arm, struggling to keep the thing in the air. She gasped. 'I think it's working.'

'*Apiqsaq*!' said Tal in a commanding voice. 'Will you answer my questions?'

'Of course I will, human,' said a deep voice that seemed to come from the thong. 'But make it quick. The girl is weak and will soon drop me.'

'*Weak?*' Light asked, offended.

'It's to be expected. You're a girl,' said the spirit.

'I'm a— *What?* I can do anything a boy can do,' said Light crossly. 'And that includes letting go of these straps *deliberately*.' She eased her grip on the leather, causing the thong to slip and descend an inch or so towards the ground. 'You wouldn't want this stone to break, would you?' She let the thong drop a little further – actually she was struggling to prevent it from falling. 'Do you accept that girls are not weaker than boys?'

'I apologise,' said the spirit. 'I was a killer whale when I lived, so I am prepared to concede that there is no great difference between girls and boys. You all taste the same, after all.'

Tal gave an exasperated sigh and said, 'Do you know where this girl's father is, *apiqsaq*? We would find him, and quickly.'

'I know where he is,' said the spirit, in the voice. 'But it won't help you. He sits by the throne of Frost, and you should give him up as dead.'

'And where is the throne of Frost?' Tal said. He had heard tell of the man of ice, and nothing he had heard was good. The old folks spoke of a man made all of ice, who could turn your heart to a snowball, who could take the lightning in your nerves and replace it with the slow cold glow of the Northern Lights.

'Don't you know?' said the spirit. 'His throne is North.'

'North is not a place. It's a direction.'

'No,' replied the spirit. 'When you have gone North all you can, and the compass can no longer direct you, that is North. It is very much a place.'

'Oh, the *pole*,' said Light, butting in. 'You mean the *pole*.'

'I mean North, but you can call it what you like.'

Suddenly, Light's fingers gave way, as they had once or twice when carrying heavy bags of shopping from the supermarket. The thong fell towards the ground and as it fell Tal shouted out a harsh, barked command. There was a quiet sound of impact – Light was amazed; shouldn't something that heavy have caused a *boom?* – and the small stone and ring rolled out. Light bent down and picked them up, slipping the ring back on her finger. The salmon stone was light as ever, but intact. She looked at it curiously and then handed it to Taliriqtug, who had walked over to her. 'The spirit is gone then?' she asked.

'It's gone.'

Tal went once more to his possessions and came back with a length of rope and a leather pouch. He handed the rope to Arnie and busied himself with inspecting the contents of the pouch.

'What am I supposed to do with this?' asked Arnie.

'Tie me and Light up with it,' said the *angakut*. 'We're going on a spirit journey through the air. A *ganjakatuq*. To try and find Light's father.'

'But we know where he is,' said Light. 'He's in the North.'

'And you think we can go there?' asked Tal. 'Greater men than I have tried and failed. So instead we will try to find his . . . what did you call it? His research station. Frost must have been there once, to capture him. Maybe he will come again. If you and I find its location on our spirit journey, then we can walk there easily in the flesh afterwards.'

'Why do we need to walk there if we can travel through the air?' Light asked.

'In a spirit journey it is impossible to go inside – to cross a threshold or a doorway. We must locate the place in spirit, then walk there, if you wish to see inside.'

Arnie tied Tal first, following his instructions. Once Light was also firmly tied, Tal instructed Arnie to throw the contents of the leather pouch on the fire. An intoxicating smell of herbs and spices filled the igloo and, as Tal started singing, Arnie crouched by Light's side. They could see that Tal had kept a small knife in his hands before being tied.

Now, as effectively as he could with his hands tied, he seemed to be stabbing himself in the chest.

'What's he *doing*?' Light asked in horror. Pinpricks of blood were appearing on the old man's shirt.

'Calling his *tuurngak*,' Arnie answered.

'*Tuurngak?*'

'Spirit helpers. Could be dead people, could be dead animals. Probably dead animals – that's why he's stabbing himself. Animals are often killed with knives, you see, so if he stabs himself he has a better chance of getting their sympathy, and luring them here.'

'Light!' Tal shouted. 'Think of animals! Any animal! You must find a spirit companion if you're to fly with me!'

Light concentrated, filling her mind with thoughts of bears and foxes. Nothing happened. She closed her eyes and pictured a seal, doe-eyed and cute. *Seals must get killed all the time up here*, she thought. *Must be a lot of dead ones around to help me.*

There was a popping sound. Light felt woozy. The room was spinning. She felt an electric pulse in her spine. Then a tugging on her umbilical cord and that made her look down because she knew she didn't have an umbilical cord, not any more. There was no flesh there but she could see a glowing tendril of light spiralling from her belly button and she thought, *so that's where I'm connected to the world.* It felt right that her middle should be the anchor that kept her tied to her body, the place where her soul connected, but then the tugging became more intense and she felt as if her stomach must turn inside out, and then the igloo wasn't there any more and she was in the sky, hanging like a snowflake in the cold black air.

Chapter Thirty-five

Walking in the air

Light looked across at Tal, who was floating in the air beside her. His beard was frosted with ice and his clothes were rippling in the breeze. It looked like he was really there, but every rational thought in her mind was trying to tell her otherwise. 'Don't look down,' he said.

She looked down.

They were at least fifty metres off the ground, suspended in thin air with nothing to hold them. She screamed.

Tal floated over to her and laid a hand on her arm. 'Don't worry,' he said. 'Your body is still in the igloo. You can't come to harm here.' Light looked around warily. In front of Tal a walrus was lying on its back in the air, looking relaxed and calm, like a fat person reclining on a sofa. On its belly she could see a red wound.

'That's where the harpoon got me,' said the walrus.

Light screamed again.

'Calm down,' said Tal. 'It's only my *tuurngak*. My spirit

258

animal. It is he who helps me to journey through the air.'

Light looked around her. 'Where's mine?'

Tal looked a little worried. 'I don't know,' he said, and the walrus shook its head too. 'It's a mystery. You're flying – you're very definitely *here* on this spirit journey with me – and yet you don't have a spirit animal.'

'I thought of a seal,' said Light, helpfully.

'Well, perhaps it's here but we can't see it,' said Tal, not sounding at all convinced. 'Let's go and see if we can find your father. If he's still alive, you should feel a slight pull in one direction, as if gravity has switched allegiances and is now pulling you to the side. Do you feel it?'

Light considered for a moment. Then she felt it – a gentle tug to the right. She nodded and aimed in that direction, doing a kind of graceless breaststroke in the air. Tal followed, the walrus leading him. Light hoped he wouldn't look down and see what she had just glimpsed as she turned.

On the snow below them, the *angakut*'s shadow was that of a normal man.

But Light's shadow was not the shadow of a girl. In fact it didn't look like her at all.

It was the shadow of a crow.

They floated for hours, Light amazed that the cold didn't seem to affect her up here.

They crossed over cracks in the ice where the sea showed through, over huge piles of snow like sand dunes. It didn't seem possible that anything could live here, but then Light saw a single polar bear, loping slowly along the ground below. She stiffened, but the bear only walked on, ignoring them, driven by animal instinct not will. This wasn't one of Frost's army.

Light still felt the tugging sensation, the pull towards her father, but they had been drifting a long time now above the ever-white snow, and had seen nothing but this one solitary bear which, even as they floated past it dived into the black sea and was gone.

Tal pointed to the ground, then began to float downwards. Light and the walrus followed and they soon alighted on the snow. Light looked at her feet. They were touching the ground, but she felt nothing – no softness of snow, no coldness. It was disconcerting.

Tal glided towards her and cleared his throat, and Light knew what was coming.

'We are travelling in a circle,' said the shaman quietly, pointing at the stars. 'This is the second time we have faced Orion.'

Light nodded. She had felt it. She couldn't navigate by the stars, but she had known somewhere inside her, had understood what was written on the endless blank whiteness below them – nothing; no one; nowhere. Her dad was not there.

'Then where is he?' she asked.

The walrus answered. 'Frost has him, and we know nothing of Frost. Perhaps his home is not even in this world.'

Tal pointed at the snow beneath their feet. 'He may live in the ice. He may live in the sky. He may live in a single flake of snow. It is impossible for us to imagine the home of a creature like that.'

'Then what do we *do*?' said Light. She gestured hopelessly at the snow, at the night sky, at the stars wheeling their course through it, burning with the light and heat of unimaginable worlds.

Tal raised his hands. 'I don't know. We should travel to your father's research station – I believe I know it. Perhaps there will be clues. For now, we must return to our bodies. If we are separated from them too long, they will grow sickly and distressed, like dogs when they are abandoned.'

Light reluctantly agreed, surprisingly tired from her swim through the air. They lifted back into the air then returned to the igloo, Tal navigating by some unknowable means, his walrus turning his flippers gracefully through the air.

When they reached the igloo, the walrus held out a flipper for Light to shake, and bowed gravely when she did so. 'It was a pleasure to meet you, Light,' he said. 'I hope you find your father. It is not good to be alone in the world.'

'I hope so too,' said Light.

'It is strange that you have no spirit animal,' said the walrus, thoughtfully. 'That is a thing I have never seen.'

Light shrugged, and the walrus seemed to smile.

'Well, what do I know?' he asked. 'I'm nothing but a dumb animal.'

Light smiled weakly back.

But what she was thinking of was the shadow her body had cast on the snow as she flew. It had not been the shadow of a girl. In fact it did not look like her at all. It was the shadow of a crow, projected onto the whiteness below. Perhaps she *did* have a spirit animal. Just one that no one else could see.

261

Chapter Thirty-six

One betrayed, two drowned

Every adult has a cream, unguent or dietary supplement that they believe to be a panacea, capable of healing anything. For Light's father it was Savlon, a very ordinary antiseptic. There was no affliction – from acne to burns – that he didn't think could be improved by judicious application of the sharp-smelling white cream. For Butler, it was the old mother's favourite: spit. He believed with passionate conviction in the curative powers of spit against all known ailments.

Tal was no exception to the rule. And while Savlon and spit are (relatively) inoffensive, Light was truly sick of seal blubber. The shaman insisted on feeding them blubber with every meal, saying that it contained vitamins they could not otherwise get in this world without vegetables. He rubbed it on Light's hands when she complained that they were tingling from the cold, and smeared it on their bodies before letting them out of the igloo. Even the lamps that lit the small round room were fuelled by blubber – which Tal said had been put in the animals of the sea by Tulugaq the Raven, so that man could have heat and fire.

Today, however, she was about to encounter something worse than blubber. After their usual breakfast of fish and blubber, Tal took out a bowl made of what looked like leather, woke up a couple of the dogs and led them outside. Light and Arnie looked at each other, puzzled.

After a few minutes, the *angakut* came back in with the bowl and brought it over to Light. 'For the skin,' he said, gesturing at the seal carcass on the floor. He and Light had killed it the previous day – or rather, Tal had killed it, while Light was sick on the snow. They'd spent hours waiting by a hole in the ice, Tal holding a harpoon ready. When the time came he threw the harpoon with deadly accuracy. It was amazing that he could still throw it with such force after holding the same position, in the freezing cold, for so long.

'I've already taken the skin off and macerated it in the brains for a night,' said Taliriqtug. 'Now you must soak it in dog's urine.'

'*Me?*' asked Light. This seal was in danger of making her sick twice.

'Yes, you. Traditionally it is a woman's job. Makes the clothes better. Warmer.' He was playing on her greatest desire – to feel less cold – and she knew it but it still worked.

'OK,' she sighed. They needed warm clothes if they were going to walk to the research station from here.

'Oh, gross,' said Arnie, peering over. 'That's really disgusting.'

Taliriqtuq smiled and handed Light the bowl. His smile faded as he saw her wrinkle her nose – not with disgust, but with recognition.

Light stared at the bowl. When she had picked it up . . . that smell . . . she saw in her mind's eye a scene she had not known she remembered – her, as a young girl, sitting with her father in the kitchen . . .

In the memory, her father seemed ten feet tall.

'What is it?' asked Tal, a little sharply.

'Nothing . . . it's just . . . This smell . . . I don't know. It made me feel like a child again.'

Tal jumped, startled, and accidentally spilled some of the urine on Light's hands. Light jumped up, wiping her hands on her jacket. '*Ugh,*' she said. If spit was preferable to blubber, then blubber was *definitely* preferable to dog's urine. Light felt nauseous again. Tal looked at her with a serious expression, ignoring her disgust at the urine on her hands. 'You know this smell well?' he asked.

'Well, if you'd asked me that before I smelled it I'd have said, *what, are you crazy?* But now . . . yes. I think I *do* know it well. It's really bizarre.'

Tal slowly stood up, taking the bowl back, and walked over to the other side of the igloo. He picked up the skin which was pegged out on the ground and started mushing it in the urine, muttering. Every so often he glanced over at Light.

'What?' she said. 'What is it? What does it mean? Is it bad?'

'Not bad,' said the *angakut*. 'Just strange.'

Arnie looked back and forth between the two of them. He didn't know *what* was going on. 'I thought you said a woman should do that?' he asked Taliriqtug.

'I did,' replied the shaman. 'But it's not so important. You two enjoy yourselves.' Light raised both her hands, palms up, in a gesture that meant, *what's happening?* and Arnie replied with a shrug and a shake of the head that said, *I have absolutely no idea.*

When the skin was done – and Light didn't know how you could tell – the *angakut* put the bowl aside and stood up. He went to Light's kit, rummaged around in it (ignoring her protests of *hey* and *that's my stuff*) then brought out her knife. Silently, he handed it to her. She was standing now, starting to get angry, feeling that once again there was a mystery she wasn't privy to, something to do with her that she wasn't supposed to know. He went over to the dogs' corner and spoke in the ear of one of the ones he'd gone outside with. Neither Light nor Arnie could hear what he said.

Baffled, Light weighed the knife in her hand.

Without hesitation or warning, the dog leaped towards her, closing the couple of metres between them in less than a second –

– and slamming Light back into the wall of the igloo. She gasped for breath, terrified, desperately holding the dog back as it snapped at her throat with its teeth.

What the—?

Light felt her arms weakening, felt the dog getting closer and closer . . . It tried to bite her and she felt the air stir on the skin of her throat.

She could feel liquid running down her chest and she knew it wasn't sweat. The dog's claws had raked her and her body was fire. Light's eyes swung wildly to where Arnie had been but she saw that he couldn't help her – Tal was holding him with his arms behind his back.

Arnie shouted, struggling against the *angakut*, but Light couldn't make out what he was saying.

The dog was big and heavily muscled from a lifetime of running over snow. It was too strong for her. Her arms were weakening already, bringing the slavering jaws closer to her neck. The beast's eyes were black holes, meaningless tunnels opening on to death. There was only one hope and that was the knife. She twisted her hand, managing to bring it round so that she was still holding the dog off – just – and the knife was in an inverse grip, pointing at the creature's chest. All she had to do now was slacken her tensed arms suddenly and the dog would go for her throat, forcing the knife into its own heart before its jaws would have a chance to do their damage. She took a deep breath, and prepared to relax her arms . . .

No.

She couldn't do it. Blood was running down her chest and her life was in danger but she couldn't hurt the dog. A voice was telling her this, in fact, a screaming voice in her head that drowned out her own panic,

don't hurt the dog don't hurt the dog don't hurt . . .

like an air raid siren in her mind. She started to cry, turning the knife slowly down so that when her arms gave way – and that would be soon – the blade could not harm the dog as it killed her.

Not for the last time in her life, Light made her peace with death.

From the other side of the room Tal shouted a single word and the dog let go, abruptly, causing Light to fall crumpled to the floor. She dropped the knife.

'You couldn't hurt the dog?' asked the shaman.

Light checked her chest. It wasn't blood – the dog had drooled on her chest. Actually, she wasn't hurt at all. Not physically, anyway.

'No, I couldn't hurt the dog, OK?' she screamed. 'What the hell do you think you're doing?' Tears of fear and humiliation ran down her face. 'Why would you do that? You're sick!'

'I did it to test something,' said Taliriqtug. 'And I am sorry that you are upset, but I find it interesting that you would not hurt the dog, even if doing so would save your own life. What you have told me with your actions is that you would rather die than cause harm to a dog. Would you agree?'

Light, slumped on the floor, looked up. She supposed, now that she thought about it, that it was a little odd. She *had* been prepared to die, rather than hurt the dog. She shrugged. 'Yeah, and?'

'I'll explain later, I promise,' said Tal.

'Fine. And another thing. Pull another stunt like that and I swear to God or whatever it is you believe in that I'll kill you. I may not be able to harm a dog but I'm pretty sure I can harm an old man. And I want you to swear by God or your bloody walrus or whatever that you'll tell me what's going on soon.'

'OK,' said Taliriqtug. He patted the dog's head and returned it to its companions, then went back to preparing skins for their walk.

'You didn't swear,' said Light.

'No. We Inuit do not believe in anything, especially not God. It is, as an *angakut* said to Rasmussen, the explorer who learned our ways in Greenland, *We do not believe, we fear.* We know that all living things have a soul, an *inua*. And yet we can grow nothing to eat here. We can eat only living things. And that means we are always afraid – because if we don't placate the souls of the things we eat, it will go badly for us.'

Light thought for a moment. 'Then swear by the soul of that seal,' she said finally.

Tal looked at her with the expression of a parent whose child has just learned some new and essential skill, like the ability to write their own name. 'I swear by the soul of this seal,' he said.

It was an odd start to a day they would never forget.

The three of them were on the ice by the sea, about to start their walk to the research station, when they were attacked.

Their gear was strapped to their backs and the dogs were pulling a sled packed with provisions. Light was marveling over the way the water encroached onto the ice, lapping at the moveable shore like pale fire – flames that fed on snow not wood. Then two polar bears and three of the spear-men, the *isserkait*, surrounded them, grabbing Arnie immediately. Tal said something to one of the men and laughed at the reply. Then he turned to Light and seized her, grinning with a new and terrifying intensity. In English he said to the nearest *isserkat*, 'You followed her admirably. But I'll deal with the girl myself.'

'Frost said we were to take her,' the man replied.

'Are you presuming to tell me my job?' asked Taliriqtug. 'She is to be *killed*.' The man looked at one of his companions, who shrugged. Then he looked at a bear and the bear shook its head.

It didn't know what Frost wanted. Its job was only to kill.

The bear growled and Light was surprised to find that she could understand what it said. *Kill her if you like. But Frost will be angry if he wanted to kill her himself.*

Tal made an impatient gesture. 'You, *isserkait*,' he said. 'Capture the boy and take him back to my igloo. I will deal with the girl, but I wish to have a moment with her before she dies. Would you give me that?'

One of the *isserkait* looked unsure. But another nudged him and said, 'You don't want to be turned into plankton, do you? I've seen the *angakut* turn people into that, and much worse.'

Still the man hesitated.

Tal sighed. 'You can stay here and watch. The others: to the igloo with the boy.' This seemed to satisfy everyone. The bears trudged towards the igloo while the men grabbed Arnie. They started marching him back. One *isserkat* stayed behind.

'No!' Arnie screamed as he was dragged away. 'You betrayed us! Tal, how could you do this?'

There was a dull *crack* and the shouting stopped. Light screamed, unable to process this turn of events.

Soon the figures were out of sight in the Arctic darkness and as suddenly as the dog had attacked, Tal whipped a length of rope from his overcoat and started wrapping it around Light's forearms, lashing her hands together. He cut her pack from off her back.

'What are you *doing?*' she shouted.

'Shut up,' Tal instructed sharply. He drew a cloth from one of his pockets and used it to gag her.

Next Tal took a small pebble from his pocket and placed it in Light's right hand. Then he used the rope to bind her fingers closed over it, so she couldn't let go. He chanted. '*Apiqsauvutit, apiqsaqarlanga*, you are the *apiqsaq*. Let me have an *apiqsaq*.'

After three repetitions of the chant, Light felt the *apiqsaq* enter the stone. This time, with her arms bound, she was powerless to counteract the enormous weight and she fell painfully to the ground, unable to put her hands out to protect herself. She lay stunned on the ground, not believing what was happening.

'Do you have more questions?' asked the familiar voice of the killer whale spirit.

'No more questions. I need only your weight,' said Taliriqtug.

The shaman dragged Light closer to the sea and, without warning, plunged her head into the water. It was unbelievably cold. Light hadn't had a chance to fill her lungs with air, and after no time at all had passed she already felt the need to breathe in. She told herself she'd only drown, but the physical instincts of her body would brook no insubordination from her mind, which was a usurper and an upstart and had not been around for as long as them.

Her chest muscles and her diaphragm began to expand, ready to fill her lungs.

Just as water rushed into Light's mouth, Tal pulled her head out. 'Before you die, I want you to tell me what you know about Tulugaq. Where is Tulugaq?'

Light spluttered. 'I don't know! I think he's my butler but I don't know where he is! I don't know!'

Light couldn't close her eyes or blink – they were held wide open. She realised that the water on her face had frozen as soon as it came into contact with the air.

Her eyes were frozen open.

Tal plunged her into the water again, not for as long this time. Then he asked once more. 'Where is Tulugaq the Raven?'

When Light screamed that she didn't know, he dunked her again.

It went on for an eternity: short dunk, longer dunk, longer dunk again. Short dunk. Short dunk.

When, finally, Tal gave up and simply kicked her body into the sea, Light felt bizarrely relieved. The water was pale blue to begin with, then darkened quickly to green, changing colour like a cat's eyes as it gets older. The stone was incredibly heavy, dragging her fast down into the crushing deep. She pictured Tal walking off with Frost's men, laughing together. How could she have been so stupid? Once more the urge to fill her lungs came, and this time there were no strong arms to pull her out of the water as her muscles inexorably tightened, beginning to create a deadly vacuum in her chest . . .

Chapter Thirty-seven
Drowning

Tal watched the body sink until he could see it no more. Then he waved a hand behind him, whispering an incantation. Surreptitiously, he pricked his chest with his knife, calling his walrus to him.

And the walrus came.

There was a wet *slap*. The *isserkat* who had stayed behind to watch looked down at his torso, aghast. Just below his ribs, on either side of his diaphragm, two tusks protruded. The white ivory was spattered with blood.

The walrus waddled backwards, shaking his head like a bull. The *isserkat* jerked like a puppet before eventually falling off the tusks and lying still on the ground. The walrus fastidiously wiped his tusks on the man's furs.

'Ugh,' said the walrus. 'Always a pleasure to relieve Frost of one of his helpers. A risky move, though, don't you think? Frost is more powerful than ever.'

'Shush,' said Tal. 'I'm thinking.'

He turned back to the sea and spoke again, keeping his

voice low. Soon a seal's head popped up out of the water, its friendly child-like face looking up at him questioningly. Tal spoke a few words and then nodded, gravely, when the seal's eyes widened. The sleek creature pulled itself out of the water and rolled on to its back, exposing its rounded stomach to the shaman.

The walrus came over to watch as Tal quickly slit the seal's belly open from top to bottom and dexterously removed the heart, still beating. Then the *angakut* knelt before the carcass, thanking the seal's *inua* for this sacrifice. He knew it had only given up its life because he had asked in *her* name. And Tulugaq's.

Any animal would die for those who opposed Frost, especially one who served Setna.

'I'll send Frost this heart,' said Tal, 'and Light's supplies. Perhaps he'll believe I really have killed her.'

In his hand, the seal's heart had gone still. In its size and shape it did look astonishingly like a child's.

'Even if he believes it, you know as well as I do that he wanted her alive,' replied the walrus. 'This stunt will get you killed.'

'Yes,' said the *angakut* simply. 'But it might buy her some time.'

'How much time can she possibly have? A minute? She's underwater, remember.'

Tal smiled. 'She does not harm dogs. I do not think she'll drown.'

Rocked by the cold water, Light's mind drifted. Something at the edge of her conscious thought was trying to make itself known – a realisation, an illumination. She wondered, idly, what it was. It had something to do with Tal, she was sure.

Then a thought streaked through her brain like electricity and she knew: when Tal had plunged her head into the water, he had done it in a pattern.

A long dunk first . . . then a short one.

Had he been using Morse code?

Another long one after that? Or was it a short dunk first?

She knew she had only seconds before the cold killed her, or the water rushed in and she drowned, so her mind ran feverishly over the sequence.

Life socket?

No, that didn't make sense.

Knife pocket.

Yes! Her arms were bound together and her right hand was bound tightly closed but her left hand could move. She was in dark water now, no longer descending, and the pressure in her ears was excruciating. She knew if she got free she'd have to ascend slowly to avoid the bends. Would she stay conscious for long enough?

It must be the front pocket of her jacket. There was no way she could reach any other pocket anyway, so it had to be that one. If it wasn't she was dead.

Twisting her wrist painfully she managed to get her fingers into the pocket and they touched something cold and hard. Her knife – the one she hadn't been able to hurt the dog with. Light pulled the knife out and her heart skipped a beat when it slipped through her fingers – but then her hand closed reflexively and snagged on the handle. She turned the knife inwards and started sawing at the rope between her arms. She felt weak, attenuated, and knew that the cold was seeping into her bones, tightening its winter grip on her heart. She no longer knew where was up and where was down – a terrifying feeling because what if she got her hands free and swam down, only to feel the crushing pressure that would trap her in the deep, preventing her from ever rising.

Moments later her hands were free. She knew she should drop the spirit stone but it felt lighter now, as if the spirit had gone from it. And who knew? It might come in useful. She tightened her hand around it and began swimming towards what she thought was the surface, where the water was lighter by a tiny increment. As she swam she prayed, something she had not done for many years.

From her abortive experience at primary school, before she was taken out for home-schooling, she remembered that the nuns had exhorted her not to pray just for herself but to ask God for things that would benefit others too.

Dear Lord, she prayed, *please help all girls who are drowning at this moment, especially those who are in very cold water . . .*

She was nearing the blue water again, the colour of kittens' eyes, when her lungs gave out and the water rushed in.

Chapter Thirty-eight
Killer whale

Light opened her eyes and saw nothing but murky green. The dull sound of deep water filled her ears. Was she dead? Was she dying?

She no longer felt the need to breathe.

And yet she was still underwater.

Then something loomed out of the green water in front of her and she screamed, filling her mouth with salty water and causing herself to choke for a moment.

Note to self: no screaming underwater.

For the moment, she ignored the fact that she'd been under the water for a long, long time without dying. There were more pressing concerns.

In front of her, gazing at her with large black eyes, was a killer whale. It was huge, its head at least the height of Light. Its streamlined body stretched behind it like a saloon car, white with messy patches of black, as if stained by paint.

Its shape – rounded with sharp fins and a grinning,

 276

tooth-filled mouth – sent a lightning-fast message of fear through Light's nerves, making her skin tingle.

The killer whale moved its head slowly and then flicked its tail, describing a long circle around Light as if it were investigating some strange new phenomenon. It moved with extraordinary grace. Where Light struggled to move effectively through the resistant medium of the water, as clumsy as an astronaut on a space walk, the whale made a mockery of the water's weight, moving through it like a bird through air.

Light felt fear like a physical presence in her stomach, heavy and dreadful.

She turned her head to watch the predator, fascinated despite herself, unable to tear her eyes away from this beautiful thing that was going to kill her.

Then Light's hand spoke.

'Cousin,' it said.

Light stared at her closed fist.

The spirit stone!

The killer-whale spirit in the salmon stone was talking. And the stone was heavy again – Light was surprised to find that the spirit was still in it and thanked the instinct that had made her keep hold of it. 'Cousin,' the stone said again, and its voice was a high-pitched song, weaving its bright melody through a series of clicks and taps, like a mountain stream rushing over and through pebbles.

In Light's ears the noise was foreign; in her mind it was mother tongue.

'Do not harm the girl,' the voice from the stone said. 'I have spoken to her, cousin. Her companion is a shaman

277

and he called me to help her. She is an enemy of Frost. I think . . . I think perhaps she will kill him.'

The killer whale stopped circling and focused its gaze on Light's hand. Its eyes seemed to widen; its muscled body tensed. Then it swam quickly forwards and Light closed her eyes, unable in the end to watch the moment of her death. She felt something soft and yet hard, like silicon, against her skin and then she was being borne through the water, smoothly and powerfully, the current silky against her skin.

Light felt vibrations through the rough-smooth skin of the killer whale, and then heard liquid melody filling the water around her, eerie and beautiful, full of clicks and trills. 'She doesn't look very good to eat, anyway,' said the killer whale.

'She doesn't, does she?' replied the stone.

Light started to say 'charming', but her mouth only filled with water, and she contented herself with squeezing the spirit stone a little harder. She supposed that looking good to eat wouldn't be such a great thing, anyway.

The water lightened quickly. Clinging to the dorsal fin, she saw the surface rushing towards her. All thoughts of the bends had gone from her mind and then she was breaking through into the air.

She should have been gasping for breath, desperate to fill her lungs, but instead she sat quite peacefully on the killer whale's back, breathing normally.

The icy shore was a hand's reach away.

And looming out of the semi-darkness, unmistakeable in its shape, was Light's father's research station. She had seen so many photos of it, on her father's blog – so many drawings and sketches – that for a moment it was as if she had been there before.

She had arrived at exactly the place where her father had disappeared, almost as if the whale had known it would be so.

What just happened? Light thought. She knew she had been underwater for many minutes – and by all rights should be dead.

Then the whale spoke.

'Return to the land, girl,' it said. 'Before I change my mind and eat you.'

The whale moved up alongside the ice and Light rolled herself back onto the ice ledge. She turned to wave but the whale had already dived, and the only signs of its passing were the ripples that disturbed the black water.

Light looked down at the heavy stone in her hand. Now that she was out of the water she had to hold it with both hands, and even then she could feel her muscles weakening, the gravitational pull towards the ground. 'How can I thank you?' she asked.

'You could release me.'

'How?'

'You say, "I release you".'

Light rolled her eyes. 'Well, that's easy then.' She spoke the words and in a moment the stone became light again – a mere grain from the head of a salmon. She cast it aside.

Light stumbled towards the research station, her wet clothes already solid with ice. As she walked she cracked and snapped, ice dust falling to the ground.

When she reached the steel door, she stood by it for a

moment, touching the cold metal. *This is the door my father opened every day, when he went to do his tests . . .*

Beside the door was the snowmobile, covered now by a drift of snow that curled over at the top where the wind had blown it, like the page of an open book, hanging suspended.

That is the snowmobile my father rode . . .

She took a deep breath, and went to open the door.

But before she could even take the handle in her hand, the door opened outwards.

Light staggered backwards, raising her hands reflexively.

'Ah, thank the gods,' said Tal. 'You're back.' He reached out to hug her.

Light slapped him.

Chapter Thirty-nine

The sea floor

Light stood in the corridor of the research station, shivering. The light was bright and it hurt her eyes after starlight and candles for so long. For a brief moment she was startled by movement behind her. But then she saw that it was her shadow, thrown starkly against the wall by electric light, elongated and thin, as if a scrap of night had clung to her as she walked in, and was being slowly washed away like mud clinging to boots in a stream.

'He's telling the truth,' said Arnie. 'He's not with them. He killed the guard with his walrus, then he took a seal's heart and sent it to Frost with one of the others, saying it was yours.'

Tal nodded. 'That is what happened.'

Light stared at him. 'What about the one you killed? The others didn't mind?'

'I told them you did it, with your dark magic. It would be as well if they feared you a little.'

'My *dark magic*?'

'Yes, well,' said Tal. 'I was thinking on my feet.'

Light pushed past them and into the station itself. 'Dry clothes?' she asked. Arnie rushed to get them for her, and when she had changed, in the privacy of one of the bedrooms, they sat down at the table in the mess.

Light looked right into Tal's eyes. 'And if I'd drowned?'

He looked down, uncomfortable.

'What – you just thought it wouldn't matter if I died?'

Tal fidgeted. 'It's not that. It's just . . . you *can't* drown.'

Light looked at Arnie, who was also looking nervous. 'What?' she asked, very slowly.

'You are an *angerdlartugsiak*.'

'A what?' Light had never heard the word.

'It means,' said Tal, 'that you are immune to drowning, and someone went to great trouble to ensure it. They would have had to surround you with dog urine as a child, probably while you were sleeping. It is crucial that an *angerdlartugsiak* should be accustomed to that smell.'

Light remembered the scene in the igloo. 'So when you were soaking that skin . . .'

'I guessed, yes. But I had to make sure. You see, an *angerdlartugsiak* would also have been taught never to harm a dog, also from a very young age. When I set that dog on you, you preferred to spare it, and die, rather than harm it. That was when I knew for sure. There's only one problem . . .' He tailed off.

'What?' Light felt as though that was the only word she could say any more, like her vocabulary had been lost in the sea.

Tal played nervously with his fingers. 'Various spells would have been made over you. Not by an *angakut* but by a god. An animal god, to be specific. This is why there are not many who have this magic any more. Where would you find a god nowadays? Where would you find Nanook the bear or Tulugaq the Raven in this world of cars and fridges?'

'I don't know,' said Light, weakly.

But she had a good idea.

'How did you know I could understand Morse code?' asked Light.

'When I found you in the snow, near my igloo, you were making the SOS signal with your torch,' said Tal. 'I had to assume that you knew more than the letters S and O.'

He and Arnie were giving Light a tour of the station. There was a dormitory with four beds, a galley for cooking and a supply room which contained the generator, a hot water heating system and a petrol pump – for the generator and presumably also for the snowmobile. The generator was running a normal household multiboard – a slapdash set-up, but it seemed to work. Light was glad the *angakut* and Arnie had got here first – the place was creepy, like the Mary Celeste.

Finally, there was the main control room, complete with comms equipment, computers and a shotgun.

And, beside the gun, something far more terrible.

Light recoiled, opening and shutting her mouth like a goldfish. On a table in the middle of the control room was a half-read book, a half-full tin cup of coffee and a plate with a half-eaten slice of toast.

'We didn't move it,' said Arnie. 'It didn't seem right.'

Light gazed at her father's last meal, and burst into tears.

*

One thing was obvious – Light's father wasn't here, and hadn't been for some time. The coffee was cold, the toast dry. Neither had gone mouldy – the air was too cold for mould – but they appeared diminished and changed, made unreal by the Arctic.

Light felt helpless. Finally, they had reached her father's research station, and it was nothing but a dead end. She'd known he wouldn't be here, of course – but she'd carried a tiny hope inside her, sheltered from the cold and the wind. Now it was blown out.

He was gone.

Exhausted, she waved away Tal and Arnie's kind attentions, and went to bed in the dormitory.

She cried herself to sleep.

The next morning, Light entered the kitchen to find Tal making scrambled eggs and coffee. He put down a plate in front of her, silently.

Light began to eat, then found that the food turned to sand in her mouth, hard and tasteless. She put down her fork. Her heart felt hard and cold within her, a smooth egg lodged in her breast.

'That's it, then, isn't it?' she said. 'I've failed. My father is lost. I'll never find him, and no one can help us.'

Tal too put down his fork. 'Well,' he said. 'That's not entirely true.'

Light felt a movement in her heart – as if a beak were breaking through its wall, the shell beginning to crack . . .

'Someone can help us?' she asked.

'Not someone. Something. Or rather . . . Setna.'

'*Setna?* Light remembered Tupilak saying that she had

 284

sent him to help her – Setna, the goddess of the sea and of hunting, most powerful of the Inuit gods.'

Tal nodded. 'We could visit her. I have never done it, but I have heard the elders speak of it. It is a spirit journey, but downwards, into the sea. I know the words to begin it.'

Light stood up. 'Well come on then,' she said. 'What are we wasting time with breakfast for?'

Moments later the three of them stood in the control room. Tal set a length of rope down beside Light and knelt. He began building a fire in the small stove.

'Do you know her story?' he asked. 'It is useful to know a little of a person, if you are going to visit them.'

'Yes,' said Light. She spoke in Inuktitut. 'Setna was a beautiful young girl. But she refused marriage offers from every young man who asked her. Until one day, when she could not resist the overtures of a beautiful sea lion, with whom she agreed to elope. In the sea lion's home, she soon realised that she had been deceived by false promises, for the sea lion treated her cruelly, and she saw her mistake in leaving the human world. In her sorrow, she sang a song to her father and pleaded with him to take her back.

'So the father came and, furious at his daughter's treatment, he killed the sea lion, took Setna in his kayak and set out for home. But the sea lion's fellows followed the kayak and with their flippers and their heavy bodies they stirred up the sea, threatening the kayak. In fear for his own life, Setna's father offered his daughter to the sea lions and threw her overboard. Since she desperately clung to the side, he took out his knife and cut off the top joints of her fingers. And it is said that the finger joints became the whales and the dolphins.

'After that, the sea lions thought Setna was dead so they swam away and the violence of the sea abated. Setna's father piloted his kayak safely home while his daughter drifted to the bottom of the sea. There she swore revenge on her father and began building a kingdom, for she had power over the animals which had sprung from her body.'

Tal, who had been nodding throughout the story, pleased by her telling of it, smiled. 'And did Setna get her revenge on her father, on the man who had hurt her, who had thrown away her life?'

Light frowned. 'It's not in the story. I guess not.'

Tal spread his hands. 'Exactly. This is your strength, when you see her. You seek something Frost has taken from you. Setna doesn't usually concern herself with such things. But she may see something of herself in you. You must remember that, when we see her. Appeal to her sense of justice, of revenge.'

Light shook her head. 'It'll be all right. Setna wants me to defeat Frost. She sent someone to bring me to the Arctic.'

Tal smiled sadly. 'Believe me, that doesn't mean she'll help you. Setna is cruel.'

Light closed her mouth. 'Oh.'

Tal busied himself with the preparation, talking things through with Arnie. Light sat staring at the floor, trying to control her breathing. She was about to visit the goddess of the sea, looking for her missing father.

The strangest thing was, it didn't even seem strange any more.

Just terrifying.

Finally Tal had finished his preparations, and he came to Light with the rope. He tied her quickly, with less ceremony

286

than the previous time. 'This is the *nakkaaniq*,' he said. 'The journey to the underworld. It is a serious business.' He turned to Arnie. 'Do you understand what you must do when Light and I enter the passage?'

'I understand,' said Arnie, who looked a little white. Then, after throwing some herbs on the fire, Tal sat down and tied himself with the remaining rope, his fingers tying the knots around his own wrists with a dexterity that Light wouldn't have believed if she hadn't seen it. He leaned back on the ground and began singing.

Igluli majja ijigivara silarjuali sunauvva manna
I look at the igloo. It turns out it's the sky.

Light interrupted. 'It's not an igloo. It's a research station.' 'Shush,' said Tal. 'It isn't important.' He started singing again.

Natirli majja ijigivara sikuliurjuarli sunauvva
manna, ijaa, ja, jaa, jaa
I look at the floor. It turns out it's the sea ice, ijaa, ja, jaa, jaa

Iglirli majja ijigivara nunarjuarli sunauvva manna,
ijaa, ja, jaa, jaa
I look at the bed. It turns out it's the land, ijaa, ja, jaa, jaa

Katagli kanna ijigivara taqqirjuarli sunavva kanna,
ijaa, ja, jaa, jaa
I look at the entrance. It turns out it's the moon, ijaa, ja, jaa, jaa

 287

Igalaarlipikka ijigivara siqinirjuarli sunauvva
  pingna, ijaa, ja, jaa, jaa
I look at the window. It turns out it's the sun, ijaa,
  ja, jaa, jaa

Igluli majja ijigivara silarjuali sunauvva manna,
  ijaa, ja, jaa, jaa
I look at the igloo. It turns out it's the sky, ijaa, ja,
  jaa, jaa

Light gasped. She was looking up, following Tal's eyes and
in the blink of an eye she saw the roof of the research station disappear.

Above them was only black sky and sparkling stars.

Akili majja ijigivara imarjuarli sunauvva manna,
  ijaa, ja, jaa, jaa
I look at the floor. It turns out it's the water, ijaa, ja,
  jaa, jaa

Light looked down and screamed. Below them was water,
dark blue. And then they were falling through it.

Chapter Forty

With Setna

Light gripped Tal's arm. The rope had disappeared and they were both descending freely through the cold water. Again, though, the cold did not seem to reach her – as if there were a cushion of air between her and the sea. A whale drifted past, its huge eye turning slowly to watch them fall. Plankton hung in the air around them, sparkling.

Light had only just got used to being suddenly in dark water, when she felt something hard pressing against her side and realised they were entering a smooth rock passage at the bottom of the sea. She struggled against the rock sides, but Tal put a hand on her shoulder and nodded at her reassuringly.

Dimly, Light heard Arnie's voice, which floated down to them brokenly, like a dimly received radio channel.

'*Uvajairuagut, uvajairuagut . . .*' he chanted.

Pass through, pass through.

With a *plop* sound Light and Tal were sucked through

 289

the passage and into a dry cavern, walled and floored with slippery ice.

'Where did the water go?' asked Light.

'This is Setna's kingdom,' said Tal. 'We are under the sea floor.' He took Light's hand and led her forward into the cavern. 'This is when it might get a little dangerous,' he said.

'Oh, fantastic.'

Soon they had to stop talking: the floor was too slick and they needed all their concentration to pick their way across it. The place was lit by some kind of phosphorescence, spreading over the walls like glowing lichen.

After a minute or two they came to a huge arch in the ice. Tal squeezed Light's hand more strongly. She took a deep breath and walked with him through the ice doorway.

She stopped, her muscles quivering. In front of them was a black abyss, falling steeply away from them into a fathomless depth. Light shook with fear. Gently, Tal placed a hand on the side of her head and moved it, so that she could see the bridge.

It was miraculous: a massive, glittering bridge of ice, providing a treacherous crossing over the chasm. 'You've got to be joking,' said Light.

But Tal only walked forwards and onto the bridge. She had no choice but to follow.

The bridge was narrower than it looked from the side. Light stepped gingerly on to it, trying not to look down.

But of course, she did.

The drop was literally dizzying, making her head feel light and her stomach tingle wetly, as if the bones of her pelvis had turned to liquid. She concentrated on putting one foot in front of the other, crossing the bridge in manageable increments of one step, then another step, then another step, then another . . .

Suddenly, Tal slipped and Light felt a stab of sudden fear, but he regained his footing and they continued, finally crossing the bridge after Light had counted thirty-four steps.

In the next room was an enormous kettle filled with boiling water, at least the height of a house. Light stared at it, surprised that she was still capable of being surprised.

From the top of the kettle, several seal heads popped out, eying them suspiciously. The seals began to agitate the vessel, swimming around so that it wobbled alarmingly.

'Run!' said Tal, pulling Light along.

A splash of scalding water hit Light on the arm, hissing when it came into contact with her skin, as if her body displeased it. She ignored the pain and kept running.

Light and Tal burst into the final chamber. At the far end, an old woman sat on a throne.

No, not a throne.

Her eyes becoming accustomed to what she was seeing, Light realised that the throne was in fact an entire whale's skeleton, laid out upside down. Setna sat on the raised pelvis, framed by the ribcage, which curved elegantly above the sitting woman like fingers held protectively around the flame of a match. The great whale skeleton stretched out in front of the goddess, culminating in the huge sieve-like jaws, which extended almost as far as Light and Tal. A gaping, bony eye socket gazed sightlessly up at them.

On either side of Setna sat two leopard seals, and as Light and Tal stood there these moved from their mistress's side and pulled themselves wetly towards the visitors. They looked aggressive.

'Setna,' called Tal. 'I believe you know me. Perhaps I could comb your hair, while my companion speaks with you.'

There was a rattling, breathy sound from the old woman. She waved a hand and the seals stopped.

'Approach,' she said to Light and Tal, and her voice was the surf on a pebble beach.

Tal pulled Light forward, stepping over the bones of the whale that was Setna's throne and throne-room all in one. They came to the pelvis and Tal stepped up beside the queen of the sea. Up close, Light could see that Setna's dress was made all of shimmering fish scales, gleaming like petrol. Around her neck was a necklace of shark's teeth – no, it was a shark's *jaw*, stretched back and worn like a neck brace.

Suddenly, as if it felt Light looking at her, the jaw snapped shut over Setna's head, the teeth coming together just over her wavy black hair. Light could still see Setna's smiling face – the jaw was hinged in such a way that it could snap shut without hurting her.

Slowly, the jaw stretched out and down again, becoming once again an unusual piece of jewellery. Setna caressed one of the teeth and whispered to it.

Tal made an urgent gesture and Light knelt, lowering her eyes. When she raised them again she saw that the shaman had taken out a bone comb and was running it through Setna's dark hair. The queen sighed with pleasure as wriggling black things dropped from the tangles, to squirm and then die on the bone floor. 'Parasites,' mouthed Tal to Light. Out loud, he said to Setna, 'My companion has a question she would like to ask you.'

'I know who your companion is,' said Setna, with a voice of infinite patience but distinctly finite interest. Light got the impression that this woman would put up with anything if it was convenient for her to do so but would kill anyone without a thought if they ceased to be of use. 'This is Light. I have been expecting her.'

Light looked into the old woman's intelligent, ruthless eyes. 'This *angakut* told me that I should appeal to you as one who has been hurt. But I don't think that would work.' Tal sucked in his breath sharply. Light continued. 'I think I should appeal to you as one who wants to be rid of Frost.'

Setna nodded. *Go on.* From the thick knots of her hair another black wriggling thing fell.

'I think,' said Light, 'that you hate Frost as much as I do, because he kills the animals of the sea without respect.'

'Your people kill the animals of the sea also, and in great number. Perhaps Frost's reign would be better for my subjects than your own?'

'But without people, who would worship you?'

Setna smiled widely. 'You are not as stupid as you look, girl. Tell me, what is it you wish to know?'

'I wish to know how to defeat Frost.'

Setna lowered her head, causing Tal to slip with the comb and scrape the skin of her forehead. She batted him aside. 'Frost cannot be vanquished by a human,' said Setna. 'I am sorry.'

Light felt a hot prickle in her eyes, the prelude to tears.

 293

'But . . .' she said, 'but . . . you told Tupilak I could . . .'

'And perhaps you *can*,' said the queen of the sea. 'Though I will tell you again that he cannot be defeated by human hand. He is the cold that inhabited this world before any animal, and he is not so easily killed.' She waved a dismissive hand. 'But you are asking questions of the wrong person, anyway. If you wish to learn your destiny, you must learn your past. Ask Tulugaq what you are. Ask Raven.'

Light pursed her lips, annoyed. Had Butler had the answers all along?

If she ever found him again, he was going to have a lot of explaining to do . . .

Chapter Forty-one

Siege

A familiar voice was intruding into Light's sleep.

'Wake up, Light . . . wake up, Light . . .'

'G'way,' she mumbled. 'Leave m'alone.'

From the other side of the room she heard Arnie say, 'Shut up!'

So it wasn't him then.

Tal groaned.

Wasn't him either.

Light's eyes snapped open. That voice was Frost's.

Light stumbled out of bed, trying to keep as quiet as possible. She moved into the control room and edged towards the window, peering out. A ring of *isserkait* surrounded the station, balloon-men floating above them. Several of them wore the uniforms of British sailors.

In the middle of his troops stood Frost, lost again behind a huge dark cowl. Several bears crouched among the *isserkait*.

'Ah, my dear Light,' he said, in his terrible, grinding

voice, the sound of the ice floes scraping against each other as the Arctic breathed its slow breaths. 'I wondered when you would make your way to your father's last working place. What a shame you couldn't find his last *resting* place. Haha! And there you are all snug in your bed while I stand cold outside. It hardly seems fair does it? Perhaps you should invite me in.'

Light wondered. What if he couldn't come in unless invited, like a vampire?

In fact, Frost could have come in at any time, and it is a mercy for Light that she did not know this.

He was simply hoping he could make her cry.

From outside, Frost continued taunting her, his voice thin and high. 'Your Butler cannot save you now, Light! Or should I call him your servant? I'm not sure how to describe him any more. Your legal guardian? Your father *in loco parentis?* Perhaps, when you're feeling sad, you call him *Daddy.*' On this word, Frost's voice took on a grotesque, cutesy tone. 'It really is too ghastly for you that I've captured your father and reduced you to living with the hired help. You could simply come out here, you know, and cry for me. If your tears are pleasing to me, perhaps I'll let your father go. He has been a source of great irritation to me – poking his nose in my business, asking questions about me, writing things down.'

The journal, thought Light.

'I have gone to some considerable effort to keep my existence secret, girl. Even the Inuit do not speak of me, such is the fear I inspire in them. And then a man from Ireland tells my secrets in a book! I know you have the book, Light. Bring it to me. Cry for me. And we will see what can be done about your father. After all, his life is of no consequence to me – you will all die soon, anyway. The whole stinking planet of you.'

Light had no intention of going out there. She knew she had to keep him talking.

'Still wanting to destroy mankind, then?' she shouted, by way of making conversation. In her mind, she was putting together a plan. She ran back to the dormitory, holding her fingers to her lips when Arnie and Tal sat up, motioning them back into bed.

'Of course, my dear. You humans are so tedious – I can't wait till you are all dead. Vulnerable to love and to revenge; ruled by hot passions and never cold logic, though you consider yourselves reasonable beings. Incapable of inaction – forever launching yourselves into ridiculous missions without thinking them through. Assuming that you know everything about this world when in fact you know nothing. You can never just be *still* and *cold*. But I will make you so, don't worry, I will make you so.'

Light wasn't even listening. She grabbed a shotgun from the storeroom and ran to the dormitory. Arnie was sitting up on his bed; Tal stood beside him.

'Frost?' Arnie asked.

Light nodded.

'Any ideas?'

Light shook her head. Then a movement at her feet caught her attention and her shadow waved up at her.

'Psst,' it said.

'What was that?' asked Arnie.

'Nothing,' Light muttered. 'Back in a sec.' She ran from the room and as soon as she was alone her shadow shivered again and then a dark girl rose up from it. She winked at Light – an unsettling effect; the smoky darkness that constituted her body formed a hole of an eye through which light shone for a moment, before closing up again just as quickly.

'Would you like some help?' the shadow asked. 'I could give you a little, before I take your life. It would be a shame if Frost got to you before me.'

'Please,' Light replied.

'Your compass. The generator. The diesel pump.'

'My what? The what?' asked Light, but the shadow was already pooling onto the ground, forming a puddle of darkness that wavered, then settled perfectly onto Light's own shadow like a tracing-paper drawing.

'Hey!' said Light. 'I don't get it!'

But the shadow didn't move again.

Light walked dejectedly back to Arnie and Tal, and was just about to say, 'let's give ourselves up' when she realised what the shadow meant.

Of course!

She reached under her bed and Arnie said, 'What's going on?' but she ignored him and pulled out her pack. From inside, she took her father's antique compass. She turned it over – there was that inscription of Franklin's.

Spero Meliora. I hope for better.

And she did.

Rummaging in the bag, she also removed the 9-millimetre, tucking it into the waistband of her trousers.

Light explained her plan to Arnie and Tal. She handed Arnie the shotgun. She didn't think he'd be able to use it but hey, she was arming her troops at least. She led Arnie

 298

and Taliriqtug into the supply room and turned off the generator. Then she cut the cable on the multiboard attached to the electrical socket and, with her knife, pared back the plastic coating on the live wires. Arnie held the petrol pump by its plastic handle and showed Tal how he could apply the bare ends of the wires to the metal length of the pump, sending a huge electric charge down it when the generator was turned on.

'You know what to do?' she asked Arnie. He nodded, smiling weakly. 'When I say the word *devastating*, that's when Tal turns the generator on.' The old man nodded. 'And you'll need this of course.' She tossed Arnie the pack of matches she'd found in the kitchen.

'Now,' Light continued, 'if this doesn't work we're all going to have to run as best we can, right?'

'Right,' said Tal. 'Good back-up plan.'

Light crept back into the control room, holding the beautiful old compass ready. She'd never thought she might need it, what with the GPS. And now she was going to have to give it to Frost. The thought was unpleasant – it had been a gift from her father. But the alternative was worse, and she couldn't help smiling at the irony of destroying Frost with an artefact of the Franklin expedition.

She called out, 'Frost! Oh Frost!'

'Yes, girl? Are you ready to weep for your father? Are you ready to cry for him?'

She ignored the question. 'You know about the journal,' she said. 'But do you know what my father was doing here when you came to kidnap him, Frost?'

'I don't know. He was putting something in the water. Polluting, I imagine. That's what you people do, isn't it?'

Light laughed, trying to sound confident. 'No, that's not what he was doing. He was working to construct a massive weapon. A weapon capable of destroying all the people on this planet. It's like ... a ... genetic atom bomb. It wipes out anything with human DNA, right across the world. And I've been looking at his research notes. He finished the weapon just before you took him.'

There was a pregnant pause. Light hoped Frost's desire to see Man dead was greater than his desire to see a girl weeping.

'Where is it, this weapon?' He was trying to keep his voice neutral, but Light could hear the want, she could hear the need.

'It's inside, I think. But if you come in, you have to promise not to hurt me or my friends.' She affected the intonation of a younger, more naïve girl. A girl who had not seen a man grinning as he died to save her.

Light went to the door and opened it. She stood back against the wall as Frost swept in, his cloak billowing, accompanied by two *isserkait* and a bear. 'Not the bear,' she said. 'He'll wreck the place. This is a *delicate* weapon.'

Frost gave a command and the bear retreated. He followed Light into the galley where she placed the compass on the table.

'That's not a weapon,' said Frost. 'That's a compass.'

'Not just a compass,' said Light. 'This is a special compass.' And indeed, with its gold lettering and its brass and wood construction, it did look special. 'This compass does not point to North. It points instead to where the weapon is. You see, my father's notes don't describe what the weapon actually looks like. But he described this method of finding it – I suppose as an extra protection against bad people finding it. It's like . . . magic, I guess. If someone whose motives are pure holds the compass, the device inside will tell them where the weapon is.'

Light hoped that Frost's knowledge of science was as weak as his knowledge of people.

Frost glided forward and lifted the compass. Of course he believed his motives to be pure. All he wanted, after all, was to rid the world of these awful people. The weapon *must* reveal itself to him. *I am pure*, he thought. *I am noble*. He did not know and could not know that he would never really understand these concepts.

He wasn't human enough.

The sight of the compass in Frost's hand – her father's compass – was disturbing, but didn't hurt as much as she had expected. Light spoke as if rambling. 'Yes, and Dad's notes say that this weapon really is quite incredibly devastating' – she emphasised the word just slightly – 'much more powerful than a nuclear bomb or anything like that.'

On the word *devastating*, Tal touched the wires to the metal of the petrol pump and turned the generator on. Instantly the pump became a powerful electromagnet and the needle of the compass swung away from North, where it had been faithfully pointing, and towards the door of the supply cupboard. Frost cooed like a child.

'It's in there!' he said excitedly, pointing to the supply room.

Light held herself back as Frost walked forwards and opened the door.

There was the popping scratch of a match being lit and

a jet of flame roared out as the door opened, engulfing Frost completely and setting his cloak alight. Arnie raked the pump from side to side, and flaming petrol doused one of the *isserkait* too, melting his skin in an instant, turning him into a brightly glaring X-ray image as the flames ate away his flesh.

'Go!' screamed Light. Tal stepped neatly out of the door as Arnie stopped the pump, transferring the sparking wires of the generator from the metal neck of the pump to the fleshy neck of the remaining *isserkat*. The man jolted spectacularly, unable even to scream, and the only sound was his spine snapping. Light pulled out her gun and waved Arnie and Tal forwards. Arnie paused for a matter of moments, fulfilling his final task. With a length of duct tape, he taped the handle of the pump down so that petrol was pouring out continuously. Flames roared. Then he dropped the pump on the floor and they ran for the door, bursting out into the frosted air.

For once the Arctic's permanent night, its crazy diurnal darkness, proved to be an advantage. The other members of Frost's band had seen three figures going in, and now they saw three coming out, so they were not immediately worried.

It was only when the first of those figures – who was pale and wearing a hood – walked briskly towards them and shot two men and three bears with casual precision that the order in the ranks broke down.

The figure pulled back its hood – it was the girl!

One of the *isserkait* threw his weapon at Taliriqtug, who sidestepped smoothly and shouted some meaningless gibberish. The *isserkat* laughed and drew his knife. The old man was mad – an easy kill. He lunged forwards but felt himself snag on something. When he looked down he saw his own spear sticking out of his stomach. In front of him, a walrus whooped with pleasure. 'A direct hit!' the sea-creature shouted. 'You know,' he said to the dying man, 'you really shouldn't throw a spear unless you intend to hit your target. Anyone could pick it up and throw it back at you.' The walrus reared up and gave Tal a high five, slapping its flipper against the man's hand.

On the other end of the intestinal line the foolish hollow man, victim of his own overriding instincts, was already sucking the stunned *isserkat's* life-blood away. The *isserkat* groaned, and fell to the ground. Another of the *isserkait* pointed to Tal, shaking. 'An *angakut*,' he called to his fellows. 'A powerful *angakut*! Be careful of that one.'

'The hunter becomes the hunted,' said the walrus to Light as she came out of a body roll and squeezed two shots into a bear's head. 'Such a delicious irony.'

'Run!' shouted Light. 'Don't stay and fight! Cut a path through to the snowmobile!' A spear flew past her right arm and she ducked to the left. She pulled off her protective amulet and threw it at the man who had thrown the spear. Instinctively, he reached out and caught it, then cried out as the amulet burned into his hand. Taking advantage of his distraction, Light raised her gun and put two bullets in his chest, then stooped and picked up the amulet again, hanging it around her neck. How many bullets did she have left?

Five? Four?

Less than the number of men and bears, anyway.

She'd paid more attention to the aiming and shooting

part than Butler's lessons about loading and cleaning the gun. She risked a glance behind her and saw Arnie blasting a bear with his shotgun. A dark shadow flitted past her side followed by another. There were shadows everywhere, now Light looked. Why didn't they help, the shadow people? Then she remembered: *they can't attack someone who can't see them.*

Light looked up as she ran. No one was guarding the snowmobile. Frost's people wouldn't win awards for strategic acumen. She picked up her pace, slipping a little on the snow underfoot, legs and heart pumping. Ten metres to go,

five metres

and then

bear.

She smacked into the bear's chest with bone-jarring force. She fell, the wind knocked out of her, but the bear reached out and held her up with its arms. It brought its muzzle down to her face and breathed foul air onto her. She wrinkled her nose. The bear's eyes were vast pools of blackness that showed no mercy – little remnants of the darkness that once surrounded mankind's campfires. Light spat in the animal's face and it roared, digging its powerful claws into her side.

Light twisted to avoid the noxious air of the roar and saw a shadow slide up to her. 'Help me!' she said. 'Please, help me. I know you're not supposed to attack someone who can't see you, but can't you please help me?'

The shadow wavered, then started to move away.

'No! Please, don't go!' Once again, Light saw her death approaching.

Then came a low voice from the moving shadow. 'I cannot help you directly, but I can give you advice,' it said. 'The bear is complacent in its strength. It has not secured your arms. Use your hands, and the amulet we gave you. It is . . . harmful to bad things.'

Light turned back to the bear. It was still holding her by the waist, letting her arms dangle free.

Well, clearly it can't understand English, she thought.

As the bear lowered its head again, jaws wide and slavering, she whipped her hands up and grabbed the amulet around her neck, pulling it off its leather thong and shoving it into the bear's mouth. She pulled her arm back, quickly, before the bear's teeth met on her hand. The bear looked momentarily puzzled, then roared. Its mouth hung open, slack and useless, dripping drool onto Light's face. Its eyes started to glaze over.

Abruptly, the bear dropped her. Before it keeled over, Light ran, leaving the beast lying on the ground behind her. It twitched and bucked, its skin sizzling as blue flames engulfed it.

Harmful? thought Light. *It set the bear on* fire.

On automatic pilot, Light ducked another spear and jumped on the snowmobile. Arnie was backing towards her, reloading the shotgun with trembling fingers. A bear and a sailor-*isserkat* were bearing down on him, the *isserkat* still armed with a spear and the horrible hollow man that came at the end of it.

'Well, well,' said the sailor, doffing his naval cap with his free hand. Barnacles clung to the skin of his face. 'Shiver me

305

timbers and all that. Reckon I've got me a pair of little pirates, here! Do yourselves a favour, loves, give yourself up. I can't promise I'll let you live, but you won't walk the plank, you have my word as a sailor on her majesty's commission. It would be difficult, you see – the plank sank with our ship!'

Light eased herself off the snowmobile, keeping her hand – and the gun in it – held low. 'Her majesty wouldn't want you now,' she said. 'There's no room in the British Navy for cannibals and murderers.'

At that, the man hissed. 'Now that ain't nice, missy.' He raised his spear and—

'Duck, Arnie!' screamed Light.

He did –

– and she emptied the clip of her 9-millimetre over his back, praying she wouldn't hit him. One of the bullets hit the hollow man, spinning him in the air and causing a high-pitched *hiss*. He spiralled off into the night air, whining as he deflated, dragging the sailor off his feet and out of the path of Light's second bullet, which was on a collision path with his face.

Damn, thought Light. *Missed.*

The third and fourth bullets hit the bear in the stomach and it roared angrily, swatting at the bullets like they were bees. The fifth was a direct hit – centre of the forehead – and the bear fell, arms still waving.

The sailor staggered to his feet, screaming. 'Damned landlubber! Fight me like a man . . . I mean, a girl . . . Just come back and fight me fair, I tell you!'

Light ignored him, grabbing the handlebars of the snowmobile and throwing her leg over.

Arnie jumped onto the back and Light turned the ignition.

Work.

Please work.

The engine roared into life and she gunned the throttle, spinning the machine 180 degrees and pointing it away from the station. 'Where's Taliriqtug?' she shouted. Arnie put a hand on her shoulder and pointed into the melee, which was considerably thinner now.

Tal was the worst armed and he could not, in fact – as some of Frost's men believed – turn a person into plankton. His best weapon was the walrus, who was even now flying into an *isserkat*, burying one of his tusks in the man's neck. Tal smiled. He didn't think the sight of a flying walrus would ever fail to make him smile. And it was as he smiled that the boy from the depths snuck up on him.

Tal turned to see one of Frost's oldest lieutenants standing with an arrogantly cocked hip on the snow in front of him. It was a boy, a terrible boy, with seaweed for hair and pearls for eyes. The boy opened his mouth and screamed, displaying a mouth full of sharp little teeth. Tal felt his legs give way with fear. Then the boy was upon him, tearing at his flesh, pummelling his body, whipping his face with his seaweed hair, such was the frenzy of his attack.

The walrus knew as soon as the *angakut* fell. He didn't see it but he felt the sudden pull back into the spirit world, felt himself dragged from the ice and into Setna's realm.

He left this world behind with human tears in his animal eyes.

Light screamed. 'Tal! No!'

Then the terrifying boy was no longer on Tal's body but

was moving like a film from which frames have been cut, flickering from one place to another until he was standing in front of the snowmobile. Arnie screeched in fright.

Light drew back, seeing the needle-like teeth and the blank, milky pearls that were the boy's eyes. A barnacle clung to one cheek, fusing sickeningly into the flesh. An anemone sprouted from under his left ear, its fronds waving gently in the breeze.

The boy smiled and Light thought,

this is it

and then she remembered something – a story Tupilak had told her in what seemed another life, when they had sat on the jetty at home. About a boy with seaweed for hair, and how he had only wanted to play but his mother had used him to take revenge on her husband. Light got off the snowmobile and walked slowly towards the boy. He cocked his head to one side and gave her a puzzled look.

'Light!' Arnie shouted. 'What are you doing?'

Light ignored him, focusing only on the boy. 'Would you like to play?' she asked in Inuktitut. The boy frowned. 'I know a game – hide and seek. It's fun. Would you like to try it?'

The boy looked from Light to Arnie and back again with frank confusion. This wasn't how things were supposed to go. Light saw the shadow of a smile on his lips – not a cruel smile of bloodlust but a *real* smile, a smile of fun and friendship.

She pushed a little harder.

'It's OK,' she said, spreading her hands and dropping her gun. 'I don't want to hurt you. I only want to play.'

308

'Light!' said Arnie.

'Shh,' said Light. 'I'm playing with my new friend.'

That did it. 'How do we play this game?' the boy said. 'This hide and seek?'

Light smiled. 'Well, you run and hide and I count to a hundred. Then I have to come and find you. If I don't, you win.'

The boy grinned. He lived under the sea – there was no way Light could find him there. He'd conceal himself under the ice – hang in the water where the seals swooshed and spiralled, waiting as long as he liked while the strange white girl searched the snow in vain. He turned and ran, giggling. 'You'll never find me!' he shouted.

Light picked up the gun and jumped back on the snow-mobile. She eased the throttle, not wanting to hit something or skid and so jeopardise their chances of escape.

Arnie pulled at Light's jacket. 'Look!' he screamed.

Light let go of the throttle, turned and saw Frost stepping out of the research station's door. The makeshift flame-thrower had not melted him: his clothes were burned off and he stood naked, his body of ice gleaming in the light of the flames. He grinned – his open mouth forming a hole through the ice of his face. Through it, Light could see the walls of the station. Frost opened his hand, revealing a dark object – a small, leather bag. He began to open the bag, looking straight at Light. Arnie groaned and she felt her eyes stinging with the injustice of it. She knew they had lost. It was hopeless.

The British sailor Light had missed with her gun watched as Frost opened his weather bag. Frost would send a wind

 309

towards the girl and her friend, a wind of such cold that they would be stunned, and their machine would not start.

Then he would have won.

The sailor hesitated. When they had been lost on the ice, after Franklin died, Frost and his tribe had seemed to be their only sanctuary, their only chance at survival.

But had they not lost all that made survival worthwhile?

The first thing Frost had made them do was kill and eat the weak. *They are only animals*, he had said. *And you are hunters.*

But they had not been animals, they had been people.

The sailor wondered. This girl, this Light, had done no harm to him or to his men – at least, not of her own volition. She had defended herself fiercely – like a sailor of the British Empire – and that impressed him.

All hesitation gone, he stepped quickly forwards. *I do this in penance for the murder of my crewmates and friends*, he thought. *When I stand before you, Sir John Franklin, my captain, in the land of the dead, I pray that you will forgive me.*

Light watched, stunned, as the sailor threw himself at Frost, knocking him to the ground. The bag in Frost's hand fell to the ground. Despite his massive bulk, the sailor struggled to hold Frost down. '*Go!*' he screamed at Light. 'Go and save yourself! For Queen and for country!'

Bloody hell, thought Light. *Good job I didn't shoot him in the face.*

Light gunned the throttle and the snowmobile leaped forwards. She kept her eyes ahead, not daring to look back.

*

Frost's icy body was slippery beneath him, and the man who had once been a navigation officer on Queen Victoria's most ambitious expeditionary force felt Frost evading his grasp. Frost got hold of his arms and pushed him back, with unbelievable force – now the two of them lay on the ground side by side, almost like lovers looking at the stars together.

Then Frost got up into a crouch and thrust his transparent face into the sailor's.

'Traitor,' Frost spat, through a mouth that was nothing but a hole. The man ceased to struggle. His death was upon him, and there was no point fighting any more. Frost raised his hands and grasped the man's face, the ice searing his skin immediately, making him cry out. He felt Frost's fingers gouging into his eyes, burning him with coldness, blinding him once more. *A condign punishment*, he thought. *A fitting end.*

The fingers pushed through his eyeballs, entering his brain.

Captain.

Hello, Captain.

I'm sorry.

Chapter Forty-two

Locket

There was something thrilling about crossing the ice in a snowmobile: the sensation of uninhibited speed was intense and exhilarating. It was also scary – they had narrowly missed two cracks in the ice already, Light swerving the machine at the last second. And soon both of them were shivering, the fast-moving air dipping into the gaps in their clothing like a pickpocket.

They were still wearing thick jumpers from the research station and when they tried to get off the snowmobile they found that the wool had picked up a layer of lint-like snow, sticking them firmly together. They struggled for a moment, like a four-armed, two-headed beast in its death throes, then managed to pull themselves apart. Arnie bent over, laughing and coughing at the same time. He smiled a wan smile at Light and she could see what he was thinking: Tal was dead and their chances didn't look good.

There were several loose mounds of snow, like alien rock formations, and the ice underfoot felt thick. Behind

 312

them the two tracks of their snowmobile ran back darkly into the distance, appearing to move gently towards each other like a stretched-out V.

It brought a tear to Light's eye.

In the Arctic, with its relentless blankness, there were no man-made structures to draw the eye and make sense of the world. This environment, completely devoid of context, a featureless *tabula rasa*, wore away at the human mind and threatened it with the endless void. To see any structure at all – even a great elongated V left by the runners of a snowmobile – was a lifeline for sanity.

'We'll dig ourselves in here,' she said, 'and get some sleep. We can hide the snowmobile behind one of those mounds.'

She gestured at a pile of snow.

Then, from behind it, she saw a shadow move, and trace a broad circle around them. Another followed.

Good: the shadow people were staking out the territory.

Light settled down to sleep. She was about to close her eyes when one of the shadows glided along the snow towards her and dropped some dried meat on to her sleeping bag. 'Thank you,' she said. She saw another piece land on Arnie.

'You're welcome,' the disembodied voice replied.

That night, when Arnie was asleep, Light felt a tap on her shoulder. She turned her head and saw no one. She calmed herself with an effort of will, forcing her pulse to slow. 'Shadow?'

'Yes?' The voice that answered was male.

'Oh . . .' Light realised this was one of the shadow

people. 'Are you the shadow man who helped me with the bear?' she asked.

'Yes. My name is Atiluk.'

The voice was clear and light but Light could see nothing more than a dark pool of shadow next to her head, melting into the darkness all around. It was unsettling. 'What do you want?' she asked.

'We want to help you. We would fight alongside you against Frost and his men but our honour . . . we are bound by it. It is a dilemma.'

Light sat up a little and tried to think. 'This honour thing. What it means is that you can't attack someone who can't see you, right?'

'That is exactly right.'

'And that's it? I mean, that's the only thing you could do that would be dishonourable?' Light was starting to see a possibility.

'I'm not sure what you mean.'

'I mean, what if your enemy couldn't see you, but you couldn't see them either? Would that even things up?'

There was a pause and Light could tell that the man was thinking. 'I think so,' he said finally.

'And how many of you are there?'

He told her.

She caught her breath.

'Then I have a plan,' said Light.

When they woke after a few hours' sleep Light shared out some corned beef she'd brought from the research station. Afterwards Arnie walked off behind one of the mounds. There was an unspoken rule between them: if one of them walked off a way, the other would not follow but would turn their back, giving the gift of privacy.

When both had finished their ablutions they took the snowmobile again, but this time Light started to sweep west in a wide circle, bringing them – imperceptibly to Arnie – back towards the research station. Light hadn't shared her plan with Arnie, and she hoped she wasn't leading him to his death. But the plan was too unformed, too vague in her mind for her to explain it just yet. She was hoping she could lead Frost and his men back to the place she and Arnie had just escaped from. She also hoped there wasn't a petrol tank under the research station, otherwise the place would have been blown off the map (always assuming it was *on* the map).

Once they were there – well, she just hoped Arnie's amulet would protect him.

When Light started to feel hungry she stopped and got off the snowmobile to stretch her legs. She took the dried meat the shadow man had given her and began to chew it silently. Arnie wandered off, sensing her need for time.

Light swallowed the meat and a huge, hard hand closed over her mouth. The arm attached to it was braced against her throat, poised to crush down on her windpipe if she screamed. The skin against her mouth didn't feel human and the arm around her neck was thick and hairy.

She had been captured by a bear.

Arnie came sauntering back, whistling. Another bear crept up behind him, grabbing him an instant after he saw Light's predicament, so that he gasped just a little before the huge arms closed around his chest. Light couldn't see the bear that was holding her but she could see the one holding Arnie: it was huge, bigger than any she had seen before, and a black mark ran down its side like a blaze on a tree trunk.

Light's bear growled in her ear but she couldn't understand it. She felt herself being lifted off the ground, the other arm around her waist, and then she was being carried swiftly over the ice. The bear crossed the terrain more smoothly than the snowmobile had. After a few minutes the bear stopped, seeming to wait. They were near the sea edge now – she could hear the waves lapping at the shore ice, their monotonous, hungry lullaby smoothing away the ice.

As Light listened, the sound became more complex, acquiring a rhythm. A splashing noise had joined the drawn-out, breathy fricative of the waves, like a beat joining a bass line. It was the sound of oars.

From where Light was standing she saw the kayak appear like a slowly-executed drawing, starting off as a light grey sketch and then darkening and shading, acquiring detail and nuance as it approached closer. The rowers swung the craft expertly around to meet the ice side on, and several *isserkait* leaped lightly out. They approached with circumspection – almost with fear – and took up positions in a semicircle. Most of them trained their spears on Light but from the way some of them aimed at a spot just behind her and to the right, she deduced that Arnie was being held there. Again the sound of the sea changed subtly. Oars. A couple of the *isserkait* turned towards the sea, visibly relieved.

Frost, thought Light.

She tensed, ready to fight and knowing at the same time

that it would be useless. She was holding her hands in tight fists and the blood of her fingers was pulsing quickly, making it feel as though she was holding two small, scared mice.

Light felt tears welling up. *It's not fair*, she thought. *Frost can't be killed and I don't know what else I can do . . .*

She was going to give up. It was time to face facts. Her father was dead, and soon she would be too.

But it seemed that there was a part of her mind that she couldn't control, for just then an idea rose up, a glistening bubble ascending from the depths. The way the bear was holding her, she was constrained so tightly – almost as if she were tied up.

It might work, she thought.

Silently, she began to recite the words, as best as she could from memory.

Akili majja ijigivara imarjuarli sunauvva manna,
   ijaa, ja, jaa, jaa
I look at the floor. It turns out it's the water ijaa, ja,
   jaa, jaa

And then she was no longer in her body; she was dropping through dark water, shapes gliding around her, schools of fish swimming through her. And then she was on the sea bed, facing Setna, who smiled at the pale girl from so far away, standing defiantly before her, one hand on the whale bones of the sea goddess's throne.

'You have returned,' said the ruler of the oceans.

Light bowed. 'I have left my body with Frost's men. I need—'

Setna raised a hand. 'I have already told you what you need. You need Raven. Call to him – he will come. And you need to understand who you are.'

Light began to cry – she was going to die and this undersea witch wouldn't help her. 'There isn't time! Frost is there and my friend Arnie is going to die too and I can't do anything . . . I'm so *scared*. I just . . .' She felt her very essence weaken and slip. 'I just can't do it any more.'

Setna seemed to consider this. Then she gestured for Light to approach. Light came closer – close enough to see the pearls that were the woman's eyes, the crabs that fled through her long hair.

'As long as you are with me there *is* no time. You will return to your body at the same moment you left it,' the old woman said.

Light shook her head. 'Please,' she said. 'Help me. I need to be stronger, I need to be harder. I feel so frightened and I miss my dad and I don't know what you want from me.'

'Only you can help yourself,' said Setna. 'Only you can see what you need to see—'

'STOP TALKING IN RIDDLES!'

Light buried her face in her hands. It was over. She was too weak.

Setna gazed at her for a moment. Then she reached into a fold of her robe, and produced a necklace. It glinted liquidly in the light – silver, Light thought, or something like it.

Setna motioned for Light to kneel and hung the necklace around her neck. Light looked down and gasped. Hanging from it was a heart locket – but not the stylised heart known to sweethearts; this, instead, was a human heart in miniature, a little closed fist of chambers and arteries, chased in exquisite detail from a lump of metal.

Setna looked at her gravely. 'There is a way to not be scared, but it is a hard path. If you choose it, your heart will be lost to you – your pity, your compassion. Frost will no longer be your nightmare. He will be your enemy, and you will hate him and wish for his destruction.'

Light closed her eyes. She thought of her father, lost for so many months in this cold and brutal world. She thought of Arnie, who was going to die any moment now if she couldn't help. She took a deep breath. 'Why would I want anything else?' she said.

Setna nodded. 'Very well.' She gripped Light's wrists and Light almost screamed – the woman's touch was clammy, smooth; the skin of some watery creature. 'Do you agree to this?' she asked. 'Do you agree to be changed in this way?'

'Yes, I do.' Light felt the weight of the words in her mouth, their formality. They had the heft of a marriage vow.

Setna rubbed her hands together and placed them, suddenly, on Light's chest. Light collapsed to the ground, feeling her heart stop.

How is that possible? She thought. *I am not even in my body.* But it was possible, and it was true – she felt it. In her real body above the ice, her heart had stopped too.

She gasped – the feeling was painful but also *right*; she felt death enter her body and she realised she would welcome it when it came for good. Ecstasy filled her – ecstasy and fear. Light felt herself slipping into a world of infinite warmth and security, a place of total bliss. With her one half-open eye she saw a mussel on Setna's skin, such a simple creature in its shell, and she understood that it was sacred. Everything was sacred.

'Quick, repeat after me,' Setna droned, her voice echoing slowly from somewhere harsh and bright, somewhere Light didn't want to go back to. She felt dizzy. Her remaining vision narrowed to a pin prick. The woman kept speaking. Kept droning. Droning crone.

Crone drone stone.

Drone . . . drone . . . crone . . .

A stinging slap woke Light up. 'Repeat. After. Me.'

Light nodded, painfully, her head lolling as her muscles lost control. She needed oxygen. As the old woman spoke, she forced herself to repeat the words.

'Pluck out my heart and in its place put a smooth, hard stone.'

Light repeated the words.

'Take away my pain and give me instead a cold, swift river.'

Light gasped out the words.

'Cut off my hurt, and give me instead a crutch of anger, to carry me through my days.'

Light whispered the words, coming finally to the end of the air in her lungs, blacking out into nothingness.

A startling cold and pain in her chest brought Light, coughing hard, back to life. The crone knelt over her, and Light saw that she had breathed her own breath into Light's lungs. She coughed again.

Setna pulled her to her feet. 'How do you feel?'

Light smiled. 'I feel hard. Like ice.'

'Yes,' said Setna. 'Like Frost.' Her voice as she spoke

sounded sad, but Light could only feel the happiness of strength, the joy of no fear and no grief.

Light turned to go but Setna raised her hand. 'Remember, girl. Sometimes the thing that makes you strong is not the thing that will save you.'

Light stared at her. Stupid old woman.

She looked up at the gleaming roof of the cavern – the bottom of the sea, seen from below. She rose to join her body.

Chapter Forty-three

Reunited

Light could feel the bear's arms around her and could hear the oars of Frost's kayak. She opened her eyes – she could see him now, only a few hundred metres away, his icy bulk catching the light of the stars.

Good, she thought. *Let him come, and let him die. I will destroy him, even if I must melt him with the warmth of my own blood.*

Arnie looked at her, fear in his eyes, and she turned away from him in disgust, from his cowardly weakness.

Ah, Butler, she thought. *If only you could see me now. I am not the cry-baby I was.*

Dimly, she knew that she *should* be afraid, but it was as if the feeling were trapped under the ice, mouthing words she couldn't hear. She ignored it, and bit down on the bear's arm, whipping her head from side to side to tear its flesh with her teeth.

'Light!' shouted Arnie but she was lost in the fight, and pummelling the bear's face now, for it had dropped her in pain and surprise. Screaming herself, she went for its eyes, fingers stiffened to gouge them from their sockets . . .

And then a movement in the sky caught her eye and she looked up.

Crows.

They careered through the air, black and crying, dive-bombing the *isserkait* and the bears.

Then another movement – a shadow, at her feet. Light looked down, expecting to see a shadow man, but this dark patch was *under* the ice, a black shape moving swiftly in the water, deep below the crust.

Moments later, the ice crust just to her left exploded and a large conical shape like a torpedo burst through, sending shards of ice into the air. The shape crashed into the first *isserkat*, sending up a spray of red blood that splattered the snow on all sides.

Then Tupilak was on his feet, shaking the dead *isserkat* in his vast shark's mouth like a dog worrying a rabbit.

A cry went up and the bear that was holding Light let go, lunging towards Tupilak. Light called a warning and Tupilak dropped the *isserkat*, ducking under the bear's attack. He sidestepped gracefully, his clawed bear feet giving him perfect grip on the ice, then swung his head in an upwards arc, eviscerating the white attacker. The bear's forward movement carried him over Tupilak's crouched body, even as the contents of its stomach fell to the ground. It sprawled on the snow, finished and empty.

One of the other *isserkait* had the presence of mind to throw his weapon but Tupilak was ready and he snapped the spear in his mouth, catching it like a dog catches a stick.

323

There are too many, thought Light, as Frost's men regrouped and sized up their opponent. *He can't possibly kill them all.*

Then there was a rustling sound and a disturbance in the air and Butler was standing by her side. Light gasped – deep inside her was joy at his return, but frozen and sluggish, kept under thick ice by the cold heart that hung at her throat.

'You called,' he said.

Light shook her head. 'No, I—'

She stopped. What was it she had thought to herself? If only Butler was here now . . .

She remembered what Setna had said. *You need Raven. Call to him.*

'Hello, Raven,' she said, and she couldn't keep the coldness from her voice, the hardness of her new heart.

Butler nodded and sighed. 'Hello, Light.'

He stepped forwards, still dressed – to Light's surprise – in the coat tails and black trousers of his butler's uniform. He rolled up his sleeves like a man preparing for a pub fight and plunged his hands into the snow, then raised them up and *flicked* them forwards, extending his arms.

The black tattoos on his forearm swirled inkily and *leaped* from the skin, streaming from his fingers like silk ribbons. In the air, the black liquid coalesced into globules that flew forward, shifting and expanding. As they flew they grew wings and beaks and by the time they reached Arnie they were a flock of ravens. Arnie covered his face and the birds separated around him like a stream around a rock, then crashed into the bear behind him, driving it to the ground.

They squabbled and cawed loudly, strutting and pecking on the prostrate bear. One of them plucked out one of the bear's eyes, and another attacked it, squabbling for the morsel.

Light smiled. Butler was powerful, and he was on her side. They were going to win.

Butler shouted a harsh command to the birds and turned back to Light. He pointed to Frost, who was now only metres from the shore, and already giving orders to his men.

'Come,' he said. With that he reached behind him and pulled his coat tails up and over, where they became a crow's head that settled neatly onto his shoulders. The black coat melted into wings, the smooth surface of it giving way to the intricate texture of feathers. Standing in front of Light was a huge raven, as tall as Butler and with a wingspan to match. It grabbed her, stepped into the air with practised grace and climbed quickly.

Light looked down, dizzy, as the ice cap spiralled away from her. She saw Tupilak pick up Arnie, who was curled in a terrified ball on the ice, and begin to run, holding the boy as if he were little more than a seal pup.

Oh, good, thought Light, distantly. *He isn't going to die after all.*

She turned to Butler – Raven – and examined the dark feathers and sharp beak of his real face. 'Take me to the research station,' she said. 'Make sure Tupilak follows.'

'Why?' said Butler, and the human words in that impossible, cruel beak seemed a nonsense, an impossibility. But Light was beyond such things now.

'Because,' she said, 'I'm going to set a little trap.'

325

Chapter Forty-four

Old Mother Moon

Tupilak put Arnie down – he had just run with him for what seemed like two miles, at a flat-out sprint, without even becoming short of breath. Butler wheeled down from the sky, Light held in his claws. He deposited her on the snow, then alighted beside them, his great dark wings folding once more into a dinner jacket, his beaked head sliding backwards to reveal his human face.

They stood in front of Light's father's research station.

Corpses – of *isserkait*, but also of a shaman who had wanted only to help, and a hundred-year-old sailor who had sacrificed himself to save someone he didn't know – littered the ground.

'We have a moment before they arrive,' said Butler. 'Tell us what happened since the ship.'

Light filled them in on the events of the last few days – and what she'd learned since they were separated. She left out her second visit to Setna, the bargain she had made – she sensed that it had been foolish, that she had given away something important of herself, though the thought filled her with no fear.

Tupilak interrupted her. 'No human can kill Frost? That's what she said?'

Light nodded.

'Useless.'

'Maybe not so useless,' said Butler. 'You and I are not human after all.'

'That's true,' Tupilak replied. 'But I do not think we could kill Frost. Do you?'

Butler didn't respond, and that was reply enough. 'I am only a god,' he said. 'Frost is something older. I could try but . . .'

'Yes,' said Light. 'You will.'

Butler looked at her with something like surprise. 'You sound . . . different.'

Light spread her hands. 'After all that has happened, what do you expect? You are my oldest friend and yet you've lied to me all my life.'

Butler bowed his head. 'I have devoted my life to you, I live to an extent in your heart. I am your guardian, your *tuurngak*, your spirit animal. I am also . . . I hope . . . your friend.'

Light shrugged. He was her spirit animal – of course he was. That was why her shadow when she journeyed in the air had been that of a crow. 'Then help me to kill Frost,' she said. And she turned and walked to the station.

'Where are you going?' asked Arnie.

'To fight,' said Light.

Arnie looked appalled. 'But what about Tal?' He gestured to the corpse on the snow. 'Shouldn't we . . . I

327

mean . . . Shouldn't we do something with him? We can't just leave him there. He deserves—'

Light hissed. 'We none of us get what we deserve. Fight, or die. There is only one choice that is useful to me, so make your decision soon.'

She turned on her heel and walked away.

While Arnie buried Tal – he had refused help from Tupilak – Butler flew off. Light only vaguely wondered where he was going, then forgot about it.

So it was a bit of a surprise when a group of British Navy marines came around the research station and stood in front of the shallow snow grave.

One of them saluted to Light and she nodded wearily back. 'M'lady,' he said. 'Your butler has told us a lot about you. This is a strange mess he's got us into, I don't mind telling you. But it's an honour to serve, m'lady.'

'Yes,' said another marine, raising his gun. 'We don't get many chances to do much up here. So I may not understand what's going on, but I'm ready to fight.'

'Thank you,' said Light. They would die, of course. But they would provide a useful diversion.

Inside, the fire from the petrol had gutted the station. Black ash lay on the ground, silt-like and fine, and all the wooden furniture and electrical equipment was destroyed. The structure, though, seemed to have survived.

Arnie had asked one of the marines to arm him with a pistol. The man wasn't keen at first – being one of those old-fashioned people who think that children shouldn't go about with powerful guns – but Arnie could be very persuasive.

'Why not?' he said to Light when he came back inside. 'We might as well fight.'

Light nodded. 'That is a good choice.'

She didn't notice Arnie frowning as she walked away, to check on her defences.

Something is wrong, he thought. *She wasn't like this before . . .*

Later, when Arnie had stretched out on one of the beds and gone to sleep, Butler came and sat next to Light. 'I imagine you're wondering . . . well, I guess you must be wondering why. Why your life is like this. Why I pretended to be your butler.'

'The question did cross my mind, Butler. Or should I call you Tulugaq?'

'You can call me Butler. To be honest, I've sort of got used to it. And first you should know that your father and I are friends. I was not deceiving him as well. Your father and I . . . have a long history. We wished to keep you safe. We performed some rituals that would preserve you from harm, make you immune to drowning, that kind of thing . . .'

'I gathered,' said Light.

'You did? How?'

'Someone tried to drown me. It didn't work.'

'Ah. Well, that's logical.'

'Keep talking,' said Light. 'Why did Dad bring you back to Ireland? More importantly, why did you come? Why would a god become a servant? It's because you're a coward, isn't it? Nothing but a big coward.'

'No. It's true that, a long time ago, I failed the human race. There was a flood and I did nothing, at first. Not out

 329

of cowardice but out of . . . uncertainty about my nature. I was a creator – I made people and creatures from clay. I was not a saviour. But a girl . . . she was a little like you, actually . . . a girl convinced me to save mankind. When I had done it I swore never to fail them again. And when you came along . . . well. Let's just say that there were signs you might be special – that you might be able to save us. Why Frost wants you I truly don't know – for centuries he has remained in the Arctic where no one saw him, and it is only recently that he has begun to attack the settlements of man.'

'He wants the journal,' said Light.

'The journal?'

Light went to her bag and took out her father's diary. She opened it and showed Butler one of the articles. 'Everything Dad could find out about Frost is in here. All written down. Frost wants it back, so that his secret is safe.'

Butler turned the leather-bound book in his hands. He breathed out, slowly. 'Foolish man,' he said, finally.

Then he put the book aside. 'I am sure Frost wants this. But it is not his only concern. You must not listen to anything he says – he wants you, whatever his excuse. He believes that you can destroy him. He believes that you are special. And he is right.'

Suddenly angry, Light stood up, knocking over her chair. '*Why?* In what way am I special?' She was incandescent with rage, all her impotence over the strange circumstances that had overtaken her life dammed by the silver heart and spilling out of her instead as anger. 'I just want my dad back. I just want him *back*. And I want Frost to suffer.'

'My darling,' said Butler, 'the reason you are special is that your mother is the moon.'

330

Chapter Forty-five

Human. Moon.

There was a moment of silence. Light broke away from the hug. 'Wait. First off: my mother isn't dead? Second: my mother is the *moon?*'

'It might seem hard to believe,' said Butler.

'Er, yeah,' said Light, sarcastically. 'Kind of.'

'Imagine,' said Butler, 'that there was a lonely young man who spent many solitary months of every year in a cabin in the Arctic. This young man amused himself, during the everlasting darkness of a night that spans half the year, by playing with the skulls of seals and pretending that they were his children. When he left the station to go out and perform his scientific tests, he would line the skulls up outside and say to them, "Be good children while I am gone and go straight into the house!" and when he found them still there on his return he would cry out, "You all seem to be deaf, did I not tell you to go back in the house?" It would be fair to say that the loneliness and the cold and the dark had made him a little mad – in moments of weakness he would also eat candles, craving the fat that they provided and its accompanying warmth.

'Once, for something to do, this young man took his snowmobile and drove far away, to where there was a great lake of seawater in the ice. The young man watched as an enormous white swan flew down from the dark sky – apparently from the stars themselves – and lighted on the lake. The swan swam to the shore and there it took off its feathers and wings, revealing a beautiful woman beneath. She laid herself out on the snow, appearing to bask in the starlight. This woman seemed to the young man to glow and if he had had more sense he would have looked up at the night sky and seen a disturbing sight: the full moon was still there, but the woman who sits in it was gone.

'Loneliness fuelling his bravery, the young man crept forwards – and stole the woman's coat of feathers. When she stood up and saw him there she was angry, but he spoke tender words to her and invited her back to his station, where she could be his wife. "I will," she said, "but only give me back my feathers. I am the Moon, you see, I am Malina, and I need them to fly there and back."

'It is not certain whether the young man believed her or not, but at any rate he did not return the feathers, locking them in a store cupboard in the station, and the woman became his wife. With time, she came to love him, and increasingly he trusted her not to fly away. They were happy together in the station for many months and then they returned to Britain.

'On their next trip to the Arctic the following year, the woman bore the young man a daughter, whom they called Light after the way that the girl – like her mother – seemed to glow, and in honour of the bright white light of the moon. The man and woman were so happy together that one day the man forgot to lock the store cupboard in which he had stored the swan's feather coat. The woman, even though she loved the man, could not overcome her nature, and so she put the feathers on.

'And then the woman – Malina – flew back to the moon, to live there unhappily ever after. And the man too was unhappy and was lonely again, and every night he would look up at the moon with tears in his eyes. Even when the moon was dark or he was in the Arctic during the endless daylight, still he would look at the sky where the moon should be, and wonder. And the woman looked down at him in return, or at least I presume that she did.'

Hearing rhythmic breathing Butler looked down and saw that Light was falling asleep.

'S'true?' she asked, slurring her words sleepily.

'Oh it's true,' he answered. 'It's true.'

In Light's mind, two words chased each other like kittens.

Human. Moon. Human. Moon.

Chapter Forty-six
Showdown

Light was woken by gunfire. She ran to the window, frosted up as always, and dimly made out the figures outside: white-clad British sailors, firing their guns at the attackers.

Butler came and stood next to her. 'I don't know how long guns will hold him off. And then I don't know what we'll do.'

'Now,' said Tupilak to Light, 'might be a good time to tell us your plan, if you have one.'

Light went to the storeroom, praying that the fire had gone out – it was so cold, after all – before ruining the electrics.

She hit the master switch, and the lights came on.

She smiled.

Heading back to the main room, she sent Butler and Tupilak to stand by the back wall. Tupilak was snapping his jaws, itching to get outside and join the fray, but Light told him to be quiet. She positioned Arnie in the storeroom.

'Frost won't fall for the same trick again,' Arnie said.

 334

'It's not the same trick. This time I just want you to turn the lights off,' Light replied. 'It is darkness I want.'

Then she went and stood in the centre of the room.

The door held for a surprisingly long time before Frost broke through. He dumped his battering ram on the floor – it was a sailor, frozen solid, his head crumpled by repeated impacts with the door. Several *isserkait* followed him in, spreading along the walls. Last in were three bears, who stood guard at the broken door. Frost's army seemed inexhaustible.

And on the floor, shadows swirled and spun – like the shadows of clouds, seen from a plane. They moved quickly into position, unnoticed by Frost or his men.

Frost spread his hands, palms up. 'I have brought your father,' he said. 'Are you ready to hand over the journal?'

'Now!' Light screamed.

Arnie threw the switch on the generator and the light cut out. Only Frost's face remained visible, flickering like a diamond from within his voluminous hood. He spoke with near-equanimity, only a touch of anger inflecting his voice. 'Kill the others,' he said. 'Spare the girl.'

But his words were answered only by the hiss of arrows from the waiting shadow people, filling Frost's ears from every direction with the sound of hatred.

He did not duck – he didn't need to – but he heard the screams of his dying men.

In the darkness, Light counted to twenty, then called to Arnie to turn the light back on. The *isserkait* were all dead, arrows having been trained on their hearts as soon as they came into the station. One of the bears was turning madly,

335

pawing at an arrow sticking out of its chest. Frost raised a finger and froze the bear where it stood, a statue of twisting rage.

One of the shadow men had been hit, against all odds, and the fact that Light could see him at all told her he was dead. His features were delicate, beautiful even, with large, elfin eyes and skin of pure white. A balloon-man was feeding on him.

Then one of the shadows on the ground moved forwards. The arrow that appeared in mid-air flew, fast and true, and pierced the balloon-man in the eye. He floated to the ceiling, dead. 'I will not allow my dead to be desecrated in that manner,' said a voice Light recognised as Atiluk's. Then the shadow disappeared.

Frost, though, still stood.

He moved his fingers as if playing a piano and in a moment the room was hung all around with icicles and frost, which glittered and shone as brightly as day.

Light saw a shadow moving towards her. 'I'm sorry,' said the man. 'We can no longer help you. Rules can only be stretched so far.'

Tupilak roared and charged forwards, slamming into Frost. But Frost, implacable and immoveable, did not budge. He knelt lithely, picked up Tupilak by one bear's foot and spun him once before throwing him into the far wall. A shelf packed with books crashed to the ground, splintering beneath Tupilak's massive body.

Butler – Tulugaq – snapped his wrists and a black stream of ravens flew at Frost's face, but Frost only held out his hands and they fell to the ground with hard thuds, like hail. He flicked his own wrist and Butler found himself imprisoned in a circular wall of ice, that surrounded him like an upturned glass over an insect.

'I am the Cold, impudent god of ugly birds. I was here long before you. Haven't you learned that by now?'

As Butler slammed his fists uselessly into the ice, Frost stepped forwards, uncoiling a length of rope from his sleeves. As he approached Light, he spotted the journal, on the floor where Butler had cast it aside. 'Ah,' he said. 'The diary. How lovely.' He picked it up, concentrated on it for a moment, then dropped it.

It shattered into frosty shards.

Light looked at the destroyed pages of the journal. 'It's gone now,' she said, her voice even. 'You can go. You can give me back my father.' Her fear of the hideous creature had disappeared, locked away inside the locket, and instead she felt only a great weariness, a desire for it to be all over.

Let him take one more step towards me, she thought, *and I will tear out his icy heart.*

Frost laughed, a sound like icicles falling and breaking. 'Would that it were so simple. But you are no ordinary girl, are you?'

It didn't seem that he had moved, yet a moment later he was standing in front of Light. He touched her gently on the arm and she felt a crippling cold shoot through her body. She sank to her knees, paralysed.

No, she thought. *No, this is not how it's supposed to—*

'Won't you sit as friends?' he asked, sitting down beside her. She tried to move but she was frozen, immobile.

'We aren't friends. We're a monster and a girl.' Her voice came out as a quavering tremolo, not from fear but from the aching cold.

337

'Well then, won't you sit as monster and girl?'

'I don't have much choice, do I?'

'Of course not,' Frost said, brisk and business-like. He looped rope around his crystal hands. 'Now, I hope you don't mind, but I think it incumbent on me to secure you.' He tied her arms to her sides, then ran a loop down her legs and tied her feet back, so that she was immobilised on the ground. 'It seemed judicious to incapacitate you before I do this.' With gentle, dexterous fingers he took a small leather pouch from a deep pocket in his robe. 'My weather bag,' he said, and then opened it. A swirling white mist rose from the open bag, twisting and curling like an icy genie from a lamp. 'I took this from a sailor who had it from an *angakut*,' Frost said. 'The sailor paid dearly for it, in more ways than one. First he exchanged his wife for it, who was very beautiful – he wanted a bag full of wind, you see, that would carry him in his boat wherever he wanted to go. Then he exchanged his life for it, when I took him in my cold embrace and stole his greatest treasure.' He stroked the bag. 'In my hands, of course, it is rather more than a toy for sailing against the wind . . .'

The whiteness resolved into a miniature ice storm, grains of hail spinning in the centre. Then it shot forwards and split into two, hitting Butler as he broke free of his ice prison, slamming him backwards into the wall, and Tupilak, as he struggled to his feet.

Arnie came running in from the storeroom, shouting, 'Light! Are you alr—' and Frost flicked the weather bag again, hitting him with a blast as his feet were off the ground, toppling him instantly. Arnie lay on the ground, covered with a rime of frost, utterly still.

338

Light stared at him. She knew she should feel pain, she should feel grief. Arnie didn't move at all – he had to be dead, and yet the tears would not come, staunched at the source by the locket.

Vaguely, this made her feel uneasy. *Is the necklace good if it takes away that sort of pain?* she thought. *Maybe there are things we* should *feel, unpleasant though they are. Maybe that's what makes us human.*

Then she dismissed the idea.

Stupid. Weak.

All that matters is that I am strong. Pain is for victims. And I am not *a victim.*

'Hurry up and kill me,' she said to Frost. 'I'm getting bored.'

The ice-creature hissed sibilantly. 'Don't you want your father? Aren't you ready to give in?' asked Frost. 'I will return him to you, do not fear. But first you must cry for me. I so hate to see a person frozen over like you – I like it when you *melt.*'

Light considered. 'I cry, you give my father back. That's it? It seems too easy.'

'Well,' said Frost. 'I'll take your life, too, of course. In exchange for his. You must understand.'

'What's the use of having my father alive, if I am dead?' she asked.

Frost looked at her, head tilted to one side. 'Ah, that self-ishness again. *He* will live, won't he?'

'He'll miss me. He'll be sad. It will be terrible for him.'

'Yes, well,' said Frost. 'I'm not very nice.' He called something Light didn't understand and an *isserkat* came in from outside. He was dragging Light's father behind him, cocooned in rope.

'Dad!' Light shouted. 'Dad!'

He didn't reply. His head hung low – he seemed unconscious.

Frost touched Light's cheek and she felt her skin burn. He turned to his *isserkat*. 'She will not cry for him alive,' he said, almost to himself. 'Perhaps she will cry for him dead. Kill him.'

Light struggled to move but it was too late. The *isserkat* knelt and very quickly, very simply – as if he were doing nothing more than drawing a line under something he wished to remember – slit Light's father's throat.

Light felt something rushing inside her, something hot and expanding – a fire ball in her chest. But it was dull, and far away. She looked at her father as the blood seeped from his open throat, slowed by the extreme cold. She looked at Arnie, motionless and huddled.

Dead.

All dead.

But the *feeling* wasn't there – she was numb. And this, finally, was too much for her. All of this had been for her father; to get him back. But to see him dead and feel nothing – that made her a monster, didn't it? She had never cried for him. For the pain of others, yes – even at films and books. But she had never allowed herself to cry for her father because that would make him gone and she couldn't stand that.

And now he *was* gone. Now he was really dead and there was nothing she could do about it.

Suddenly, she couldn't stand it any more. She turned to Frost. 'Around my neck,' she said. 'There's a locket. Take it out.'

Puzzled, Frost reached into Light's jacket, his fingers burning her skin when they brushed against it. He pulled off the locket, snapping the thin chain around Light's neck.

She had thought she was being strong. But she understood now that she was not strong – only protected, and that was not the same thing. She herself was broken, she realised, and had been since her father's disappearance. She was not Light. She was a dull and lifeless doppelganger that saw only half the joy in the world that the real Light used to do. How long was it since she'd last laughed? She felt like a usurper in her own skin.

'Open it,' she said.

Frost examined the finely carved silver heart for a moment, then shrugged and opened it.

There was an inrush of air in her lungs and a hot, choking pain and then she was crying, really crying, the tears feeling like something burning to get out. She huddled instinctively against the pain, even though the pain was inside.

One thought blocked out all others – *my father is dead* – and yet at the same time she couldn't touch that thought; its edges were too sharp. There was a ringing in her ears and she could hear the *whoosh-thump* of the blood in her head and she was dimly aware that these two sounds were the same thing.

That anything other than a mortal wound should hurt so much seemed a betrayal on the part of life itself; that her heart should continue so stubbornly to beat seemed an abomination.

Frost leaned down and looked her in the eyes. 'Good girl,' he whispered.

Chapter Forty-seven

Bargain

There was one shadow that the shadow people shunned, not knowing what it was. They could see each other, the shadow people, though humans could not see then. Yet they could not see the person this shadow belonged to.

This shadow had come a long way, following Light – anxious for revenge on the last heir, the sole remaining scion of the man who had killed her. It would be fair to say, though, that the shadow was becoming more than a little confused.

Light was brave and fierce, intelligent and unyielding. She appeared to be kind.

If Mad Eric, the man who had walled her up, had an heir in this room, it was not a blood heir. She saw his traits only in one figure here:

Frost.

The same cruelty, the same desire for power. The same casual disregard for human life. Even now he bent over the curled-up figure of Light as she wept, and he smiled.

342

The shadow crept closer towards Frost, moving inkily along the ground like a manta ray. Something odd was happening and it wanted to get closer, to see the change up close.

Light was glowing.

Light did not know how much time had passed when Frost said, 'That is enough now. Take her outside. It is only fitting that she die in the cold.'

She sank into the red darkness behind her eyelids. *Good*, she thought. *Soon it will be over.*

She felt rough hands lifting her up, as one of the *isserkait* carried her towards the door. She sank into his arms as if he were a friend come to rescue her.

And, in a way, he was.

But just as she was locking herself once more into the dark room of her mind, the *isserkat* let out a surprised grunt and stumbled, dropping Light to the floor. She opened her eyes just in time to put out her hands, and break her fall. She looked around her, eyes misted with tears.

The *isserkat* stood at an unnatural angle, one of its legs sunk into the floor. The concrete there was dark, viscous – as if oil had been spilled, but Light thought:

shadow.

The shadow spooled inkily along the floor, leaving the *isserkat* behind. But his leg was still halfway trapped in the concrete, where it had sunk, and he tried to move but only fell onto his face with a breaking sound. He began to scream, pulling at his leg, part eaten by a world that had turned against him.

The shadow-girl melted up from the ground, coalescing into human form. She nodded at Light.

'What creature is this?' asked Frost, doubt creeping into his voice. He held his hand up, ready to send out a blast of ice.

The shadow-girl smiled. 'A creature of darkness. Your cold cannot touch me.' Then she turned to Light. 'I find that I am softening towards you, lady of the house. And so, once again, I offer you my aid.' She leaned forwards, the smoke of her form touching Light – where it did, Light felt her skin go numb.

'Answer me this riddle, Light,' she said. 'I am emeralds and diamonds, left by the moon. I am found by the sun and picked up again soon. What am I? Then answer me a second riddle: if a human cannot kill Frost, who can?'

And with that, the shadow-girl disappeared.

Frost looked blankly at the space in the air where the girl had been. Part of Light wished simply to lie on the ground, close her eyes – to make all of this go away. But again that traitorous part of her mind – the animal part that wanted above all to survive, began to whisper its ceaseless litany.

Slowly, she stood. The *isserkat* continued his wailing, clutching at the leg he would never free from the ground. Distractedly, she waved towards him. 'Shadow – set him free.' Darkness unspooled from the floor.

'You're sure?'

Light nodded.

Out of the corner of her eye, she saw the *isserkat* free his leg in wonder from the ground, then run whimpering from the room. She concentrated.

 344

Left by the moon . . . found by the sun. What did the
moon leave? Tides? They had something to do with the
moon, didn't they? No . . . wait. Emeralds and diamonds.
Glinting. Picked up again – gone.

Dew.
The answer to the riddle is dew.

She looked at Frost and there it was: a trickle of water run-
ning down his hand, from the sleeve of his robe. Another,
running down his face. He was *melting.*
Why?
Light looked down.
A blue glow surrounded her, faint but visible, like an
aura. For a moment, she stood senseless.
Then she realised.
The glow was coming from *her.*
She was making the light – it shone from every inch of
her skin, shot from her eyes in sharp, bright slants that
raked the floor and the walls like searchlights.

I am . . .
I am emeralds and diamonds
Picked up again . . . I am . . .

Then, more slowly, with growing wonder, Light thought:

I am not human. My mother is the moon.

Despite her pain she smiled faintly and imagined a light
bulb growing gradually brighter, until you would have to

avert your eyes or go blind. She felt a heat inside her and the blue glow increased in intensity, and when she could look no longer she half closed her eyes. In the flood of blue light that came from her body she saw Frost melting, sinking into the ground, a snowman in spring. His cloak and hood were crumpling, collapsing.

'You don't understand,' he hissed. 'I am the cold and I have been here on this planet since before your kind were *walking*. I cannot be defeated! I will be chilling your bones in your grave long after you are dead.'

Light ignored him because he was wrong; he was nothing. And she did understand. What was it Setna had said? *What makes you strong is not always what will save you*.

And it was true. It wasn't the locket that made her strong, or anything like it. It wasn't weapons or people or armour. It was her own being, her own essence.

Her light was blinding even her, and she knew no one could withstand it. Frost would die. She was the moon, and the moon was made to reflect the light of the sun. Though the sun was far away to the south, she was drawing in its light – and then she was pouring it out again, flooding the station with it. She looked down again – buttery blue light was shooting out from her in thin, needle-like rays.

But she could also feel her energy betraying her, robbing her legs of substance, threatening to make her collapse under the strain of her heavenly light.

Rasping with a startling sound, animal in her human throat, she fell to her knees, unable to stop the light from blazing, feeling her strength ebb away. She looked up at Frost, still melting but still standing. He began to reach out towards her, water dripping from his ice-carving hand. In his eyes Light was shocked to see fear.

And she was even more shocked that his fear made *pity* rise in her – in even the short time that she had possessed the locket, she had forgotten this sensation, the sheer sickening horror of another's suffering.

If anyone felt what I feel now, this suffering – and I could take it from them and into myself, to spare them – then wouldn't I do it?

And if that's the case then can I truly destroy this creature, when I know it is not necessary?

She looked at Frost and understood that she could not kill him.

'Shadow!' she said and blackness slid up into existence before Light, coalescing from cigarette smoke into a black and smiling girl. But something about the shadow-girl was different. Her blackness was greater, too perfect. What did it make Light think of? Something important.

Oh yes, she thought, her mind snagging on something unpleasant – as when you explore your mouth with your tongue and find that one of your teeth has been chipped. *That is death I'm looking at.*

'Shadow,' Light said, praying that her idea would work, praying her energy would not run out. The light continued to pour from her but she was weakening still – soon she would not even have the strength to kneel. 'Would you take another in my place, if he were willing?'

The shadow nodded very slowly, not in agreement but pensively, as if weighing up a matter of grave import. 'You wish me to take Frost instead?' she asked. 'And *is* the great Frost willing?' she asked, turning towards the melting figure.

Frost looked at Light imploringly. He had to look up now, his body shortening by the second as the pool of water grew wider. 'What is this?' he asked.

'Will you agree to take this shadow's place?' asked Light. 'You will be condemned to walk the corridors of my house for ever – you will become the soul of the house. But you will live.'

Frost closed his black eyeholes, his face becoming a mask of glassy ice. 'I accept, if the shadow will take me.'

The dark girl turned to Light. 'I do not see much of Mad Eric in you, Light. But I see him in Frost. I accept your new covenant.'

The shadow dissolved from its girl-shape into a black circle on the floor which moved under Frost and stayed there. The circle spread, and Frost's feet started to disappear into the floor.

There was a brief sound of damp resistance – a plughole being unblocked – and then Frost's melting body dropped into blackness, followed in its descent by a tapering, echoing scream. Immediately the circle started to close, a pupil contracting in the light.

And then there was nothing in the room but the living and the dead.

Light stumbled to her father's body. She knelt beside him, turned him to face upwards. She leaned in close, putting her fingers to his neck.

There was no pulse.

Light pressed her fingers to the skin again, held her ear to his mouth, listening for his breathing, but there was none, and her tears splashed his face. She clung to him as if drowning. She thought:

No no no no no no you can't be dead you can't be I came to save you and I defeated Frost and now you can't be dead

and she thought:

When I was a child you had to cover my eyes if there were fireworks – they scared me, but always I wanted to see them anyway, I knew you would put your arms around me and everything would be OK everything would be . . . would be . . .

and then she thought:

"   "

and that was worse.

She pressed her palm against his chest, breathing in panting gulps, her throat tearing, pushing *one two three,*

one two three

Then a breath from her lungs into his.

Again: her palms pressing hard down over his heart, her breath in his body.

She had no more concept of time but a moment (an hour?) later she felt strong hands pulling her back.

Butler.

'He's gone, Light,' he said.

'No,' said Light. 'No, he's not.'

'Yes.'

'No. Fetch me a rope.'

Chapter Forty-eight

My mother, the moon

Hundreds of miles above the earth and looking down on it with a kind of breathless vertigo, Light stepped off the dog sled that had carried her up through the night sky, through the clouds and through the earth's atmosphere, where colours as bright as the Northern Lights burned on the sled's surfaces. Behind Light, the earth hung like a bauble in the blackness of space, startlingly blue and green, seeming delicate and precious in a way that sent a thrill through Light's heart. A woman stood before her on the sugary surface of the moon, in front of a hall that glowed with inviting light.

Her mother.

Light's mother – beautiful, with a rounded face and a glowing body in a blue dress – gestured to the hall's door, inviting Light in. Behind her was a group of shining people, watching Light curiously.

One of the people stepped forwards, and Light saw that it was the Captain. He nodded to Light deeply, a bow almost. 'Thank you,' Light whispered. 'I am glad that you have come here, to this good place.' Tears filled her eyes, spilling hotly down her cheeks.

Light felt and did not hear the Captain's words, which seemed to come from the shimmering of her starlight. 'I am glad that you still live,' he said. 'And I am happy here.' Then a troubled look passed over his face. 'But you shouldn't be here,' he said. 'This is where the dead live. Aukjuk is coming, the stealer of souls. She will try to make you laugh, and if you do she will eat your stomach and you will be neither alive nor dead for evermore.'

'I'm not afraid of that,' said Light. 'I just want my dad back.'

'Oh, Light,' said another voice, a familiar voice, a voice Light had not been able to conjure in her dreams but which now rang out across the dusty surface of the moon. 'You were always my brave girl.'

The Captain stood aside, and there was someone behind him.

Light's father.

She screamed with joy, and would have run to him, but Malina raised a hand and she found herself unable to move. 'No,' said Light's mother. 'Not yet. You will be united when you die. For now, you will return where you came from.' But her eyes were not as hard as her words, and when she looked at Light's father it was with a tenderness that broke Light's heart.

Light took a deep breath – she had defeated Frost, she had shone with the light of the moon. She was raised by gods.

'Not without my father,' she said.

*

Butler didn't know how long he had sat for.

At his feet, lying tied up on the ground, was Light. Her eyes were shut, her body motionless. Her feet and hands were bound tightly with rope.

'Do you think—' began Tupilak.

Butler cut him off with a wave of the hand. 'No thinking. No talking.'

The shark-man was over by the stove, sitting with the boy, Arnie.

The boy had not spoken since they revived him. He only stared at Light, rocking slightly back and forth in his chair.

And then, in one of those endless instants – just one –

Light's eyes snapped open.

She took in a great breath, the sound so violent it seemed the air attacked her, filling her defenceless lungs.

She smiled at Butler. 'Untie me.'

A moment later Light was crouching once more over the corpse of her father. 'Listen,' said Butler. 'I don't know what you were doing but you can't just—'

And then Gordon Fitzwilliam's eyes opened, with the same suddenness as his daughter's and he looked on his Light.

'Dad,' she said.

'Light,' he replied.

And that was all – all that Butler had wanted for Light, all that could have been expected, and all that in that moment was needed.

As Arnie leaped from his chair and Tupilak rose beside him, powerful and quick as the sea, Butler turned away.

Such reunions – such tears – were not for his kind. In time, he would greet his young charge, his old friend, and talk with them into the night.

In time – because there would be lots of time. But for now, he turned away.

As we will, too.

Epilogue

Light was woken by the pleasingly familiar *whoosh* of the message tube, and the less pleasingly familiar impact to her abdomen as the heavy cylinder of metal and glass landed on the duvet. She opened the tube and read the message inside.

You'll get through this. Love, Dad.

Light grinned and got up. She looked out of the window – spring sunlight shone down on the lough, making its surface sparkle. Swans led their cygnets, Indian-file, across the clear water by the shore.

Light thought of the endless ocean and her adventures on the ice – there was a time when she had thought Lough Neagh was enormous, but now it seemed small and safe. In fact, the whole place seemed different. Someone seemed to have come to Neagh House in her absence and taken all the furniture away, replacing it with items that were almost but not quite identical – the angles seemed wrong, the sizes smaller and less imposing.

There had been a real change, too, in the character of the house – in its soul, one might say. Where before it had been snug and sometimes malevolent, as if nursing a secret resentment, now it had a more expansive feel, even if its rooms and corridors were colder than before. Light's breath misted in the air before her and she saw a shifting in the grey half-light of the far side of her room, where the light from the window didn't reach.

'Hello, Frost,' she said. 'Lovely day, isn't it?'

'I suppose so,' he said, his shadow elongating up the room till his head reached the ceiling. 'Though a little warm for me. I'm not a sunshine person.' He laughed, and the sound shivered like struck crystal.

Then his shadow contracted and slid along the ground, and Light sensed that he was gone.

Light put on a pair of jeans and a T-shirt. She wasn't going to dress up this time. She ran downstairs to the kitchen, where her dad was waiting for her. She ran to him and jumped into a hug, wrapping her legs around him. She was getting a little heavy for this, and her father grunted with something approaching pain, but he said nothing and she hung on for a second longer.

'Ready?' he asked.

'Ready,' Light said. She held his hand.

Together, they stepped into the drawing room. A banner was stretched over the fireplace, reading

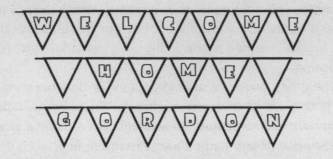

There was a series of bangs as guests let off party-poppers, covering Light and her father with stringy bunting and confetti.

From the other side of the room, Butler waved them over. He was standing next to Maeve, who was dressed in a stunning silk dress. Light noticed that his arm was wrapped around the cook's waist. Light smiled at Butler and raised her eyebrows.

'Maeve and I have . . . that is to say, Maeve and I—' said Butler hesitantly.

Maeve cut him off by lifting herself up on her toes and kissing him. 'Maeve and I have waited too long for each other for that kind of dithering,' she said. Light giggled and Maeve pulled her into a hug, the three of them wrapping their arms around each other.

'You know, Butler,' said Light, 'there are some things you should probably tell Maeve if you're going to be a couple.' Maeve pulled away from the hug a little, looking suspiciously at Butler. 'Oh, no!' said Light. 'Nothing bad. But I think you might find it interesting.'

'Yes,' said Butler, smiling at them both. 'It'll be interesting, all right.'

Light's father's fingers beat a tattoo on the skin of her arm.

-.— — ..- / -.. .. -.. -. / - / - . .-.. -.. / — . / ... . /
.— .- ... / ... — / -... . .- ..- - .. ..- .. -.. .-.-

You didn't tell me she was so beautiful.
She grinned and tapped her father's hand.

-.. .- -.. . . ..- .. .- -.. .--.- / — ..- / .— . / -... -.. / .-.. —
- ... . / -.— — ..- / — -. / .—. .. -. .—. — . — ... . /
- .... / - .. — . .-.-

Careful. Or we'll lose you on purpose this time.

Acknowledgements

I'd like to thank my agent, Caradoc King, and my editor, Venetia Gosling, for seeing something in this odd little tale. (Well, OK, not little. In fact it's probably far too long. But definitely odd.)

Judith Evans and Elinor Cooper at A.P. Watt gave invaluable early comments on the manuscript, as did my wife Hannah. If there is anything a bit rubbish in this book, it reflects only my pig-headedness, not the expert guidance I received from them and Venetia.

The designer, Nick Stearn, has made the book look more beautiful and arresting than I could have hoped, with the aid of Liane Payne's stunning illustrations.

And finally – if you've read the book and you're STILL reading now, then I'd like to thank you too.

NL